DEATH SPRINGS

DAVID J. GATWARD

DG CREATIVE LTD

Death Springs
by
David J. Gatward

Copyright © 2025 by David J. Gatward
All rights reserved.

No part of this book may be reproduced in any form or by any electronic or mechanical means, including information storage and retrieval systems, without written permission from the author, except for the use of brief quotations in a book review.

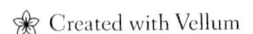

❊ Created with Vellum

To the Vobster Lobsters

ONE

Five years ago ...

TONY MILLS WAS HAVING one of those days where, given the chance, he'd have happily set fire to every last bit of it just to watch it burn.

The building company he'd set up in his twenties had, over the years, grown from just himself and a mate zipping around the Somerset lanes taking every job they could, to a permanent workforce of a dozen labourers, and too many contractors to mention. Priding himself on doing not just a good job, but the best, and charging accordingly, had ensured the kind of lifestyle that had allowed him to pursue interests he had, all those years ago, only ever dreamed of. Now in the dying embers of his forties, he had already amassed a decent little collection of classic sports cars, which included a Triumph TR4, a Lotus Esprit, and for some reason, a Vauxhall Nova. Fitness was another interest, and he was happy to admit that he perhaps had a problem with buying too many bikes, all of them expensive, none of them comfortable. The priciest of the lot was akin to riding a razor blade. Bloody fast, though. Although he wasn't one for taking much time off, when he did, he spent it well, either on the slopes or in the sun, in the best resorts the money he'd earned could buy. Life was, in many ways, very, very good. But today? Well, today was doing its best to prove otherwise.

It had actually started the night before, when three things had happened in quick succession, none of them good. Not that Tony was all that superstitious; he didn't carry around a lucky rabbit's foot or anything, but he had grown up with a mum who most certainly was. She would pepper her day with phrases like, 'See a penny pick it up, all day long you'll have good luck,' and one that now seemed more than a little portentous, 'Bad luck comes in threes.' She would throw salt over her shoulder, salute magpies, touch wood, and take great pride in the fact that she'd never, not even once, opened an umbrella indoors. She also had a thing for crystals, was particularly enamoured of a dreamcatcher she had hanging in her lounge window and was a very enthusiastic believer in ghosts. Tony didn't believe in the paranormal, superstitions, good or bad luck, that crystals had energy, and especially not ghosts. He believed in what his five senses told him was real. Anything else? Well, that was all just bollocks, wasn't it?

After a long day at work, Tony had decided that what he really needed was a damned good feed. Courtesy of his recent marriage breakdown, there was no one at home to share a meal with, and he really didn't fancy eating alone, so he'd headed to his local pub, The George Inn, in Norton St. Philip. The evening had been a windy one, and as he'd been blown along through the village, he'd remembered being a kid and lifting his jacket up behind his head as a sail. He'd lived in Norton St Philip his whole life, and the ancient pub was as much a part of his DNA as the colour of his eyes. So, after his brisk evening walk, he'd gone to The George and greedily tucked in to a large stilton, steak and mushroom pie, with mashed potatoes and peas, all washed down with a couple of pints of beer. He avoided cider and had done since a bad experience at the age of fifteen where, after a few too many cans of something cheap and strong and apple-flavoured; he'd been so ill he'd felt sure he was going to die.

Meal over, and forcing himself to leave the George before he was tempted to have more beer, Tony had strolled home and walked right under a ladder that he felt sure hadn't been there earlier. He'd hurried along, thinking nothing of it, though he had questioned the sanity of anyone who thought it was a good idea to clean their gutters out as night was drawing in.

Stepping off the kerb, the squeal of car tyres had made him jump so violently that his dinner had very nearly reintroduced itself. The vehicle had swerved to avoid a black cat, which had then dashed across in front of him with a violent hiss, as though to imply what had just happened had been entirely his fault. Tony had stared at it and heard the voice of his mum start to whisper something about bad luck, which he ignored and pushed on for home.

Having arrived home, and with all thoughts about the ladder and the black cat forgotten, Tony had shuffled through to the kitchen, made himself a large mug of tea, then retired to the lounge. With no desire to waste what was left of the evening flicking through the TV channels, he'd chosen instead to listen to a relaxing jazz album from his growing vinyl collection. Then, as he'd turned to slump down in a large armchair, he'd tripped over a rug, spilled his tea, lost his footing and fallen headfirst into the wall. It was only when he'd come to his senses a few moments later, a headache blurring his vision, that he'd noticed the mirror. He'd picked it up at some antiques shop, goodness knew when, but it was now useless, lying as it did on the floor in a thousand deadly pieces.

With a headache almost as large and painful as the growing lump on his forehead, Tony had decided that enough was enough and had headed up to bed. He'd eventually drifted off to sleep, refusing to accept that bad luck did indeed come in threes, because that was superstitious nonsense, wasn't it? And there was no way in hell that he was going to find himself thinking like his mum.

Just a few hours later, Tony was woken by the sound of sirens outside his house, followed by a loud thump on his front door. Falling out of bed, to what he had hoped would be just a normal day working on a rather extensive renovation of a crumbling farmhouse, he had half fallen downstairs to open his front door. He'd been greeted by the very unimpressed faces of two firefighters. It was only then, while he had tried to pull himself out of being half asleep, that he'd realised the day had barely even woken itself up, never mind the people who would soon be going out to work in it. Staring past the firefighters, the street beyond his drive was still lit by streetlamps, the world blissfully asleep beneath a thick blanket of night.

'There's no fire, then, Sir?' one of the firefighters had said, then added, 'Nasty bump you've got there, by the way.'

'What?' Tony had yawned, too tired to even cover his

mouth, and only then remembering what had happened earlier that evening.

'No fire, Sir?' the other had offered. 'In your house. You know, big orangey stuff, very hot, very dangerous, plays havoc with anything flammable?'

Tony had been none the wiser, and the sarcasm hadn't helped much either.

'Yes, look, I know what fire is,' he'd replied, still barely awake, his head now throbbing from the knock against the wall, 'just not what you're talking about. Why are you at my front door? Why have you woken me up?'

The first firefighter had then given Tony such a foul look that he had taken a step back.

'We had a call, Sir. Not just one, either, but three, all claiming that this house was on fire.'

'Which is why we're here,' the second had added.

'To put it out.'

'What with us being firefighters.'

Tony had been somewhat baffled. So much so, that he'd stepped out of his house far enough so that he could turn around and have a jolly good look at it. And yes, the firefighters had been right, there was indeed no fire. Which didn't really help much in explaining why they were there ruining his morning.

'I'm sorry, can we start from the beginning again, please?' he'd asked. 'Why are you here, exactly? I mean, there's no fire, is there, and yet you've woken me up.'

For a moment or two, neither of the firefighters had said a word. Instead, they'd just stared at Tony, their eyes narrow, jaws set hard.

As he'd waited for one of them to say something, he'd found his attention drawn again to his house. Its windows were dark, the only light being that spilling out from the hall, and yet, for the briefest moment, he'd had the distinct and unnerving sensation of being watched.

Yawning once again, so much so that his jaw locked just long enough to cause the two firefighters to go rather wide-eyed at the sight of him, mouth jammed open, teeth bared, and moaning, it was Tony who had broken the awkward silence.

'Look, I didn't report a fire. I know you clearly think I did, but I promise you, I didn't.'

'Well, Sir, someone did, otherwise why would we be here?'

'It wasn't me.'

'Who was it, then?'

'I don't know.'

'The call came from this house.'

That same sensation had hit once again, the feeling of being watched, and he'd looked again at his home, his eyes narrowing on his bedroom window. And why was it he felt a sudden waft of blistering heat from the place? That made no sense at all.

But of course it doesn't, Tony had thought; there was nothing there, because of course there wasn't. He was just tired, and that bump on the head had clearly done him no good at all.

'It can't have done,' he'd said. 'I live on my own, I'd know.'

'Exactly.'

'Exactly what?'

A moment's silence, then ...

'You do know that it's a criminal offence to prank call the fire service, don't you, Sir? You are aware of that fact?'

'I didn't prank call the fire service,' Tony had replied, taking a very large dislike to the constant use of the word *Sir* as a term of condescension rather than respect.

'And yet, here we are, Sir, having answered a prank call, made by someone from this very house.'

'But, like I've just said, I live alone.'

'Exactly.'

Tony had rubbed his eyes, half hoping that in doing so he would wake up, find himself in bed, and realise that it was all a weird, slightly irritating dream. Then, on opening them, he'd stared past the two firefighters at the large, red fire engine parked in his driveway.

'There must be some misunderstanding,' he'd said, working hard to sound calm, collected, patient even, which wasn't easy considering the hour. 'There has to be. I live on my own. There's no one else here. No one called you from my house. No one.'

And so, the argument had continued, until, at last, the two firefighters had left, leaving behind a raft of threats of legal action, piled high with numerous accusations about wasting time and money, and that surely someone like him had better things to do with his time (*Sir*).

With the fire engine no longer sitting in his driveway, and with all thoughts of something in the house watching him having vanished, Tony had given up on the idea of going back to bed. Instead, he had taken a long shower, then sorted himself out a lazy breakfast high on protein and healthy carbs and seasoned with just the right amount of healthy fats. Didn't make it taste any better though, and he really was growing so very, very tired of eating so many spinach omelettes fried in coconut oil. But he enjoyed taking his time over it all, not being in a rush, and even made himself two lattes on the fancy coffee machine he'd bought a few months back.

Arriving at their current job early, Tony had pulled into what had once been a farmyard and was now a driveway beautifully laid in brick, only to receive messages from the two lads working with him that day that they'd both been hit by some god-awful bug doing the rounds. Explosive from both ends, one had decided to tell him, which was a detail he could have well done without, not least because it had been delivered with frighteningly realistic sound effects.

For once, though, Tony hadn't been all that bothered, had wished them both a quick recovery, and immediately looked forward to having the day all to himself, especially considering the way it had started. Then he'd made his way into the farmhouse, and the day had turned sour quicker than his long-dead father's face when he'd told him that, no, he didn't want to follow him into the Army, if that meant ending up being anything like him.

The first problem he encountered was that there was no power to the building. Tony checked the fuse box, found nothing wrong there, and eventually ended up spending a couple of hours on the phone with the energy company trying to establish what was wrong and how it could be solved. They didn't know, but sent a young man with too much gel in his hair to investigate. He turned up only to tell Tony it wasn't his job and that the energy company had sent the wrong contractor. He did, however, point out that the fuse box was burned out, and was surprised that Tony hadn't checked that first. Which he had, and said so, only to receive the dirtiest of looks before the young man had driven off.

Luckily, Tony had a portable generator in his van, so he had been able to get on with a few tasks regardless, such as mixing up some concrete to crack on with repointing some of the external walls, of which there were plenty, not just of the house, but the numerous farm buildings that sat around the yard in front of it like children at story time.

Then, while he was doing that, the rain had come. He'd not checked the forecast, what with the Fire Brigade waking him up at What-the-Hell o'clock. Postponing the repointing, while praying that the rain didn't ruin what he'd already done, Tony had headed inside the house to see if there was anything else he could be getting on with, only to find that overnight, something had managed to get into the house and set up shop. That *something* being a large family of rats and their numerous relatives. At the sight of Tony they had scattered, a good number of them throwing themselves directly at him in an attempt to escape, and he'd found himself running from the building like a very poor and somewhat panicked version of the Pied Piper of Hamelin.

And yet all of this paled into insignificance when compared with what had happened next.

Standing in the rain as rats scattered through the numerous puddles now populating the farmyard, his head thumping again from the night before, Tony found himself to be suddenly, and for no reason he could think of, very short of breath. All he'd done was sprint a few yards to escape the rats, so he knew that he shouldn't be out of breath and yet there he was, barely able to pull in enough air to fill his lungs. He could smell burning as well, and that made no sense, because there was no fire anywhere. Was he having a stroke? Panic gripped him, and he had an awful thought that perhaps he was going to go out the same way as his father and die of a heart attack in his forties.

Forcing himself to stay calm, Tony tried to focus on the

rain, the cold wind blowing it into him like wasp stings, anything that would help him not panic that he was about to die. When, at last, the tightness in his chest started to ease, he had just a few seconds of relief before an ear-piercing scream ripped the air in two and the world around him stopped.

The scream came at Tony with such violence that he clamped his hands over his ears, dropped to his knees, and found himself screaming back, as though the sound of his own voice would repel it.

It didn't.

The scream not only grew louder, but closer, and Tony realised then that he was cowering, though from what, he had no idea. He was crouching on the rain-drenched ground in the yard of an old farm he'd been employed to renovate, he was alone bar the rats, and above him, grey clouds hung so low in the sky he felt sure they would soon be resting on the roofs of the farm buildings. There was nothing here to cause him to feel like this, to react like this, yet something unseen now had him so torn with terror that it burned.

The scream stopped as suddenly as it had begun. Tony, sucking in air with the desperation of a man close to drowning, relaxed, wondered if the whole thing was just some odd echo of the knock he'd taken the previous evening, that perhaps what he should've done that day instead of going to work, was take a trip to the doctor. Then the hairs on the back of his neck and arms, stood on end, his ears popped, and inside his head, and from somewhere in the world around him, he heard a voice call his name.

Tony instinctively looked to where he felt that the voice had come from. And there, not three feet in front of him, stood a young man and woman, their ragged clothes blackened and burned, the charred skin on their skeletal faces showing bone beneath, their hair gone, the left side of the young man's head crushed flat. Then rats, their fur alight with bright tongues of fire, swarmed from behind the couple and threw themselves at Tony.

From that day on, when the ghosts had come a calling, Tony's life was never the same again.

TWO

Three days ago ...

GAIL CARPENTER HAD BEEN a member of the open-water swimming group, The Ebb, since its inception over ten years ago. She had seen it grow from just a handful of members to what was now thirty-plus. She couldn't quite recall whose idea it had been to set it up in the first place, though she had a faint recollection of it possibly being hers. Regardless of the finer details, the whole thing had come about one summer's evening over a few pints of cider at Tucker's Grave, a pub with a history, a campsite, fantastic cider, and one hell of a name.

Those first members had all gathered at the inn, each having arrived on their bikes, keen to spend a couple of hours chewing the fat, quite literally at points, thanks to the plentiful supply of pork scratchings. The cider had been good, the food simple and tasty, and sitting outside on that particularly warm evening, which hadn't even cooled as the sun had gone to bed, and with the moon rising high and bright, one of them had said something about how nice it would be to go for a dip. The conversation had explored this idea with gusto, and soon a list of various known swimming spots had been drawn up, from the swimming club over at Farleigh Hungerford, to a rather secret pool only Charlotte, it had turned out, knew about.

Having woken the next day with a rather fuzzy head, and aching legs from the bike ride, Gail had completely forgotten about what had not only been discussed but arranged. Then, while she was tucking into a rather delicious plate of bacon, egg, and black pudding, Marg had called to double-check the location for their planned dip later that day, and history had been made.

That first foray into the world of open-water swimming had been a joyous affair. Like teenagers again, she, Margaret, Mike, Terry, and Charlotte, along with Dolly Parton, Marg's lazy Labrador, had turned up at a riverbank and spent a glorious afternoon together. They had all brought various picnic items, and Mike, being the most outdoorsy of them all, had arrived with a little gas camping stove to heat some soup, and fry off some bacon for the butties they had quickly demolished.

Gail could still remember the gasps and the laughter that had filled the air as they had all dipped their respective toes in the calm waters of the river, eventually slipping fully into its embrace. The water had come as a blessed relief on that hot day, and instead of just splashing around in one place, they had explored the river a little.

She had been so taken with the serene beauty of the

place that she had known immediately that open-water swimming would be her new obsession. It wasn't just the soft, cool water against her skin that hooked her into it either, but the whole experience. Back then, the health benefits of swimming in cold water were known but not promoted as openly as they are now. In many ways, she wondered if it had been better back then, when the joy of swimming in a river had been the innocence of it, the sense of absolute abandonment to nature, a shunning of the modern world for an hour or two, to sink into the wildness that could still be found if only you took a few minutes to look for it.

Though she was a keen regular at the quarry diving centre near the village of Vobster, Gail would jump at any opportunity to drive to the coast and throw herself into the sea. But it was river swimming that she loved most of all.

Rivers, Gail felt, offered a deeper, perhaps even spiritual, experience to anyone who decided to venture cautiously into them. She loved the slow movement of the water as it wound its way through the countryside, which was so often hidden in thick shade by the silent watchers of trees that lined their edges. She enjoyed the sensation of both pebbles and mud on her feet as she left the solidity of land, walking slowly into the depths.

Then there was the sense of exploration, that around the next bend a heron might be seen, perhaps even an otter; she had seen only one in all her time of swimming in rivers up and down the country, and to this day she held that moment close as her most treasured. She had drifted around a corner in a small river somewhere in Wales to find the beautiful creature resting on a log, as a wide blade of sunshine had cut through the tree canopy above to bathe it in gold. She had trodden water in the middle of the river, perhaps for too long, just watching it clean itself and stretch in the warmth of the sun, then it had dived beneath the surface of the river, and to her amazement, swum within just a metre or so of where she was.

Right then, she was standing on the bank of the River Avon, just a short walk out from the small and exceptionally pretty town of Bradford-on-Avon. She had considered calling The Originals, as she referred to them, but had preferred the idea of a solo swim. Unfortunately, that was not to be; she was not alone, something she found wasn't allowed very often in modern-day life.

Within minutes of her arrival, others had turned up, all having had the same idea that a swim that afternoon was just the ticket. But then who could blame them? thought Gail. Early autumn was blessing them with the perfect day, the sun bright in a clear sky, the air just warm enough to mean a brisk walk would have you unzipping a jacket, but not so warm that wearing a T-shirt was sensible.

She could give Margaret and the others a call she supposed, but then there would be all that waiting around for them to turn up, assuming any of them would want to or even be able to, for that matter. Still, she sent them a message on their little group chat, just in case.

Driving over, Gail had taken things nice and leisurely, by way of narrow, winding lanes. Window down, she had sunk deep into the smells of a world busy with harvest. Delays due to the many tractors filling the roads like worker bees had simply made her smile and relax even more. It was, she thought, a lesson in slowing down, which was another reason she loved to slip beneath cool waters; life was fast, too fast by far, and rivers, ever so gently, gave her space to just be.

Gail recognised some of the new arrivals as members of The Ebb.

'I would've messaged you to say we were going swimming, invite you along,' said Paula, who was in her late thirties, and who had embraced the open-swimming lifestyle with such enthusiasm, that she rarely spent a day not wearing her dry robe; Gail had even seen her wear it to the supermarket. 'You work Tuesdays, though, don't you? That's why I didn't. Nice to see you, though.'

'Took the day off,' Gail explained, and left it at that.

'Pulled a sicky, you mean?' winked Simon, a retired accountant who, like Paula, had been in the group just a few months. Not that you would know that from how he talked. He had even fitted a tiny roof rack to his Porsche just so he had somewhere to strap his unnecessarily huge waterproof holdall, which contained all his gear.

Why he needed so much of it, Gail had never quite understood. He even had two dry robes. Two! What on earth for? She'd seen him offer one of them to Charlotte a number of times, but never anyone else, even though Charlotte, like herself, was happy with a couple of towels. She knew he was flirting with her, even though he was married, but the notion that he might have bought an extra dry robe just for that purpose seemed ridiculous. Though she did remember him at that barbeque she'd had for the group round at her place a couple of months ago; he'd been up close to Charlotte then as well, hadn't he? Odd man.

As for herself, she had eventually bowed under pressure and replaced the beach towel dance she would do after every swim with a dry robe, which was much cosier and had considerably less risk of a boob flash. That was about it, really, as far as she was concerned when it came to equipment. She had a tow float, a cap and goggles, but she'd never gone so far as to purchase a wetsuit, because that was cheating, wasn't it? And really, did she look like someone who did triathlons? To his credit, although he owned one, Gail had never seen Simon actually wear his wetsuit. Not that it was a competition to see just how much cold you could bear, but also, it kind of was, wasn't it? He might need it come winter, and he wouldn't be the only one. Gail, though, had never bothered, and doubted that she ever would.

'No, I don't mean that at all,' Gail replied, perhaps a little rattier than she had meant to, so added, 'I've a few days carried over from last year, and I need to use them up.'

As well as Paula and Simon, two other new members had turned up; Eric and his wife, Izzy, were there now, and although Gail was, in the end, happy to share the swim with them all, she lamented the absence of that original group.

But that was the way of things, wasn't it? she thought. Times change, and she knew full well that you had to bend with it a little, or you might just snap. She would've liked Margaret and Mike to be there, and Terry and Charlotte, because at least then she'd have had something to talk about. Not that they were all the same age, but that added something to their conversations; it was so dull to always talk to those who had grown up in the same decade, much better to see life through different eyes and experiences.

'Can't wait to get in the water,' said Paula, and she then proceeded to strip down to her underwear without a care, before wrapping herself in her robe to complete her transformation, with relative modesty, into a swimmer.

Such behaviour was not Gail's way, not anymore anyway, and she envied her a little. Charlotte could still get away with it, but she was a decade younger than her at least.

'I've a few chaps at the golf club who want to come along and give river swimming a go,' said Simon. 'I've invited them along.'

'What, now?' Gail said. 'And how many, exactly?'

'Oh, I can't remember,' laughed Simon. 'I mentioned coming along this morning, and to the Saturday morning swim. They're a hoot!'

Paula laughed. But then she laughed at everything Simon said, or certainly seemed to, thought Gail.

'Open water swimming's not really about being a hoot, though, is it?' she said. 'Have they done it before?'

'Can't say that I know,' said Simon. 'They'll be absolutely fine, though, I'm sure. They've heard me talking about it and just want in on the action! And I said that everyone would be happy to give them a bit of help and advice, which is right, isn't it?'

Gail took a few deep breaths. She wasn't sure who had invited Simon to join the group in the first place, but whoever it was, clearly hadn't explained a few things.

'They can't just turn up,' she said. 'They need to be able to swim four hundred metres with ease, be confident in deep water, have the right kit ...'

Simon dismissed Gail's points with a wave of a hand.

'They'll be fine,' he repeated.

'He wouldn't invite them if he didn't think they were up to it, would he?' said Paula. 'You need to stop taking everything so seriously.'

'My point exactly, Paula,' said Simon. 'And they're just what the group needs, I think; a few more people to lighten things up a bit.'

'How do you mean?' Eric asked, and Gail was relieved that someone else was finding Simon's attitude a little taxing.

'About what?'

'About how the group needs to lighten up,' said Eric. 'In what way?'

Simon paused for a moment before answering, and when he did, the words he uttered made Gail's blood boil.

'Well,' he shrugged, 'it's just swimming, isn't it?'

THREE

Charlotte Apperly had arrived in Frome bright and early, and that went for herself as much as the hour. The market had been set up, and she always liked to have a stroll around before she headed to work. She'd usually pick up a nice bit of fish for dinner, perhaps some fancy cheese as well, to nibble on while sipping a nice glass of red, and it was always fun to have a chat with the stallholders. At least today they weren't battling against the weather, as the day had started well, with bright sunshine playing hide and seek behind cartoon clouds.

Leaving her car just far enough away from the centre of town to force her to have a nice, brisk walk, she wandered down through some houses to a path leading along the river. Few things caught her imagination like running water, and though the River Frome was, at this point anyway, hardly the most attractive of waterways, she still enjoyed sharing her time with it. Brown though the water was, ducks were still playing about on its surface, and sunlight decorated its glistening surface like glitter.

Crossing over a road, she continued on the path, walking

between a weir and a playground, and then alongside a bike track. Even at this time of the morning, children and teenagers were enjoying it, riding their bikes with such disregard for risk that Charlotte hurried along, fearful that if she stayed, she'd witness someone coming a cropper.

The path became darker, with trees waving their long branches high above, as though trying to reach over it to fish in the river. Then she was in the main car park, and there ahead of her, was the market. It was still too early to pop into the Cheese and Grain, a large event space that had witnessed everything from top names doing warm-up gigs before Glastonbury, to disco yoga. Today, it was the flea market, and she thought she might nip in there at lunch, just for a potter, really, because there was nothing she wanted to buy. Still, it was fun to mooch around, just in case.

Arriving at the market, Charlotte grabbed a nice piece of salmon and treated herself to some other tasty bits and bobs, including a dressed crab. Instead of her usual dinner, she was heading out as soon as work was done and taking a picnic with her. What she'd bought would be a delicious addition to everything she had already packed and placed in a cool box in the boot of her car, though the large slab of salmon would be saved for later in the week. She'd need white wine for both, she thought, and would grab some on the way home. Either that, or pop to the little organic wine shop opposite the cinema. Today, she decided against cheese, so had enough time to drift through the market and on into town for a coffee.

Heading past the library, and over a footbridge, she wasn't quite sure where to go for caffeine, when a shout caught her up short. She turned around to see a familiar face approaching.

'Mike.' She smiled, sending a little wave his way with her free hand.

'Lovely morning, isn't it?' Mike said, stretching his arms out to the sun. 'Been shopping? Anything delicious?'

'Everything from the fishmonger's is delicious,' Charlotte smiled.

'Might pop there myself, now you mention it,' said Mike, then asked, 'Have you seen the messages from Gail?'

'Messages?'

Though Charlotte had just used her phone to pay for what she'd bought, she had her notifications turned off, because sometimes, she just didn't want to be interrupted by other people.

'She's at the river.'

'On her own?'

'I think she wanted to be, but now she's very much not.'

'Oh.'

'Oh, indeed.'

Mike shoved his hands into the pockets of his dungarees. That they were bright red gave him the look of an oversized toddler about to be sent into the garden to run around and burn off some energy. Though he lacked the chubbiness of someone in their early years, no doubt due to his healthy lifestyle and meat-free diet, there was a childish glee to him which was, Charlotte thought, rather addictive. It was impossible to be with the man and not want to do something a bit silly, whether that was climbing a tree, spinning on the spot until dizzy enough to fall over, tumbling down a hill, or skinny-dipping. And of those four things, it was only the skinny-dipping she had avoided. Well, certainly in the company of others, anyway.

Hard to believe he's in his late fifties, Charlotte thought;

Gail must be mad to not want to take him up on the obvious affection he had for her.

'Who's with her?'

Mike took out his phone.

'You're not going to check yours, then?'

Charlotte shook her head.

'Don't want to get sucked into anything, not today.'

'Why not today? Is today special?'

'Not especially, no,' she said, noting a narrowing of Mike's eyes as he looked at her. 'It's just that sometimes, the last thing I want is my time taken up with, you know ...' She waved her hands around in front of her. 'Stuff.'

There was something else though, thought Charlotte. But that wasn't until later, and it wasn't any of Mike's or anyone else's business, was it? Just a private thing she did every year, had done since The Ebb had started, not that those two events were exactly connected.

'I hear you,' said Mike, and standing beside her, pulled up the group chat for The Ebb, the swimming group they were both members of.

Charlotte read Gail's message.

'Oh.'

'You've already said that.'

'I think it was worth saying again. Did Simon really say, *It's just swimming*?'

'I think we can both hear him, can't we?'

Reading Gail's message, Charlotte rather felt for the woman. It was obvious that she had headed to the river for a bit of quiet time, and she fully respected that and understood Gail's frustration. To have it ruined by the arrival of others seemed a real shame. Simon was a weird one for sure, and clearly thought he was God's gift. She'd rebuffed his advances enough herself, and he'd eventually got the message, not least because she'd told him that perhaps that spare dry robe he had would be better given to his actual wife than her. That had certainly made him back off, albeit with a good deal of false laughter and brash dismissal that there was anything at all behind his actions. There was though, Charlotte thought. Not that she would've ever acted on them anyway, and not just because he was married.

'I can't go,' she said. 'Work, I'm afraid.'

'Same,' said Mike.

'You don't work.'

'I have an allotment.'

'That's not work.'

'If you had an allotment, you wouldn't say that. And I'm helping Margaret and Terry with theirs as well. They're a bit clueless about it all.'

'How long have they had it now?'

'Two years. It's mainly weeds. Well, weeds and some kind of mutant crop I think might be part potato, part carrot, and all menace.'

'Sounds delightful.'

Margaret and Terry, deciding to get an allotment between them, had taken everyone by surprise. Neither of them could profess to be a gardener, and nor could their respective partners, for that matter. Though Margaret's husband, Jim, had been very enthusiastic about having another shed to sit outside while drinking beer of an evening. Terry's wife, Elaine, the most prim and proper person Charlotte had ever met, had made it quite clear she would have nothing to do with any digging, planting, sowing, or harvesting. However, she would be very happy to cook whatever produce they managed to grow, which, so far, was nothing at all, not really, anyway. Certainly not enough of anything to throw into one of her fantastic stews.

Charlotte read Gail's message again, then a flurry of other messages pinged into the chat, from Margaret and Terry, and she read a couple of them out loud for Mike.

'Listen to this,' she said, and attempted to do an impression of Terry's voice, which was deep and sonorous, like he was speaking from the far end of a tunnel. '"Simon needs to wind his neck in."'

'That's Terry.'

Then she tried with another voice, this time more feminine and with a sharper edge.

'"It really is about time we had some rules written down,"' she said.

'And that's Marg,' Mike guessed. 'She does love rules.'

'There's more,' Charlotte said, handing Mike his phone back. 'You can read them yourself, though. Terry goes off on one about Simon and his Porsche and how he thinks he can just order everyone around and take over. Marg just says more about rules. Don't think they're very impressed, though. Simon's a right one, isn't he?'

That got a quizzical look from Mike.

'One what?'

'Not sure, but whatever he is, Gail's clearly not happy about what he's doing. Which is such a shame, really, as this was all her idea, wasn't it?'

'It was,' said Mike. 'We owe her a lot. I don't think people realise how grateful they should be.'

Charlotte said nothing for a moment or two, then gave a shrug.

'Nothing we can do about it. The whole point from the off was to just accept people as they are. That's what it's still about, isn't it? We can't just bin people because they don't fit in, especially when we're about everyone fitting in.'

Mike laughed.

'What, even Simon?'

'Yes, even Simon.'

'I do feel for Gail, though,' said Mike.

'Same,' said Charlotte, then watched as Mike dropped a finger to his phone and hit *Call*.

FOUR

No, it isn't *just* swimming, Gail seethed, struggling to hide her annoyance at what Simon had just said, and Paula's resultant, crow-like laugh. She agreed to a point that there were those in the group who took it more seriously than others, and she was probably one of them, but at no point did that mean what they needed was a few clowns turning up with jokes and laughs and whoopee cushions courtesy of the not-so-delightful Simon.

Gail waited for someone, anyone, to say something in response to Simon's throwaway comment, but no one did. She refrained from doing so herself, knowing that arguing with Simon, even disagreeing with him a little, was a waste of what little energy she had. So, with the brief and slightly awkward chat thankfully concluded, she set about getting herself ready to venture into the river.

The water was dark, its surface mirror-like in places, and in others rippled by the dance of the softest of breezes on its surface. The current, though not strong, still provided a tough swim upstream, but then the trip back was little more than a glide. A number of small craft were on the river further up: a couple of kayaks, and a stand-up paddle board.

Gail had never tried either and had no urge to. Kayaks, she thought, looked like the perfect way to drown, because there was just no way she would ever fit in one, she was sure, not with her ample hips. As for SUP boards, she found them to be little more than a blight on the waterways and seas she knew and loved. Simon had one, because of course he did, and he could really go on and on about the damned thing, given the chance, talking about it like it was some kind of adrenaline-fuelled extreme sport, which it most surely wasn't, Gail thought.

Gail couldn't let go of what Simon had said about it being *just swimming*. She failed to see how what was to her, and a good number of others in the group, the deeply spiritual nature of being in the water, could in any way be improved by floating around on it in a bright pair of swimming shorts, but then to each their own. She liked Simon's enthusiasm, but only in small doses, and he was really pushing his luck now with this seemingly open invitation to a bunch of his cronies. She would try very hard once they were in the water to distance herself from him and the others as well.

Gail's phone pinged, and once in her swimsuit, she checked the messages. They'd all replied, and none of them could make it. The question had also been asked of who was there with her, and her answer had received plenty of emojis; face slaps, looks of irritation, one green-faced and ill, and she'd done well to hide her laugh. It was comforting to know she wasn't alone in feeling annoyed by some of the new members. Anyway, The Originals would all be there on

Saturday, so that was something to look forward to. Then the phone rang.

'You okay there, Gail?'

Gail smiled on hearing Mike's voice. He was a gentle soul, and he always listened to her, took her seriously. Fancied her, too, had done for years, but she'd always stayed away from any of that. He wasn't her type, or at least that was what she told herself. They'd had the occasional fumble, and that had been fun, but she didn't want anything more complicated, and that's what relationships were, really, at the end of the day; complicated.

Another voice came on the line: Charlotte, as cheery as ever.

'Sounds like you're having a great time!'

'Could do with you here,' Gail replied, realising then that she was on speaker, and appreciating Charlotte's sense of humour.

'Sounds like it,' said Mike. 'Thought we'd best check-in, though, just in case.'

'What are you two up to?'

'Bumped into each other in town,' said Charlotte. 'I'm off to work. Mike's trying to convince me that going to his allotment counts as the same.'

'Well, it doesn't.'

Mike attempted to protest, but Charlotte talked over him.

'If you're not into it today, you can always just bail. You know that don't you, Gail? There's nothing wrong at all with just packing up and going home. Sometimes it's more sensible, anyway; you don't want to be getting into the water if you're not fully into it.'

'I'm here now, though,' said Gail.

'You're being stubborn,' said Mike.

Gail sighed.

'Just not good with change, that's all,' she said, then added something she'd mentioned a few times before. 'I'm so close to leaving the group. It's not like it used to be, is it?'

Gail heard both Charlotte and Mike gasp.

'You can't leave!' said Mike. 'It was your idea in the first place.'

'You're the *original* Original,' agreed Charlotte. 'You can't go. If you do, we'll all have to leave!'

'I second that!'

A smile curled its careful way across Gail's face.

'Well, it's either him or me!'

'Him!' Charlotte and Mike said in unison.

'But joking aside,' Gail continued, 'it's not the same, is it? The group, I mean. It's not like it used to be, when it was just a few of us.'

Mike's reply was firm.

'No, you're right, it's not. Not sure what to suggest, though; it's not like we can ban people from joining, is it? We're not an official club, really, just a group that seems to keep on growing.'

'It can't just keep growing, though, can it?' said Gail. 'It's like a rosebush that's got out of control; it was beautiful to begin with, but now it needs a really good pruning.'

Charlotte and Mike both laughed at that, and Mike said, 'Love the analogy, one I very much approve of.'

'But we can't just go drowning people just because we don't like them, can we?' added Charlotte.

'It's tempting though, isn't it?' said Gail. 'Anyway, I need to get in the water. I don't want to get caught up with the others splashing around and making all that noise.'

'See you Saturday,' said Charlotte.

'You will,' said Gail, and though she wanted to keep talking, hung up.

Securing her phone in her bright orange, waterproof tow-float, Gail was first in the water.

'It's not a race, you know, Gail!' Izzy had called over to her, and Gail had responded with a laugh and then kicked out strongly to head upriver.

For the next thirty minutes or so, she pushed on, not waiting for anyone to catch her up, happy to be alone in the wide waterway, her only company the numerous water boatmen skimming the surface for food, dragonflies cutting across from bank to bank in zigzag lines, ducks laughing at each other's antics, and a brace of swans gracefully gliding along like lovers lost to time.

Turning around, Gail met the rest of the group coming the other way, exchanged greetings and exclamations about just how wonderful it was to be out in the river, then drifted on back to where she had entered the water. Wading out of the river, she noticed that the light breeze had upped its game, and she was shivering by the time she pulled on her dry robe, her skin covered in goosebumps. Quickly removing her swimsuit, she allowed the robe to do its work and effortlessly dry her with the heat of her own body, as she rummaged around in her bag for the small flask of hot chocolate that she always carried with her when out for a swim. The hot, sweet drink toasted her from the inside, and she smiled to herself as happy in that moment as she had ever been.

By the time the rest of the group had arrived back on the riverbank, Gail was dressed and warm and tucking into a tasty ham and cheese sandwich she'd brought along, just in case she got the munchies. Before she had set off for the river earlier that day, she had thrown a couple of packets of biscuits into her bag, which she now offered around in a moment of mad charity. They were gratefully and greedily received by shivering hands.

Then Simon had bellowed, 'How bloody marvellous!' and she'd turned around to see two men approaching, one a little behind the other, both carrying small rucksacks.

'Who's this, then?' Eric asked, looking at Simon over the nibbled edge of one of Gail's biscuits.

'Rupert!' Simon said and walked over to the men, shaking the first by the hand. 'Thought you couldn't make it, old chap?'

'Change of plan,' the man replied, dropping his bag on the ground in front of him. 'Not too late, I hope?'

'The water looks wonderful,' said the other, stepping away a little from Simon and Rupert, and swinging his bag from his shoulder.

'We've all just got out, but I'm happy to dive back in again,' said Simon. 'Anyone else?'

Gail politely declined. As she left the river to head back to her car, the three men were already venturing into the river, the two new arrivals making more noise than a pair of newlyweds on their wedding night. Not that Gail had any idea at all what that was like, but such was life.

Back at her car, and dropping herself in behind the steering wheel, she threw her bag on the passenger seat and sent a flurry of messages to the group, unable to contain her irritation at the late arrivals. That done, and with the replies of yet more annoyed emojis flashing up on the screen of her phone, she started the engine with a twist of the key and muttered a few choice swear words.

Heading home, she found herself wondering again if perhaps people like Simon, even people like Paula, weren't really right for the group, and how things had been so much better at the beginning. Not that she would do anything about it, because she never did, but really, why did things have to change so?

FIVE

Simon Miller was not a happy man. He had been excited to introduce some more of his kind of people to the swimming group. Now, after the response he'd received from some of the more seasoned members to him inviting some of his golfing friends along, and with the frosty reception Rupert had got that morning, he knew who was to blame: Gail Carpenter.

She was a sneaky one, that Gail, wasn't she? he thought. Quiet, kept herself to herself, but not exactly the most welcoming. A little too full of her own self-importance, and all because she supposedly set up the group in the first place. Left early, too, but not before she'd said just enough to make everyone feel a little awkward.

So-what if she was a founding member of the group? Simon had only been in the group a short time, that was true, but who was she to say who could or couldn't join? Not that she'd said that at all, but she'd implied it, hadn't she, with that pinched look she'd given him at the river when he'd said how he'd invited some friends along? He'd seen her checking her phone as well, no doubt messaging those other founding members, that little exclusive clique, who seemed to regard themselves as gatekeepers.

Thinking about it, Gail wasn't really the worst, was she? Were any of them? He liked Terry, because everyone liked Terry, but he didn't trust him, mainly because he was on the local council. Margaret was just a bit odd, what with her jam-making obsession and the constant chitchat about what was happening at church.

Mike was the unofficial treasurer for the group. Unofficial, because the group wasn't an official group, with a committee or meetings or any of that, though Simon couldn't help thinking that would make things a lot easier. All Mike really did was take money in for things like Christmas parties or swimming trips to the coast.

And finally, there was Charlotte, who he found rather attractive. He'd tried to butter her up with his trademark charm, but that had been shunned, which was a good job, really, because his wife, Maria, hadn't been all that happy about it, had she?

Together, though, that little group has far too much power, he thought, and if he could ruffle a few feathers, then that was no bad thing.

What happened to inclusivity, welcoming everyone, no matter what walk of life? After all, the group was a band of misfits anyway, wasn't it? As far as Simon was concerned, they all needed cheering up a bit, and he'd seen himself as the one to bring that necessary ingredient to their weekly get-togethers. He'd managed to laugh off Gail's grump and encouraged his friends into the water. There had been a lot of howls, a lot of laughter, and they would be coming along on Saturday, too.

Simon had joined the group because his counsellor had advised that cold water therapy might do him good. Retirement really hadn't done him any favours, and the growing sense of being of no use anymore, coupled with the appalling reality that the days left between him and his eventual death were hollow things devoid of meaning, had sent him spiralling. He'd taken himself to see a counsellor as a last-ditch attempt before he lost his mind completely and drove his car into a brick wall.

He'd initially pooh-poohed the notion that cold water would help; who in their right mind would want to ruin their morning with a freezing blast of icy water? But then he'd read up on it, thought it sounded interesting, and given it a go.

Awful, had been his first conclusion, quickly followed by bloody horrific. But for some reason, he'd persevered, perhaps because, after that first cold shower, he had actually felt a little more lift throughout the day. He'd wondered if it was merely a placebo effect, if he was telling himself, subconsciously, that the cold shower had done him good. The only way to find out was to test the theory, so he'd continued with the showers for a week, then another week, before stopping them completely. His mood had plummeted and it was Maria who had noticed first.

Simon listened to Maria, always had done. She was the only person he'd ever met who had the innate ability to have him shut up and hear what she was saying. She cared about him. She loved him. And he loved her, too, in his own way. Which was why nothing would ever happen with Charlotte, because that had never been his intention.

He'd flirted with plenty of women over the years at work, but only ever because it helped him get things done, get what he wanted, and that was just the way things worked, wasn't it? He'd not put up with any of that 'woke' business, that was for sure, which was probably why it was a good thing that he was now retired. Still, Maria had come down on him rather hard about Charlotte, hadn't she? That she was so jealous had actually shocked him. But he'd made it up to her; diamonds really were a girl's best friend. Gold, too.

Simon had never been entirely sure if he was fully in love with Maria, but after thirty-four years of marriage, thankfully without any children to get in the way of things, he knew that he definitely respected her. Love, the stuff that poets went on and on about, was, Simon felt, over-rated, possibly even something people only imagined that they felt. It could not be depended on.

But respect? Generosity? Those he understood, and he had always treated Maria with both, generously seasoning their marriage with plenty of gifts and luxury holidays, as well as a very nice house and a rather full wardrobe. He'd even paid for her membership at that rather exclusive spa and gym, over in Bath, hadn't he, and for that personal trainer? That had certainly been beneficial, what with Maria's body responding rather well indeed to all the exercise. And that had encouraged him to take health and exercise more seriously, too.

When Maria had told him he had grown dark again, and that she was worried he might do something stupid like the last time, Simon had listened. Because *like the last time* covered a multitude of events, one of which had seen him come to in his car, reeking of booze, some three-hundred miles away from home, with no recollection of the journey, or why he had taken it in the first place.

Back under the cold shower he had gone, and seeing the

impact that the water had on him, he decided that he needed to take it further. He purchased an ice bath and a machine to make ice and started using it every morning. At first, it was the most god-awful experience of his life, but he grew used to it, and his days seemed to grow ever brighter. Soon, he found that he wanted more, that sitting in a very expensive, oversized bucket of ice was growing a little tiresome, so he did more research and stumbled on the world of open-water swimming.

Simon had quickly become obsessed. The cold shower was good, the ice bath, even better, but open water? It was all-consuming. He signed up to do a course, because if he was going to do something, then he was going to do it properly. Then he'd bought all the gear: swimming shorts, tow float, the as-yet-unused wetsuit, the little furry mat to stand on when getting dry, a couple of very large microfibre towels, some ludicrously expensive prescription goggles, a thick swimming cap, two dry robes, and a huge waterproof holdall to stuff it all in. He'd topped it all off with the snazzy little roof rack for his Porsche.

As to reason behind having two robes rather than just one—he wanted to be prepared for every eventuality. Like what would he do if he decided to go swimming twice in one day? What then? He certainly wouldn't want to pull on an already damp robe, would he? God, no. And that thought pushed a rather smug smile onto Simon's face, as he grabbed his spare robe, threw it in the holdall with everything else, and marched out of the house to his vehicle. Maria was away for a few nights with some old college pal he'd never heard of, never mind met, staying down near the coast for a little university reunion, so he was going off on a little solo adventure of his own. After the debacle at the river that morning, he didn't feel like he'd got enough out of the swim, so he was going to rectify that. Once that was done, he'd be posting a message on The Ebb's private chat group to say just how disappointed he was with what had happened that morning, and perhaps even suggest a few ways to improve things.

As to his destination? Well, he'd heard mention of the secret little pool before, from one of the original Ebb members, he guessed, though he wasn't entirely sure which one, now that he came to think about it. It was somewhere along the Old Wells Road, which eventually became the Old Frome Road, connecting the two towns by way of a lovely drive through rolling Somerset countryside. So that was where he was heading.

Simon could think of nothing better than a late evening dip somewhere, not only rather secret, but sacred as well, apparently. Tonight was the night to be in such a place it seemed—something to do with the autumn equinox. Not that he was into any of that kind of thing, but it was interesting nonetheless. He hoped that by going late enough in the evening, but not too late, he'd avoid bumping into anyone else popping along to worship the sun and moon. There were bound to be some of those hippy types who would want to throw themselves in at midnight, and he wanted nothing to do with that at all.

Once the dip was done, he would follow it with a good meal and an expensive bottle of wine or two. With Maria being away, there was no reason he could think of that he shouldn't have a bit of a treat.

The drive over to the small parking area, which itself sat about half a mile's walk from the secret pool, went by in a flash, as Simon pushed the Porsche's engine just hard enough to make the trip over the Mendips exciting. He wasn't a fast driver as such, but he did like to experience just enough speed to give him the sensation of being almost on the edge of things without tipping over completely. The car handled like a dream, and when he came to a stop, then climbed out and grabbed his bag from the roof rack, he could feel the smile on his face. His job had certainly allowed him to have some of the finer things in life, hadn't it, so why not enjoy them?

Car locked, Simon pulled out his phone and turned on the torch to navigate his way to a small path. Then, halfway across a field, he left it to head for a narrow ravine hidden from view by skeletal trees. In the distance, he heard a car on the road and hoped it wasn't someone who'd had the same idea about the pool.

The ground was dry, the evening warm, and walking through the trees Simon was overcome by a sense of such extraordinary peace that he almost wished Maria was there to experience it as well. She hadn't joined in with his new obsession, however, saying that she thought it better if he kept it as his thing, because that made it more special. She didn't want to break the spell and ruin it, but she'd been very encouraging, which was nice. Kindly, she always provided him with a little pack-up to take with him swimming: a few sandwiches, some slices of her astonishingly delicious chocolate cake, and a flask of hot chocolate. The hot chocolate would certainly warm him up after the swim. As for the cake ... Well, he'd nibbled on that on the drive over and then ended up finishing it on the walk to the pool. That was mainly because it was not only damned delicious, but it always made him feel better about things. Simon had never really believed that chocolate could influence one's mood, but Maria's cake certainly seemed to. So much so that sometimes he wondered if she laced it with something just to chill him out a bit, though that notion was beyond laughable.

When Simon finally came upon the promised pool, he was rather lost for words. Sitting at the base of a low cliff, around which the trees of the small woodland stood like guardians, the water was deep and clear. The surface was mostly still, except for the faintest of ripples emanating from somewhere close to its centre, directly above its source, Simon guessed, the spring which fed the pool.

He could see how such a place as this was regarded as sacred. By whom, exactly, he had no idea, and didn't really care, but he sensed the deep history of the place and could well imagine, in ancient times, people coming here to pray, or to cleanse themselves in some pagan ritual. As for their modern equivalent, the thought made Simon shudder; he had little time for the kinds of people who got all spiritual about things. Yes, he understood the obvious physical and mental health benefits of immersing himself in cold water, but anything else was poppycock.

No wonder then, he mused as he readied himself for his dip, that so many of those types of people were into such things as having their cards read, and why on Earth did they have to wear those awful clothes, all patchwork and tie-dye? Wouldn't harm them to wash once in a while either, would it?

The swimming group had its fair share of such types, but Simon kept away from them; he had zero interest in discussing after each swim how his aura had been cleansed. This was another reason he believed the group needed new blood, to counteract the influence of that kind of thinking, especially from the more seasoned members.

The pool welcomed Simon with an embrace considerably colder than he had expected, and he let out a bright gasp, which got caught in the trees and came back at him on the edge of a sudden, sharp breeze. He laughed, enjoying the sting of the water on his skin, and as he ventured deeper, the silvery pool's surface burned its way up his body.

By the time he was in the middle of the pool, Simon could no longer touch the bottom, so he floated there a while, adrift to thoughts of nothing at all, then to what he would be eating that evening. That done, he attempted to swim, though the pool was too small to do much more than a couple of strokes before the water was too shallow to go any further. So, he swam in circles for a while, letting the peace of the place, of the water, of the moment, cover him like a blanket. Then, to finish the evening off, he floated on his back for a good while, his eyes closed, just enjoying the peace.

Later, and with the cold just starting to get to him, Simon began to feel a little off. Dizziness crept over him, and as he lay in the water, willing his body to get moving again and push through the stiffness from the cold now upon him, it soon turned to nausea.

Keen to get out of the pool, and a little worried he'd spent too long in its chill embrace, Simon was about to stand up to wade back to dry ground when a splash by his head made him twist around, and gulp a mouthful of water. This didn't help with the nausea. Coughing, he looked up, guessing that something had fallen from a tree, perhaps a small branch, maybe an acorn mishandled by a clumsy squirrel. That thought turned his cough into a laugh, but then the nausea reminded him that perhaps laughter wasn't a good idea.

Still, the thought of a squirrel throwing things at him did seem particularly funny. Funnier than it should be really, he thought, and he started to giggle, then laugh, almost uncontrollably. Why on earth he was finding it so amusing? Simon had no idea, but it certainly wasn't helping with his churning stomach. Then came another splash, just as close, only larger, and this time, Simon had the distinct and disturbing feeling that whatever had caused the splash had been thrown, and not by a squirrel.

'Hello?'

Simon's voice sounded desperately alone, the shape of the place deadening it, stealing it away before it had a chance to be heard.

He called again, this time louder, knowing that he was being absolutely ridiculous, that of course there was no one out there throwing things at him, because why would they, and who would do such a thing anyway? Then something else landed in the water, close enough this time to not only splash him but hit him under the water, and before he knew what he was doing, Simon was racing for the shore.

Another splash broke the surface, this one so violent that Simon felt sure it must have been a boulder somehow dislodged from the small cliff. That wasn't possible though, and he knew it, because he was too far away from the cliff. And how would a boulder leap of its own accord?

Stumbling out of the water as fast as he could, his legs weren't working as they should. It was as though the muscles and bones had been replaced with jelly and rubber, but Simon took no care of where he was placing his feet, so desperate was he to get out of there. In his haste, he stepped on a sharp rock that sent him stumbling back into the water.

He caught himself, but not soon enough, stood on another stone, heard another impact in the pool behind him, and knew he needed to get back to the tree where he had changed. Not that he was going to be doing any of that. God, no, he thought. He was just going to grab everything and get the hell away from whoever else was here, taking potshots at him. He knew that he was being silly, that he was letting his imagination run away with itself, but right then, the rational part of his brain had shut down completely, and animal instinct had taken over. This was fight or flight, and Simon was all about flight.

Close to the water's edge, Simon once again fell, this time hard, and since he was in shallower water, he landed painfully on his knees. Vomit filled his mouth, but he swallowed it back down.

Swearing, he tried to push himself back up to his feet, but the cold of the water had seeped into his bones, and his body wasn't working like it should. Then, as he went to try again, a shadow flashed in the corner of his eyes, and before he had a chance to work out what it was, something hard crashed into the side of his head. The force of it sent him face-first into the water like a puppet with its strings cut.

Momentarily unconscious, Simon was unaware of time passing, of just floating, face down, in the shallows. He was oblivious to being turned over to face the tree canopy above, the touch of a hand at his neck, then more time passing, as his oxygen-starved brain started to shut down. He didn't even sense his body being carefully floated out like a pontoon into the middle of the pool, before being turned face down once again, and for good measure, pushed under.

When Simon did come to, it was already too late. He immediately, and quite understandably, panicked at finding himself pinned to the bottom of the pool by someone with the strength to keep him there. This reaction, in turn, caused him to suck sufficient water into his lungs to hurry along his end rather more quickly than he undoubtedly expected. But he had no time to think about any of that, as the endless darkness came for him, and his life light flickered, then died.

When he was eventually released, Simon stayed where he was. He did not rise gracefully to break the surface in some sad and poetic scene. Instead, he lay on the bottom of the pool, as the trees stared down in sombre silence, and the spring continued to feed that ancient place with cool waters.

SIX

Present Day ...

DETECTIVE INSPECTOR GORDANIAN HAIG was sitting in her car, her right hand on the car door. She was gripping it so tightly that her knuckles were white and the strain was starting to make her forearm ache.

'You'll be fine, it's just an evening, that's all, no pressure, no expectation, Anna would want you to go, so just ...'

Gordy tried to force herself to pull the door handle. She'd managed to unclip her seatbelt, so that was something, and her keys were in her other hand, rather than still in the ignition, so that was progress surely.

'Just ... just do it! Open the damned door, come on! Open it!'

The strain in her arm and hand muscles evolved into a strange heat and she gave the door handle a sharp pull.

The door opened.

Gordy slammed it shut again.

'No, I can't, it's too soon ... I can't go in ... I just can't ...'

For a couple of minutes, Gordy just sat in the dark, staring blankly through the windscreen. It was early evening, her stomach had twisted itself into knots, and all she wanted to do was put the keys in the ignition, fire up the engine, and sod off home. If what she was doing was making her feel this bad, then surely that was a sign? It had to be. She should never have listened to Patti; what did she know, anyway? She was young, considerably more carefree, and was probably a lot more used to evenings like this.

Swearing under her breath, Gordy hammered the heel of her left hand against the steering wheel, swore again, only this time louder, then rammed the key into the ignition and gave it a sharp twist.

The engine burst into life and as she reached up for her seatbelt, she drew back in fright seeing a face staring at her through the window in the door.

'Holy hell!'

Her heart in her mouth, Gordy took a few seconds to calm down, as the face smiled and was then joined by a hand that waved, before it was turned around to rap a knuckle gently against the glass.

Gordy, with the engine on, sent the window down into the door, her heart still thumping hard.

'Hello, Patti,' she said. 'You fair made me jump there.'

'Sorry about that,' Patti replied, though from the glint in the detective constable's eyes, Gordy didn't quite believe the apology.

'What are you doing here, anyway?' she said, 'Or am I better to not ask?'

'A bit of moral support,' smiled Patti. 'Thought I'd sign up for tonight as well, tag along.'

Gordy's eyes went wide.

'What? You can't be serious.'

'It'll be fun, and anyway, it's not like my social calendar is packed with exciting distractions.'

'A date night, though? Is such a thing ever fun? And a speed-dating night at that!'

'Try not to see it as that, then,' said Patti with a shrug that was, to Gordy's eyes, a little too nonchalant. 'Instead, think of it as an opportunity to meet new people, maybe make a new friend or two. Don't see it as any more than that, otherwise you're putting a lot of pressure on yourself, aren't you? All you have to do is just go in and be yourself and keep an open mind.'

Gordy frowned.

'You sound like you've done this before.'

'I'm not an old hand at it, but yes, I have. It's why I suggested it. I'm not about to just send you into something without knowing what it's like, am I?'

'That's very thoughtful. Have you ever had any success at these kinds of things, though?'

Patti winked.

'That would be telling! Now, how about you get yourself out of that car and we head on in?'

Gordy's stomach did a flip, but before it had a chance to do a performance worthy of an Olympic gold medal, she turned off the engine, yanked her key from the ignition, then opened the door and stood beside Patti.

'After you,' she said, heaving the car door shut.

When Gordy had checked out the website for the bar they were heading to, it had described itself as 'small and intimate', which kind of terrified her; there would be no escaping once she was inside, nowhere to hide. It sat down one of the numerous, picturesque, historic streets in the city of Bath. Gordy had popped in a couple of times since moving south from Wensleydale, just to have something to do on a day off, but had found it a little overwhelming, not least because of the many coffee shops and cafés to choose from. She had been impressed with the place though and enjoyed simply soaking up the atmosphere of such an ancient city still so very much alive.

As they walked down the narrow street, she noticed how the evening light suited the architecture, made it seem almost cosy, if that was at all possible. There were plenty of people strolling around, and their excited conversations tumbled through the air, mingling with each other and with the sounds of a city come to life as it embraced the night.

'Actually, in answer to your last question, I met Jonathan at an event exactly like this,' said Patti, as they came up to the door of the bar. 'Lovely bloke, you'd like him, everybody does. But it was probably a bit soon for me, really, as I'd only just broken up with Maddie.'

Gordy hesitated at the door, Patti's words starting a fire in her mind.

'That's exactly how I feel right now,' she said. 'That this is a wee bit too soon, after Anna's death. I didn't know you had a boyfriend.'

'I don't,' said Patti. 'Nothing happened. We just got on really well, but I realised I wasn't ready for anything, and we just sort of ended up keeping in touch. Which is kind of what I'm saying, isn't it, about just taking this as it comes, and not getting stressed about it? He's a really good Salsa dancer as well, is Jonathan. He invited me to an evening to give it a go. Had an absolute blast!' Patti rested a hand on Gordy's forearm and added, 'You should absolutely come along with me to that sometime. You'd love it, Gordy, I promise!'

That suggestion made Gordy laugh out loud.

'I'll no' be doing that,' she said. 'I can't dance.'

'Everyone can dance.'

'Not me.'

'Trust me.'

'No, you trust me,' said Gordy. 'I learned Scottish dancing as a child at school and spent most of my time tripping over myself. Thankfully, I never progressed enough to do any of the sword dances.'

Patti's chuckle at that was bright and clear and Gordy found that she was grateful that she had joined her.

'Well, we'll just see, shall we?'

'You've got me to a date night,' said Gordy. 'Don't push your luck.'

Patti reached out and put her hand beside Gordy's on the door and gave it a push.

Once inside, Gordy had to really focus to force her stomach to not do flips and twists again. She wanted to run but now that she was inside with Patti, her surprise chaperone, she knew she could do nothing of the sort. The bar was already rather full, and seeing so many faces gave Gordy an odd sense of claustrophobia, like the walls were closing in around her. She did her best to stay calm, focusing on her breathing for a moment, and the sensation eased a little, but not entirely, as though the walls were holding off for now, but at any moment could come rushing in.

A woman at the bar waved them over, took their names and contact details, and ticked them off a list on a clipboard she was holding. She then handed them each a card, a small pencil, and a sticker with their name on it.

Gordy looked at the card to see that it was printed with getting on for twenty names.

'Now, have you ever been to an event like this before?' the woman asked, smiling at them both with the brightest teeth Gordy had ever seen.

'I have, but Gordy hasn't,' said Patti. 'I've told her not to worry, though, there's no pressure, is there?'

The woman's smile grew wider, and Gordy could see that it was genuine.

'None whatsoever; there is nothing to worry about at all,' she said. 'Everyone's in the same boat, aren't they? It's very simple, really.'

Gordy held up the card and pencil.

'Is this everyone here?'

'Exactly that, though not everyone is here quite yet. When they are, and we get the thing started, I'll gather everyone together, do a quick welcome, then ring this.' She pointed at a bright red hand bell, which immediately took Gordy back to her one true love, Anna; her church in the Dales had had a small bell-ringing group, and Gordy had, once or twice, gone along to give it a go. The memory squeezed her heart tight enough to make her gasp, and both Patti and the woman glanced at her, concerned.

'It's okay,' the woman said, reaching out to Gordy with a caring touch of her hand. 'You're allowed to be a little nervous. But I promise you, you'll be fine.'

'What happens when you ring the bell?' Gordy asked.

'You spend five minutes having a chat with someone on the list, that's it. Then I'll ring the bell again, every five minutes or so, and you just move on, until you've spoken with everyone here.'

'Five minutes isn't very long,' said Gordy. 'And why the pencil?'

'No, it's not long, is it?' the woman agreed. 'But we've all had those awkward dates where we're sat having a meal with someone who, after five minutes, we have nothing in common with, or no interest in, haven't we? This hopefully goes some way to help avoid that. Which brings me to the pencil. Basically, if you like the person you've spoken with, you put a tick next to their name. At the end of the night, I'll gather all the cards, and if there's a mutual match, I can provide the contact information to both parties, and then it's down to you.'

'What do you think?' asked Patti.

Gordy looked at the list of names, then across to the people milling around in the bar. She thought of Anna, and wondered what she would say about what she was doing now. Despite the pain that came with the memory of her face, she could see it smiling encouragingly.

'I think,' Gordy said, 'that I need a drink.' And with that, she marched over to the bar.

SEVEN

The first two speed dates were, in Gordy's mind, a total disaster. The first one, because she was so nervous, she overcompensated a little and hadn't given the other woman a chance to get a word in edgeways. When the bell had rung, bringing it to an end, she had apologised profusely, and even suggested they should meet up after the event and try again. The other woman had smiled, and walked away, as firm a no as Gordy could've expected.

As for the second, well, that went no better, but for exactly the opposite reason. Instead of talking too much, she said hardly a word, and the pauses between them both talking had become so pregnant that they had birthed an awkwardness so stark it had made Gordy's skin crawl.

To her relief, the third date was considerably better, and by the sixth, she was on a roll. Not that any of those she had met with so far had caught her eye and mind enough to consider placing a tick next to their name, but at least she wasn't feeling the urge to sprint out of the bar and drive home.

She wondered if driving had been a good idea, that maybe she should've made use of public transport; one drink to get her going was fine, but she knew that one or two more would certainly have helped with her confidence. Still, getting from the little village of Evercreech all the way to Bath by bus, train, or both, and probably with a taxi ride thrown in as well, would have undoubtedly made the evening logistically impossible. Instead of alcohol, she would have to rely on her own charm. Though what that actually was, she had long forgotten.

Moving onto her ninth date, Gordy caught sight of Patti, who gave a quick thumbs up. Gordy smiled back, turned that smile round in greeting to the next person she was to talk to, and introduced herself.

'You're from Scotland, then?' the other woman said. Then she hurriedly added, 'Oh, God, what a stupid thing to say. I'm sorry, I'm not used to this at all. Oh, and I'm Charlie, by the way, just so you have a name that you can immediately forget.'

Charlie, Gordy guessed, was somewhere in her forties, though where, exactly, it was hard to tell, thanks in part to the low lighting in the bar, but also how she seemed to mix the wide-eyed innocence of someone in their twenties with just enough wrinkles here and there to betray that more years had passed. She had bright eyes, a wide smile, and her wavy, black hair was cut in a shortish bob. She was dressed much like Gordy herself, in denim and a loose top and jacket, but wore considerably more jewellery around her wrists and neck, with more hanging from her ears. Gordy wore no jewellery at all, never had.

Gordy introduced herself, going with the shortened version of her name, and held out a hand for Charlie to shake, only to have Charlie lean in and offer the quickest of air kisses by her cheek.

'Sorry, I've no idea why I just did that,' Charlie said, leaning back with the faintest of giggles. 'I've not done that with any of the others. What the hell is wrong with me? I should go home.'

Gordy laughed.

'Please don't,' she said. 'You're the first person to make me laugh tonight, and I kind of feel I need it.'

Charlie visibly relaxed.

'You're feeling it too, then?' she asked, then clenched her fists and did a little shake. 'That awkwardness? I don't know why I thought this was a good idea.'

'Well, it's not exactly easy to meet people when you get a bit older, is it?' said Gordy. 'Not the right ones, anyway.'

'That's so true,' Charlie replied. 'I've not dated anyone for nearly two years. Don't know what I'm more afraid of; getting my heart broken again, or just the awful awkward ickiness of the whole thing.'

'Like tonight, you mean?'

'Worse, actually. The last date I went on was in a pub. Not just any pub, either; turned out the person I was meeting was a close, personal friend of the owner. They'd cleared an area of the restaurant area for us to be alone. There were flowers on the table, romantic music, and for the whole two hours everyone in the place, all of them locals, just stared at us.'

'That sounds horrific.'

'It was.'

'Why are you in Somerset, then?' Charlie asked.

'Work brought me here,' answered Gordy.

'Really? I ended up here for the same reason. I'd been

made redundant, found a new job, but it was nowhere near where I lived at the time. Had no choice but to pile everything in a van, up sticks, and move.'

'Where did you live before?'

'Margate. Couldn't exactly commute from there, so I had to move.'

'You been here long, then?' Gordy asked.

'Nine years. No idea where they've gone. Wouldn't mind finding them and getting them back and maybe giving some of them another go, if you know what I mean? What about yourself?'

'Same, really,' said Gordy. 'Haven't been here so long, though; just over six months, I think.'

'And how are you finding it? Somerset, I mean.'

'It's okay. I've no' been here long enough to judge.'

The first moment of silence pushed its way into the conversation, but it wasn't given long to hang around, as Charlie said, 'I'm a librarian, by the way, you know, books, that kind of thing?'

Gordy's eyes went wide at this.

'You are? I love books!'

The look Charlie gave Gordy told her that she wasn't entirely convinced.

'I'm serious,' Gordy continued. 'My perfect evening is to sit in front of a fire, underneath a blanket, and to just read, maybe punctuate the page turns with a sip of wine. Pity I don't have a fire, but there we are. You can't have everything, can you?'

Gordy saw Charlie's eyes widen, and she felt as though she'd said too much.

'That does sound like Heaven,' Charlie said, much to Gordy's relief. 'What is it you do yourself, then?'

So far that evening, Gordy had managed to keep her job to herself, none of the conversations having had the chance to reveal that little detail. Not that she was embarrassed about it. Quite the opposite, actually, but she knew that it could make some people feel awkward.

'I'm a police officer,' she said. 'Detective Inspector, if you want to know my official title, which I'm sure you don't, but there it is. Sounds grander than it is.'

'You're not!'

'Is it that hard to believe?'

Charlie smiled.

'Sorry, no, that's not what I meant; I wanted to join the police, many years ago.'

'What stopped you?' Gordy asked and saw a faint look of concern flash in Charlie's eyes. 'Actually, that's far too personal a question for right now, isn't it? Forget I asked.'

'Anxiety,' Charlie said. 'I'm not very good with stress. Being a librarian suits my personality a little better than chasing down criminals.'

'And that's literally all I do, you know,' Gordy said. 'I'm constantly dashing through streets and alleyways, jumping over car bonnets, crashing through doors, just to bag me another bad guy.'

'Just like in the movies?'

'Exactly like in the movies.'

'How exciting! The worst I have to deal with is tracking down late returns and trying to get people to pay a fine here and there.'

Gordy gave it a second or two, then laughed.

'If only,' she said, 'though I'm rather glad my life isn't like that. Sounds exhausting, doesn't it?'

The bell rang.

'Oh, that's us, then,' said Charlie. 'Lovely to chat. Hope the rest of the evening goes well for you.'

She went to turn away, then stopped, before reaching out a hand, which Gordy shook willingly.

'And you,' Gordy said.

Watching Charlie move on to her next date, Gordy put a tick on the card next to her name. The evening, it seemed, had taken a turn for the better, and she approached her next date with a genuine smile on her face.

When the last date came to an end, Gordy handed in her card and met Patti at the bar.

'How did it go, then?' she asked. 'Any luck?'

'Don't know yet, do we?' said Patti. 'Got to wait to see if our cards match with anyone else's, haven't we?'

'You found someone you'd like to meet again, then?'

'A couple. What about yourself?'

Before Gordy could answer, the woman who organised the event came over and spoke with Patti first to confirm if she would be happy to exchange contact details with the two women she had matched with. Patti said yes, and Gordy was sure that the woman was then going to turn away and go speak to someone else in the room, but to her surprise, she looked at her and smiled.

'You have a match as well,' she said.

'I do?'

'Don't sound so surprised!'

'But I am surprised,' Gordy replied.

'You happy to share your contact details?'

'Who was it?' Gordy asked, remembering that she had put a tick next to three names, though of those, really there was only one she was interested in.

'This one,' the woman said, and pointed to the name on the card.

Gordy beamed, and as she did so, caught sight of Charlie who was standing on her own near the door staring at her phone.

Charlie looked up and Gordy caught her eye. To her delight, Charlie smiled, then lifted a hand and gave a wiggly fingered wave, before leaving the bar.

'Well?' the woman asked.

Gordy's reply came without any hesitation.

'Absolutely,' she said. 'One hundred percent, yes.'

Giving no consideration as to whether she was acting too quickly and thus coming across far too keen, she quickly sent a text message to the number she'd been given.

The woman moved on, and a reply to Gordy's message pinged its arrival on her phone a minute later.

'A successful evening, then?' Patti asked, as Gordy read the message.

'Yes,' said Gordy, and to her own surprise, felt her stomach do the very smallest of flips.

EIGHT

Detective Constable Peter Knight had arrived at the police station in Frome, his head considerably colder than it had been when he'd first left his house that morning. But that served him right for deciding at the last minute to change his hairstyle.

Instead of the usual spiked affair he sported, which made him look rather like he was wearing an angry sea urchin on his head, he'd decided to get the whole lot buzz cut at the barber's the previous evening. The resulting lack of insulation for his head had made him shiver as he'd left the barbers to go grab some fish and chips for dinner, and he'd headed home as quickly as possible, to shower off all the clippings, and to find a hat.

The rest of the morning had been spent round at his dad's, helping him with jobs around the house, and a weekly shop. His dad, as always, attempted to protest, but living alone, and with his health as bad as it was, there wasn't much of a fight he could put up. Pride forced him to try, though, but Pete was used to it, and the grumbles bounced off him like corks from a popgun.

After a quick lunch of toast topped with eggs from the three huge hens his dad kept in the garden, Pete had left the house with the usual feeling of guilt, but also of sadness. He worried about his dad more than he would ever admit, but then who else was there to look after him? His mum, who was twenty-five years younger than his septuagenarian dad, was happily re-married, and neither of them had spoken in the five years since the divorce. There were no siblings to count on, with both Pete and his dad being only children. As for friends, Pete's dad had a few, but they were mainly from his days in the merchant navy and they now lived all over the world; he knew of few who lived close by, but he had little interest in getting to know them beyond a polite, 'Good morning,' should he ever bump into them.

Pushing through the door, Pete strolled into the reception area of The Hut to find Vivek, the receptionist, staring at him.

'Have a fright, did you?' Vivek asked.

'What?'

'Your hair,' Vivek clarified. 'Something must have scared the hell out of you to have that happen.'

Pete rubbed a hand over his scalp, enjoying the fuzzy sensation against his palm.

'I did this by choice, Vivek.'

'By which you mean for charity, yes? Or as a dare? Which one was it?'

'Neither.'

Vivek laughed.

'Suits you. Better than all that, you know ...'

He mimed messing up his own hair, then turned his hands upside down, his fingers all pointing upwards.

Pete frowned.

'It didn't look anything like that.'

'You'll save a fortune in hair product,' said Vivek.

'Who's in?' Pete asked.

'Just Helen. She's just taken a call, so you'll be able to sneak in without her noticing.'

'Oh, she'll notice alright,' said Pete, and made for the stairs. 'Nothing gets past Helen.'

'True enough. Patti is out and about, and Gordy's off-duty for a couple of days, isn't she? So Patti's running things. I'll bring you a coffee up in a few minutes if you fancy?'

Pete hesitated.

'Any, er, baked products at all?' he asked, unable to hide his overly keen tone. 'Only it's gone midday, and the lunch I had with my dad wasn't exactly huge ...'

'How's he doing?' Vivek asked.

Pete gave a shrug.

'He'd be better off if he let people other than his only son help him out, but he won't be told, and he won't listen even when he is.'

'It's difficult, I'm sure,' Vivek said, and Pete heard the understanding in the man's voice. 'As for baked goods, I've got some veggie sausage rolls.'

Pete screwed up his face.

'Veggie sausage rolls?'

'Trust me, you'll love them.'

Pete headed upstairs, pushed through the main doors into the office, then made his way over to his desk.

'What the bloody hell happened to your head?'

Helen Kendrick's loudly pronounced question shot

across the office with such force that it nearly knocked Pete off his feet.

'Nothing happened to my head,' he replied, turning around to glare at the PCSO. 'As I explained to Vivek, I did this by choice.'

'No one does that by choice.'

Pete dropped into his chair.

'I like it.'

'Someone has to, and who better than you?'

Pete could think of no witty retort, and was glad to hear Vivek push through the door. He turned to watch him walk over.

'Here you go,' Vivek said, presenting both Pete and Helen with mugs of fresh coffee, and a small plate on which rested a couple of tasty-looking treats.

'I've already had one of those,' said Helen.

'Then you must have another,' said Vivek.

Helen laughed.

'You're a feeder.'

Pete sipped his coffee, then bit into one of the veggie sausage rolls.

'Crikey, Vivek,' he said, 'that's delicious.'

'Told you,' Vivek winked, then turned on his heel and left the office.

'You'll be wanting to hurry that up,' Helen said, as Pete tucked in. 'Just took a call about a Mr Simon Miller. Missing apparently, so we need to go and speak to his wife. I was just about to pack up and head out when you arrived wearing that fuzz for hair, so I was immediately distracted.'

Pete stuffed the rest of the veggie sausage roll into his mouth.

'You want the other?' he asked, pointing at it.

Helen shook her head, then stood up.

'You can eat it on the go,' she said. 'Bring your coffee as well; you've got a travel mug, right?'

'In the kitchen downstairs, yes,' said Pete.

A few minutes later, his coffee decanted into a travel mug, and a few crumbs still clinging to his uniform, Pete followed Helen outside and over to one of the vehicles.

'Where are we heading, then?' he asked.

'Mells,' said Helen.

Pete raised his eyebrows at that.

'Ooh, posh,' he said.

Mells was a small village a few miles outside of Frome. It comprised, in the main, large, expensive houses, even larger manor houses, a few thatched cottages, and various other dwellings, the not-so-grand ones sitting back from the main lanes the others occupied. It had a village shop and café, a good pub, and the surrounding fields and footpaths were popular with dog walkers. Pete though, only ever went there to eat the pizzas at the Walled Garden, a pretty little haven that during the summer months was responsible for him eating out a little more frequently than he would ever dare to admit, even to himself.

Arriving in the village, Helen turned left, opposite the shop, hopped over the bridge, round a sharp bend, then pulled left into a driveway. The house at the end of it was as perfect a looking cottage as could be, Pete thought, and just the kind of place he very much doubted he would ever be able to afford.

Climbing out of the car, Pete followed Helen over to the front door. She'd given him the scant details on their journey over; Simon Miller was missing, though for how many days they weren't sure, as his wife, Maria, had been away with friends, and they'd not been in touch.

Helen rang the doorbell.

'Ready?' she asked.

'I'm never anything else,' Pete replied, just as a scream came from inside the house.

NINE

Helen hammered her fist against the door.

'Maria, this is the police!'

The scream came again.

Pete joined in with Helen and they both thumped their fists against the door.

'Maria, you need to let us in! Maria!'

'I'll go round the back,' Pete said, and with a quick look left, then right, spotted a path and followed it.

Around the back of the house, which sat comfortably in the embrace of a neat, well-tended garden, Pete spotted a tri-fold door standing open. He ran towards it, stepped into the house, called for Maria, and heard Helen do the same.

Another scream.

With little idea as to what he was going to find, his mind gifting him too many options, none of them pleasant, Pete raced through the house to where the scream had come from.

He crashed through a door and found himself in a small, cosy lounge. Curled up on the floor was a woman, her face in her hands.

She screamed again.

When Pete spoke, he did everything he could to keep his voice calm.

'Maria? I'm Detective Constable Peter Knight. I'm here to help.'

Helen called from the front of the house.

'I've got her,' Pete called back. 'Come round the back of the house; there's a door open.'

While Helen made her way around, Pete focused on Maria. He could see nothing around her, nothing in the room, which would have caused her to scream. And though she was curled up on the floor, foetal almost, he couldn't rightly see that anything physical had happened to her either. So, just what the hell had caused her to scream like that?

Pete dropped to his heels.

'Maria?'

He waited.

Maria started to shake, and Pete heard sobbing.

'Maria, I'm here to help. I'm a police officer. You're safe. But I do need to make sure you're okay, that you're not hurt. Can you help me do that?'

Helen jogged into the room.

'What happened?'

'No idea,' Pete replied, not turning to look at the new arrival. 'Found her like this.'

Helen snapped around to look back through into the hall.

'Is there someone else here?'

'I didn't see anyone,' said Pete. 'I came straight in here.'

'I'll check …'

Before Pete could call her back, Helen dashed out of the room, returning a minute or two later. 'No one here but us.'

She dropped down beside Pete.

'Maria? I'm PCSO Helen Kendrick. We spoke earlier, about your husband, remember? You called to tell us that—'

Maria shuddered, then snapped her head around to stare at Pete and Helen. Her eyes were so wide that Pete thought they looked like cue balls on a pool table.

'Maria?' Helen repeated, then she reached out and rested a hand, ever so gently, on Maria's leg. 'You screamed. What happened? Was someone here? Did you fall?'

Maria continued to stare, first at Helen, then Pete, then back at Helen again. She tried to sit up, but her arms gave way, so Pete and Helen joined forces, first to make sure she was okay, then to help her off the floor and into a comfy-looking armchair.

'I'll go make some tea,' Pete suggested, making his way to the lounge door. 'You'll be okay?'

'I'm good,' Helen replied, and Pete was out of the door and through the house, remembering then that the doors he had entered opened into the kitchen.

Waiting for the kettle to boil, Pete allowed his eyes to wander around the room. This was a neat house, a tidy house, with nothing out of place. And the things which were in place, well, they weren't cheap, that was for sure. Not overly expensive either, but certainly pricier than the norm.

The fridge caught Pete's attention, and heading over to it to find some milk, he examined a neat array of photographs pinned to it with small, circular magnets. They showed Maria and a man, who he assumed to be her husband, in various locations, all of them abroad. They were smiling in the photographs; happy, he thought.

The kettle boiled. Pete found tea bags, a teapot, three

mugs, and soon enough, had a tray to take through to the lounge.

Arriving back in the room, he found Maria still sitting in the armchair, with Helen beside her on the sofa. The look Helen gave him was somewhat baffling, her eyes briefly very wide, a slight downturn of her mouth, and the shallowest of shrugs.

Pete set the tray down on a small table, poured everyone some tea, then handed them out.

'Thank you,' Maria said.

They were the first words Pete had heard the woman say since arriving at the house, a scream not really counting as such, he decided, as he sat himself down beside Helen.

'How are we doing?' he asked.

Maria sipped her tea and said nothing.

'Good tea,' said Helen.

'Well, there are few things worse than a bad mug of tea,' said Pete, feeling somewhat constrained by the small talk, which he'd never been very good at.

The three of them sipped their tea in silence for a moment or two, then, at last, Maria spoke once again.

'I'm sorry,' she said. 'I don't really know what came over me.'

'Maybe you can just start from the beginning?' Helen suggested. 'From when you called about your husband?'

Pete took out his notebook. Helen did the same.

Maria rested her mug on her knees, both hands clamped around it, like she was afraid that if she let go, it might spin off across the room to smash into a wall.

'I've been away,' Maria said, a nervous smile barely allowing her voice out of her mouth. 'Reunion with an old university friend. I saw Simon a few days ago, just before I left. When I came back, his car, well, it wasn't in the garage, was it? I tried to call him, but there was no answer. I'm probably being silly, but it's not like him at all, to go off, I mean.'

'How many days exactly?' asked Pete.

'Since I saw Simon?'

'Yes.'

Maria fell quiet again, looked thoughtful, then said, 'Three. I saw him in the morning, then later that day, in the afternoon, before I went away, just to say goodbye. He was heading off to go swimming in the river at Bradford-on-Avon. Don't ask me why, I've never understood it. But that's Simon; he gets into things, you see? Becomes a little obsessed.'

'Do you know where, exactly?' Helen asked.

Maria shook her head.

'I think Simon was meeting up with some of the people from this swimming group or club that he's joined, The Ebb I think they're called. He's not been with them very long, really, maybe three months? Feels like longer, though, with the amount of time he spends talking about it.'

'Do you know how we can get in touch with anyone in this group?'

'There's a card on a notice board in the hallway. A couple of them provide lessons, to help people get into outdoor swimming or wild swimming or whatever it is they call it. Can't see the attraction myself; if I go swimming, I want warm water and a nice shower to hand, not the potential threat of being poisoned by whatever pollutants are in the rivers, hypothermia, and the possibility of being attacked by an angry swan.'

'Not a fan, then?' said Helen.

Maria shook her head.

'Simon is, though. But like I said, he does get obsessed

with things very quickly, evangelical, if you know what I mean? I tune out after a while, but it's who he is, and I'm used to it. I'd rather this than his last obsession.'

'And what was that?' Pete asked, before he could stop himself.

'Model aeroplanes. Filled the garage with them. And before that, it was judo. And before that, squash.'

'That's a lot of hobbies.'

'And that's only in the last couple of years,' Maria sighed. 'He's very good at getting into something, by which I mean really, really into something, then before you know it, he's onto something else.'

Helen said, 'Sounds exhausting.'

'He club hops,' Maria continued. 'Turns up all interested. Suddenly he's on this or that committee, running things, then he's pissed everyone off, and he leaves. He's a funny bugger, really.'

'Did you speak to your husband while you were away?' Pete asked.

Maria shook her head.

'We're not really a couple that misses each other,' she said. 'We're not into calling each other a lot, sending text messages, that kind of thing.'

'So, you saw him three days ago, and that was the last time you spoke or had any contact at all?'

Maria hesitated at this question, and Pete noticed her pale a little.

'Maria?'

No answer.

'Maria ...'

'Pardon?'

Pete glanced over at Helen, who had also noticed that Maria was acting off again.

'The last time you spoke with your husband,' Helen prompted.

'Was when I last saw him, before I went away,' Maria nodded, composed again, though Pete could tell she was still a little on edge.

'Are you able to give us the details of where you were, and who you were with?' he asked.

'Really? Why? They won't know where Simon is either.'

'It's just to confirm what you're telling us, that's all,' said Helen. 'You know how the police like detail.'

'No, I don't,' Maria replied. 'I've never dealt with the police in my life, not even a speeding ticket. This is all very new to me.'

Helen asked, 'Do you know if your husband took anything with him?'

'What? How do you mean? He went swimming. What else would he take other than a towel and whatever he was going to wear while in the water?'

Pete could see a flicker of confusion in Maria's eyes at that question.

'You said he headed off to go swimming; do you think he could have gone somewhere else, perhaps?'

'Like where?'

'Maybe he has a favourite pub or something?' Pete suggested.

Maria laughed at that.

'Simon isn't one for pubs, not really. He thinks he is, but only certain types of pubs, if you know what I mean.'

'Not really, no,' said Pete.

'They need to be of a certain standard,' explained Maria.

'He checks their websites, the reviews, only likes the kind of pub that serves very expensive food to people who aren't going to complain about the cost.'

'Posh pubs, you mean?'

'Posh pubs, nice hotels, but never your more honest pub, if that makes sense. Half the reason we live in Mells is because he approves of the pub.'

'Any hotels spring to mind?' Helen asked. 'Maybe, with you away, he decided on a last-minute trip himself.'

Maria shook her head.

'That's not like Simon at all,' she said. 'He never goes away on his own. Well, he used to, with work, but not since he retired.'

'So, there's no hotel or anything that springs to mind? We're just trying to cover every avenue. If there's a chance Simon has gone away somewhere ...'

'Without telling me? Why would he do that?'

Neither Pete nor Helen said anything.

'Simon likes to go abroad,' Maria said. 'He likes us to take trips, holidays, have proper time away, that kind of thing. He's not a fan of just a night here or there, a quick break. It always has to be something grand. In fact, the only hotel I know that he's ever been to for a short stay is the one he booked us into for our wedding night, and that was decades ago, obviously.'

'And which hotel was that?'

'The Swan, it's over in Wells,' Maria said.

Helen took out her phone and pulled up the details for the hotel.

'Looks nice,' she said, and stood up. 'It's a long shot, I know, but I'll give them a call. At least it's somewhere to start, isn't it?'

Maria shook her head.

'He won't have gone there,' she said. 'Why would he? There's no reason for him to.'

Helen walked out into the hall. When she returned, she popped her head around the lounge door and gave Pete a nod, beckoning him to join her out in the hallway.

Leaving Maria alone for a minute, Pete joined Helen.

'Is there a problem?'

'The Swan Hotel. Simon was booked in to stay there three nights ago.'

'And?'

'And he didn't.'

'Didn't what?'

'Stay there. They've not seen or heard from him. Room was paid for in advance on his credit card, so they didn't think anything of it, just took the money and assumed there must've been a reason for him doing a no-show.'

'So, where the hell is he, then?'

Helen gave a shrug.

Pete led the way back into the other room to find Maria pushed back into her chair, her eyes wide with terror. Her hands were clamped hard onto the seat, her knuckles white.

'Maria?'

Maria didn't move, but her eyes did, focusing on Pete and Helen. She opened her mouth to speak, but no words came out.

Pete and Helen walked over, and Helen sat beside Maria, reaching out for her hand.

'Maria? What's wrong?' she asked.

Maria's mouth seemed to quiver, then at last, words tumbled out, as though dazed and confused by what they were trying to say.

'When ... when you asked earlier, if the last time I saw him was before I went away ...'

'And you said that it was,' said Pete.

Maria shook her head, and the strangest of smiles slipped across her face, a nervous thing, terrified to be there at all.

'That's ... Well, it's not quite true.'

At this, Helen said, 'You mean you've seen Simon since then? When, Maria? When did you see him?'

Maria was still shaking her head. Her nervous smile was becoming gradually more disturbing, Pete thought.

'Maria,' Pete said, 'Simon booked to stay at The Swan Hotel three nights ago. We've checked, and he never turned up. If you know something that might help us find him, you need to tell us.'

Maria lifted her arm and pointed a shaky finger into the middle of the room.

'There.'

Pete looked to where Maria was pointing, saw Helen do the same, but couldn't work out what she was trying to show them.

'What's there, Maria? What are you trying to show us?'

Then, once again, Maria screamed, only this time, instead of just a sound, it was a word: 'SIMON!'

TEN

A whole day had passed since the evening spent speed dating in the bar. Not wanting to come across as too keen, Gordy had stayed away from messaging Charlie. She was also nervous, and not simply from the expected butterflies of rather fancying someone. She was also deeply unsure as to her own readiness for even dipping a tentative toe into the world of relationships again. Her mind was doing somersaults, one moment telling her she was a fool to even consider it, the next pushing her to understand that life was short and that ignoring an open door was never a good thing.

Instead, she'd put Charlie's number in her phone, done her best to forget about it all for a while, and got on with the normal things everyday life comprised. Most of that was normal police work in the station in Frome, leading the team on various cases, initiatives, and mountainous piles of paperwork. Things had been quiet of late, and that was no bad thing, she thought. They'd dealt with a few break-ins, a disturbance of the peace, and were currently taken up with a good bit of community work in the local schools, and various other bits and bobs, including the reporting of a missing person, a Mr Simon Miller, which had come in as she'd headed home, having done an early shift. She'd left it with Patti to deal with, as the following day she was off duty, and she had been looking forward to it very much indeed. She certainly didn't fancy getting caught up in anything she didn't need to. And a MISPER was a simple thing to deal with, so she felt sure that there would be no problems. If there were, she felt confident they wouldn't be big enough to get in the way of a good bit of simple relaxing.

Beyond all that, Gordy had her life over in Evercreech, and although the village had welcomed her, she found the place increasingly troubling. Even if she managed to ignore a recent case involving members of a particularly extreme cult, all of whom had been hiding in plain sight in the local church of all places, what she couldn't ignore was how, no matter where she went, the place echoed with the absence of Anna.

Gordy had done her best to just get on with her life, to learn to live again, and for a while, she'd done okay. She had a lovely little flat, a decent pub only a walk away, and she was already well-known enough to be able to stop for a chat on the street with various locals.

Something was off, though, and she knew that deep down. What to do about it was the issue. Moving again seemed somewhat out of the question, because that had been stressful enough. She hadn't just moved house, though, had she? She'd moved from the North of England to the Southwest, started over, really, and under circumstances that she now realised she'd never really given enough weight to. Instead, she had just got on with things somewhat bullishly, pushing on with little if any regard for her mental well-being. Her broken heart was the one constant through it all, but as healed as it now was, the wounds had still not become scars, which would fade in time. Instead, Gordy was starting to wonder if by staying where she was, all she was doing was constantly picking at the scabs as those wounds did their best to repair. Or was she over-thinking it? Did she just need to knuckle down and get on with things? All of it was harder than she would ever admit, but something inside was giving her a sense that if she didn't do something soon, her already fragile recovery might be smashed to pieces.

With all this running through her mind, Gordy had been distracted enough that evening to answer her phone without first checking who the caller was.

'Oh, you're in! I didn't expect you to answer, actually, and now I ... er ... Oh, God, I'm rambling ... Not thought this through at all. No, I mean, I have, it's just that ...'

The voice on the end of the line died and was replaced by the faint sound of breathing.

'Charlie?'

'Yes?'

Gordy didn't know what to say next, so went with something simple. 'How are you?'

'Me? I'm good,' Charlie replied. 'Yourself?'

An honest answer was probably not for the best, so Gordy said, 'Oh, you know, busy with work, that kind of thing.'

'Of course, yes, I'm sure.'

For a moment, neither spoke.

'It's ... it's good to hear from you,' Gordy ventured at last. 'Sorry, I had been meaning to call, but I wasn't sure what to say, and ...'

'Same,' Charlie said. 'I'm not good at this.'

'I don't think anyone is.'

Another moment of silence, then Charlie said, 'I was just wondering, you know, if you were interested that is, and I'll completely understand if you're not, I mean, it's fine, really, but—'

'I'd love to meet up,' Gordy said, before she'd really had a chance to think about the repercussions of such an admission.

'You would? Really?'

Gordy heard the surprise in Charlie's voice and laughed.

'Yes, I would,' Gordy said, reinforcing the point. 'Anything you fancy doing?'

'Actually, yes,' Charlie said, firing back quickly. 'Would you fancy doing an escape room?'

Gordy had never done an escape room, and she had never had any interest in doing one, either. She'd spent her working life dealing with criminals and having a hand in rooms they were very much not supposed to escape from, so such an activity had always felt a little bit too close to home.

'That would be fun,' she said, doing her best to hide the lie behind a smile that Charlie couldn't see.

'You would? Really? I wasn't sure, but I just thought it might be fun to do something a bit out of the ordinary, you know? Something that isn't sitting in a bar or a restaurant and hoping that the conversation doesn't get all awkward.'

'I think it's a great idea,' said Gordy, even though she was fairly sure that it wasn't. But then, if she'd never actually done an escape room, how could she judge, really?

'Are you free tomorrow? If you're not, then that's fine, and I know it's very short notice, but I thought it was worth asking, just in case.'

Well, that's keen, Gordy thought, and yes, it was worth asking.

'Actually, I am.'

'Really? You are? That's great! Shall I pick you up? Oh, you might not want to give me your address. I totally get that, it's fine. We can meet there, if you want? I'll send you the address, would that be better?'

'Either is fine,' said Gordy.

'You're sure? I mean, if you're not, then ...'

'It'll be fun.'

'Right, I'll send you the details now. Oh, and once we're done, would you like something to eat?'

'Go for lunch somewhere, you mean?'

'That, or, well, I've got a nice bit of fish stew I made. It's in the fridge, but I could do that with some potatoes?'

'That would be lovely.'

'Really? That's amazing! Right, I'll send you the details now for the escape room. See you then!'

Conversation over, Gordy waited for Charlie's message to arrive. When it did, she saw the location and did a double-take; it was the prison at the nearby market town of Shepton Mallet, and the more she thought about it, the more she laughed.

NOW THAT THE date had come around, and somewhat sooner than Gordy had expected, she arrived in the prison car park not entirely sure what the day held in store. She'd read up on the place, having flicked through the website over a coffee. The prison had closed over a decade ago, and since then had been turned into a visitor attraction. At the time, of its closure, it had been the oldest operating prison in the country and was generally regarded as the oldest prison in the world. It was also, supposedly, the most haunted, not that

Gordy held much truck with that sort of stuff. As well as guided tours of the prison, visitors could also spend an evening behind bars, take part in a ghost hunt, and try to escape from a locked cell. It was the latter of these Gordy was going to be experiencing with Charlie. As she locked up her vehicle to make her way around to the entrance, she wondered what she had let herself in for.

The prison entrance was about as welcoming as Gordy had expected, but then, when was such a place ever required to be such? She'd been in plenty of prisons over the course of her career, though she had to admit that this one really was quite ferociously bleak. A grey edifice, sunk behind an impossibly tall wall, and approached through a confusing mass of metal fencing, Gordy felt as though she wasn't so much walking into a prison as a film set. The history of the place was palpable, as though the brickwork breathed with it, and it was all too easy for her to imagine the prison busy with prisoners and the wardens employed to keep an eye on them.

Standing to the side of an open door, Gordy saw a woman waving at her. At first, she had no idea who it was, having momentarily forgotten why she was there in the first place. Then she realised it was Charlie, returned the wave, and walked over to join her.

'You made it,' Charlie said. 'What do you think?'

She made a sweeping gesture with her hands at the prison.

'I'd like to say I've been in worse places, but I'm not so sure that I have,' Gordy replied. 'Brings back memories, though, that's for sure, and few of them are pleasant. The company's better though, I can tell you that for nothing.'

A shocked gasp, and a mutter of, 'What, really?' came to Gordy from her left, and she glanced over to see a man and a woman standing close by who she hadn't noticed at first, her focus having been on Charlie. She then saw Charlie's eyes flick between her and the couple.

'And this is ... Oh.'

Gordy raised an eyebrow.

'Oh?'

'I didn't tell you, did I? Sorry, I must've forgotten.'

'Forgotten what?'

'That this was a double date. Well, it's not, I mean, it's not like that at all, I just thought it might take the pressure off if we came with friends. Sorry, I thought I'd said on the phone, but I must've said it in my head, not out loud. Something like that, anyway.'

The man, Gordy noticed, was shuffling awkwardly, and the woman was now looking at her expectantly.

Gordy, hearing the concern in Charlie's voice, decided to take a first step to ease it. She looked at the couple and held out a hand.

'Gordy,' she said, introducing herself. 'Bet you're pleased you've a police officer with you in a place like this, aren't you? 'Left my handcuffs and truncheon at home, though, I'm afraid.'

'YOU'RE NOT!' the man said, as he reached out for Gordy's hand and gave it a shake. 'I'm Gavin, and this is—'

'Melonie,' the woman said. 'Call me Mel, though, please. Are you really, a police officer, I mean? Have you arrested anyone famous?'

'Infamous, perhaps, but no celebrities or anything, if that's what you mean.'

Gordy gave no further details as to her role.

As Gavin and Mel worked out how to respond to that, Gordy took a second or two to take in the two new additions to what she had originally thought was going to be a considerably more private affair.

Gavin was thin, maybe five foot eight, with a high forehead, noticeably protruding ears, and a broad, if not entirely convincing, smile. For some reason, he looked to Gordy like he was dressed to go for a run at any moment, in a thin, close-fitting waterproof jacket, a pair of shorts, and trainers. Mel, who was just a couple of inches shorter than Gavin, had shoulder-length, light brown hair, bright eyes, and a warm smile. She was wearing a fleece jacket, lightweight trousers, and walking boots.

'Do the police really still carry truncheons?' Gavin eventually asked, and Gordy could tell that he had been desperate to ask the question.

'No,' said Gordy. 'Shame, really. Nothing like a quick thwack on the head to get someone's attention.'

That answer made Gavin's eyes go so wide, Gordy was sure they might pop out of his skull.

'Joke,' she clarified. 'Have you done anything like this before?'

'An escape room?' said Mel, then shook her head. 'No, never. Charlie suggested it just the other day, and we thought, why not?'

Charlie leaned her head into the conversation.

'Best we get on,' she said. 'Don't want to be late for the booking.'

Inside the prison, and once through the reception area, where they'd collected their tickets, the four of them went through to a waiting area where tables and chairs were cheek by jowl with a few shelves of branded gifts, and some display cabinets.

While Gavin and Mel had a look at what was on offer, Gordy took a seat, and Charlie joined her.

'I'm really sorry,' Charlie began, but Gordy cut her off before she had a chance to finish her apology.

'It's fine,' she said. 'It'll be fun with the four of us. And what better way to get to know strangers than being locked in a prison cell? I can't see why more people don't do it.'

Charlie laughed and seemed to visibly relax.

'They're really nice, Gavin and Mel,' she said. 'I'm sure it'll be fine.'

'How do you know them?' Gordy asked.

Charlie went to answer, but as she did so, a bell rang, and Gordy looked over to the front of the room to see a prison warden standing, staring at them all.

'Well, from the looks of you alone, I reckon we'll be doing society a favour by locking you up, and none too soon, neither.'

What laughter there was, was awkward and scant at best.

'Let's have you all lined up over here, then, come on! Nice and neat now, and no talking!'

Along with Gordy, Charlie, Gavin, and Mel, about a dozen other people made their way from the waiting area to where the man was standing. They all did their best to get into a line.

'What was that I said about no talking?' the man shouted. 'Oh, yes, that was it, no talking! You're not here to have fun, you know? This is a prison, a place of punishment, and you horrible lot are right where you belong, if you ask me!'

He was laying it on thick, Gordy thought, but then why not? And the way he held himself gave her the sneaking suspicion that it wasn't just an act; this was someone who had genuine experience of the prison life. She just wasn't entirely sure on which side of the bars his came from exactly.

After a quick explanation of what was going to happen and where they were going, the man walked to the front of the line. On the way, he stopped a number of times to stare at a visitor, and managed to elicit a squeal or two and some nervous giggles from the handful of children who had been brought along by adults who, Gordy thought, were beginning to wonder exactly what they'd let themselves in for.

'There will be no talking,' the man called from the front. 'Neither will there be any pushing or shoving, tripping up, or attempts at escape. The Kray twins didn't escape from this place, so trust me, neither will you! Now, move it!'

And with that, he led them on, and to Gordy's surprise, she found Charlie's hand reach for hers and give it a squeeze.

ELEVEN

It was while Gordy and Charlie, and Gavin and Mel, were in the middle of almost giving up on escaping from the stark and depressing prison cell, that there came a knock at the door.

They had been struggling with seemingly random codes found in various places around the room, and what they might have to do with a written clue that they'd found in a box. None of it made any sense, but Gordy had to admit, she, at least, was having a lot of fun. Charlie had a quirky sense of humour, was easy to get on with, and Gordy was beginning to feel that perhaps she might like to get to know her a little better. To what end, she wouldn't want to say, because it was far too early for anything like that, and she was also still very damaged, very broken. Even so, Charlie was easy to be with, and her smile didn't half light up the room. And if there was one thing that Gordy was a sucker for, it was a killer smile.

At the sound of the knock at the door, Gavin barked a 'Yes?' And Gordy was sure she heard hope in his voice that their ordeal was over.

They had all been surprised by how difficult the puzzles were, the one they were currently on seeming even more fiendish than the rest. Gordy had noted a distinct air of disappointment from Gavin in particular, that she hadn't been able to use her police skills to help them. She had explained that there really was quite a lot of difference between an actual criminal investigation and what they were currently doing, but it was quite clear he hadn't been convinced.

A voice from the other side of the door replied with, 'Ms Haig's phone is ringing.'

They had all been required to leave their phones with the prison warden to avoid any possible cheating. As Gordy needed to still be contactable by the team, she'd given instructions that should hers ring, then she should be informed immediately. She'd had no reason to think that it would, but as she walked to the cell door, her stomach twisted. A disturbance on her day off was always ominous.

The door was unlocked and heaved open to reveal an outstretched hand holding the phone.

'You do know you can't have outside help, don't you?' the prison warden said. 'There's no phoning a friend or anything like that. That's what's known as cheating, and—'

Gordy took the phone out of the man's hand before he could finish what he was saying. She then stepped out of the cell and shuffled far enough away to ensure some privacy.

'This is Detective Inspector Haig,' she said.

'Gordy? It's Patti.'

'I'm going to assume this is important, Patti, seeing as I'm not on duty.'

'It's about the missing person, Mr Simon Miller.'

Gordy's heart sank.

'What about him?'

'His car's been found.'

'Well, that's good to hear, but I'm not sure why you need to tell me, Patti; you and the team can handle following it up, surely?'

Patti didn't reply straight away, and that worried Gordy.

'There's something else, isn't there?' she asked.

'Yes, I'm afraid there is.'

'What?'

'We haven't had anything confirmed yet, because the call only just came in. A man was out running with his dog, and it ran off into some woods, like it had caught the scent of something. He said that usually it doesn't run away, but this time, it just went, and he had to chase after it.'

'Well, you're no' calling me about a missing dog, are you, Patti? So, what's happened, exactly? You need to get to the point.'

Gordy knew she was being perhaps a little too sharp with Patti, but she was keeping her tone calm, making sure that the focus was on encouraging Patti to stick to the details, and that it wasn't in any way personal. And neither could it be, either; Gordy had a lot of time for Patti, and had really appreciated her turning up for the night of speed dating. That had been very much beyond the call of duty, and rather unexpected, too.

'Well, I've not spoken to him yet,' Patti said, 'but what we know right now is that when he found the dog, it was barking at something floating in a pool.'

Gordy knew exactly where this was going and she sensed the prison growing darker around her, closing in, as though it, too, knew what was coming next.

'And by something you mean ...'

'A body.'

Gordy gave herself just long enough to absorb that unexpected piece of information.

'I'm sensing there's an *and* coming up, isn't there, Patti?'

'Yes, I'm afraid that there is,' replied Patti. 'The pool the body was found in, well, it's close to where Simon Miller's car was discovered.'

Gordy closed her eyes, rubbed them with a thumb and index finger, then sighed heavily. So much for not being on duty, she thought.

'Send me the details and the location,' she said. 'I'm at the prison over in Shepton Mallet right now, and I'll be as quick as I can.'

'The prison? That's not too far from the location. Are you doing an escape room?'

'Yes.'

'Who with? Charlie? It's Charlie, isn't it? It has to be, I mean, who else would you be doing an escape room with? That's brilliant!'

Patti's excitement at what Gordy was doing seemed to be a little misplaced considering why she had called.

'Not sure this is the time or the place to be talking about it, really,' she said, 'but yes, I'm with Charlie and a couple of her friends as well. And now I've to cut it short, haven't I? I'll see you in a bit. Like I said, I won't be long.'

Conversation over, Gordy walked back to the cell and rested her eyes on Charlie.

'I'm really sorry,' she said. 'Something's come up. I have to go.'

She saw disappointment flicker in Charlie's eyes, but she hid it well with that smile Gordy found herself liking more and more, and an understanding nod.

'Does that mean we're done here, then?' Gavin asked.

The prison officer stepped in.

'Have you finished all the puzzles?'

'No,' said Mel, 'we haven't, but—'

'Then it looks to me like the answer to that question's a fat big no, isn't it? Honestly, criminals these days, they think they can just walk out of jail whenever they want!'

The shocked look on both Mel and Gavin's faces made Gordy smile, but not half as much as the wink she received from the prison officer, who clearly had a mischievous streak.

'I'll call you later,' Gordy said. Then, as she waved to Charlie from outside the cell, the prison officer shut the door with a resoundingly ominous clang.

'Anything I can do to help?' he asked, as Gordy stuffed her phone into her pocket, ready to leave.

She shook her head.

'I wish you could, though. Sometimes, this job, it really does get in the way of life and lots of things I'd much rather be doing.'

'Well, I'll mention it to the manager that you've had to leave early; I'm fairly sure we can give you and a friend a free pass for another time if you want. You could even do a ghost hunt.'

'That's very kind, though I'll pass on the ghost hunt, I think, not really my thing.'

The prison officer stuffed his hands in his pockets and gave a shrug.

'To my mind, that's really all the world needs, isn't it, everyone to just be a little more kind? Seems to me that's what's lacking more than anything.'

Gordy nodded her agreement, because right then words just didn't seem enough considering the sentiment. Then she set off back through the prison and to her car, wondering what was waiting for her at the end of her journey. Not kindness, she thought, though, because it never was, not when a body was involved.

TWELVE

The journey from the prison to the destination Patti had messaged through to Gordy didn't take long at all. Barely twenty minutes. It would've taken considerably less than that, however, had it not been for what the traffic comprised of, rather than simply the sheer volume of it.

Having left Shepton Mallet to make her way up to the Old Wells Road, Gordy had been unfortunate enough to get stuck behind a trio of vintage campervans coughing and spluttering their way across the Mendips. Overtaking them wasn't an option either, as the road, though straight enough in places, was beset by blind summits. Gordy had been left with little choice but to hang back far enough to stay out of their exhaust fumes and to just be patient. Right then, however, she was feeling anything but that; she had been enjoying her time with Charlie, had found the ever-present gloom she still battled with from the loss of Anna fade just a little, so to have that interrupted hadn't put her in the best of spirits. She would have to be careful to not let it show once she arrived at the location. Wouldn't be easy though.

The campervans stayed ahead of Gordy the whole way to where she then parked, having spotted Patti's vehicle on the opposite side of the road. Another police vehicle was also parked there, and Gordy was only just able to squeeze herself into the small amount of space left in the parking area.

The layby itself was a place of shadow, sat as it was beneath the low branches of a collection of wizened trees, bent into painful shapes by years of harsh weather and wind. As she pulled over into it, the gloom of the place only added to Gordy's sense of dread at what was to follow.

Climbing out of her vehicle, she saw Patti make her way over to meet her. As she did so, Gordy spotted another vehicle, a black sports car, barely visible in the darkness beneath the trees, and tucked behind the other police car. From where she was standing, she couldn't tell what it was, though she remembered something about the missing man owning a Porsche.

'That his car then: Mr Miller's?' she asked, nodding towards the other car as Patti came to stand with her.

'It is,' Patti replied. 'Numberplate checks out with what we got from his wife.'

Gordy asked, 'When was it she called in about him being missing?'

'Yesterday, late afternoon.'

'By which time I'd already headed home. The last time she saw him was when, exactly?'

'Four days ago, three when she called.'

'Today's Sunday, so that makes it Wednesday, right? Seems to me like a suspiciously long time to leave it to report her husband missing, don't you think?'

'She'd been away with friends,' Patti explained. 'She only

realised he wasn't around when she got back that afternoon to find his car gone and him not home. She got home first thing in the morning and he wasn't there. By lunchtime, she was worried, had tried calling him, but nothing. No message from him either to say where he had gone, nothing in the house to give any clue.'

Gordy walked over to the car.

'It's a pretty thing, isn't it?' she said. 'Not that I'm into cars like this at all, seeing as I'll never be able to afford one, but I can see why some people are. What do we know about Mr Miller?'

'He's retired,' said Patti. 'Clearly has a good bit of money to his name as well. No children. Pete and Helen visited his wife yesterday, following up her call.'

'They learn anything?'

Patti's response to that question caught Gordy off guard as, rather than provide a simple answer, she instead wore an expression of bewildered amusement. It seemed horribly out of place considering what it was they were doing and where it all might lead.

'Not sure pulling a face like that is either appropriate or in any way an answer to my question,' said Gordy.

Patti's expression fell away as quickly as it had appeared.

'The last time she saw him, he was heading to the River Avon, over by Bradford-on-Avon. There's a footpath you can follow through the fields. It's a lovely walk, if you've not done it.'

'Why?'

'Why's it lovely?'

'Patti ...'

'Oh, Simon, right, yes ... He's a member of an outdoor swimming group. They call themselves The Ebb.'

Despite herself, and how she was feeling right then at having her day off broken in two, Gordy laughed, and with a warmth that took her a little by surprise.

Patti frowned.

'Why's that funny?'

'It isn't,' said Gordy. 'Well, not the name; that's actually quite clever, isn't it, The Ebb? I rather like it. Nice and gentle, no threat of joining a group that's all about competing and being faster and better than everyone else.'

'Then why the laughter?'

'Would you think it strange if I told you I was laughing because I was remembering spreading Anna's ashes?'

The look Patti gave Gordy said yes, she would, so Gordy explained just to set her mind at ease.

'We did it down by a river in Wensleydale, a favourite little place of hers, and she'd go and have a dip there. So, once she'd joined the wind and floated off heavenward, we did exactly that, went for a dip, me and her close friends.'

'You went for a swim in the river?'

'It was bloody freezing,' Gordy laughed. 'Felt like it was burning my skin. Anna, I'm sure, was looking down and weeping with laughter. Unlike the rest of us, who were screaming.'

Patti smiled.

'You're a strange one, you know that, don't you?'

'It's better that way, I think,' Gordy agreed. 'Be the weirdo the world needs, that's what I say.'

'Do you?'

'Not on a daily basis, obviously, but I think there's wisdom in thinking like that now and again, don't you? And on the subject of weird, Patti, you've not yet explained why my asking what Pete and Helen learned from Simon's wife made you look at me so strangely, like I'd said something funny.'

'Oh, you'd not said anything funny at all,' said Patti.

'Then what?'

Patti paused, then said, 'You're not going to like it.'

'What I like least of all is being kept in the dark. Not a good place to be.'

Patti took a deep breath in and then slowly exhaled, as though to prepare herself for what she was about to say.

'When they arrived, Simon's wife, Maria, well, she was screaming. Pete ran round the back, found an open door, went in, and she was on the floor. Helen came round then as well, and they managed to calm her down.'

'What had happened? Was it an intruder?'

Patti seemed to consider that suggestion for a moment before saying, 'They managed to calm her down, and then had a little chat over some tea.'

'Tea always helps.'

'It does. They found out about the swimming, and also that, unbeknown to his wife, Simon had booked into a hotel in Wells for the night.'

'You're kidding.'

'Nope.'

Gordy shook her head, rolled her eyes.

'So, not only do we have the wife not reporting her husband missing for three days, which regardless of where she's been, seems a little odd, we've her missing husband having booked a room at a hotel in secret. That doesn't sound suspicious either, does it?'

'It's definitely odd.'

'Was he meeting someone?'

'That we don't know. However, Helen called the hotel; Simon never arrived.'

Gordy pondered this information for a moment.

'But again, none of what you've said explains that look you just gave me.'

Another pause.

'Well,' Patti explained, 'she said that although she hadn't seen her husband since that morning, she also had. Seen him, I mean. That morning.'

It was Gordy's turn to look bewildered.

'She hadn't seen him, but she had? How's that, then, Patti? Doesn't make any sense at all. Sounds like gibberish to me.'

'This is the bit where it gets weird,' said Patti, and Gordy could tell from her tone that she really didn't want to say why. 'And it's pretty weird already, isn't it?'

'Go on ...'

'It was why she was screaming when Helen and Pete knocked at the front door. She told them that she had just seen her husband, right there, in the house, just as they'd turned up.'

'He'd gone back to pick something up, you mean, and spooked her?'

'No,' said Patti. 'Not that at all. There was no one else in the house. Helen checked.'

Gordy's head was starting to hurt as she tried to work out what Patti was saying. And she couldn't.

'I'm no clearer.'

'She said that her husband appeared in front of her, right there, in the house. She was in the lounge, waiting for Pete and Helen to arrive, having called about him being missing, and then there he was, like a ... Well, you know ... Like a...'

'Like a what?' Gordy asked, hurrying Patti along.

'A ghost,' said Patti. 'She said he appeared in front of her like a ghost.'

THIRTEEN

Gordy was fairly sure her expression said more than words ever could in response to what Patti had just told her.

'There's a very simple explanation for that,' she said. 'What she saw, it was a hallucination. Firstly, she was thinking about her husband, correct? Secondly, she'd phoned the police because she was worried, so she was in a heightened state of stress. And third, she then sees something in the room, and because of where her mind is at that moment, what she sees quickly becomes something else, and that something else is her husband.'

'Pete and Helen, they both said Maria was terrified.'

'Being terrified of something doesn't make it real,' said Gordy. 'You know that, don't you? It's like sleep paralysis.'

'What's that?'

'You've never had it?'

Patti shook her head.

'Never heard of it, never mind had it. Can't say I want to either, sounds awful.'

'I have and it is. It's damned scary, even when you know what it is. You're in sleep mode, but your brain is active. So, you wake up, but you can't move, you can't speak. You end up in this state where you're fully alert, but also partly still in a dream state, and you'll see things, feel things.'

'Like what?'

'Like someone's pushing you down, preventing you from getting up out of bed. Sometimes, you'll even see someone either on the bed, or on your chest. I remember having my leg pulled so hard that I ended up falling out of bed. Clearly, that's not what actually happened, but that's what it felt like. It was all just a hallucination. Ever heard of pareidolia? If you've not had sleep paralysis, then you'll definitely have experienced that, because everyone has, I think.'

'Para what now? What's that?'

'Pareidolia. The brain likes patterns, likes to make sense of things,' Gordy explained. 'It's all part of the fight-or-flight system, I think; some ancient, primitive need to recognise a threat from the smallest signs and then react accordingly. So, our brain can jump to conclusions, turn shadows into people, into ghosts, anything really, just to help us survive. It's a primal thing, deep-seated. If you've ever stared at a cloud and thought how it looked like a teddy bear or a face or a whatever, that's pareidolia.'

'How do you know any of this?'

'Not a clue. Also, I'm old and wise.'

'You're not old.'

'Older, then. Anyway, sleep paralysis is caused by insomnia, disrupted sleep, post-traumatic stress disorder, anxiety, panic, anything like that. Sounds to me like Maria was and is experiencing a good number of those, thus she thought she saw her husband. She did not, under any circumstances, Patti, and I can't make this any clearer, see his ghost.'

'She said he looked wet.'

'You could tell me she saw him carrying his own head while riding around on the back of a pigeon; it would still be a hallucination. I'm certainly not going to entertain the idea that she saw the spirit of her husband floating around in front of her in the lounge. For a start, we don't even know that he's dead, do we?'

'The body, though.'

'Could be anyone right now, couldn't it? For all we know, Simon's buggered off somewhere with whoever he was supposed to meet at the hotel!'

'I guess,' said Patti, then added, 'You don't believe in them, then? Ghosts, I mean?'

'It's not a case of believing in ghosts, is it?' answered Gordy, cleverly avoiding answering that question. She then pointed at the Porsche. 'Anyway, let's get back to why we're here, and thinking back to some of what you've just said, if Simon had booked into a hotel in Wells, but never turned up, then why's his car parked here?'

Patti gave a shrug, shook her head.

'Haven't the faintest. And, like I've just said, his wife didn't even know that he was going to be out.'

'Maybe he didn't want her to know,' Gordy suggested. 'Plenty of reasons why that might be the case.'

Patti glanced around.

'Secret liaison does spring to mind, doesn't it?'

'Unfortunately, yes,' said Gordy. 'Wife's out for the night, he nips over here and meets someone in the woods for a little bit of slap and tickle, with a plan, perhaps, to then head to the hotel to make a night of it and have a lot more of the same. Only he doesn't make it either to the hotel, or back home, though we don't know why that is, where he is, if the body is him or someone else. There's a lot of unanswered questions right now.'

Patti's eyes went wide.

'Didn't take you long to come up with that sordid tale, did it?'

'Been in the job a long, long time,' Gordy sighed. 'Comes with the territory, I guess. But that's only one of any number of possible reasons for him being out here, isn't it? Could be entirely innocent. An accident. And we don't yet know that the body found by the runner is Simon Miller, do we? For all we know, it's someone else, and our Mr Miller is somewhere else entirely. Maybe he's buggered off completely, eloped with whoever it was he was meeting in secret at the pool, and the hotel was a ruse.'

'I suppose.'

Gordy took a walk around the car, noticed nothing out of the ordinary about it.

'What about the man who found the body?'

'He's back at the station with Jack and Helen. Obviously, he's in a bit of shock from it, but I'm sure some of Vivek's coffee and biscuits will help.'

That little detail made Gordy smile. Vivek Ramesh, the receptionist, was, for whatever reason, a world-class baker, and seemed to get a great deal of enjoyment from providing the team with various treats throughout the week. He'd even come out to Gordy's flat in Evercreech to teach her to make lardy cake, a local delicacy, if something flavoured with lard could be called such.

Jameson had joined her. He was an old friend of Harry Grimm, the DCI she had worked alongside while living up in the Dales. As he lived locally, he had taken it upon himself to provide Gordy with a little bit of additional support, which had then developed into him offering his services as a retired DCI. With decades of experience behind him, his role as a civilian consultant had already proved hugely valuable. Gordy, however, appreciated just as much his insistence on meeting up one evening a week at the Bell Inn, her local pub, for a couple of pints, some food, and a good chinwag. She knew Harry had been instrumental in having Jameson get in touch, but she was still rather touched that he had. He wasn't much of one for saying what he felt, but when it came to demonstrating it, few could match Harry, that was for sure.

'He's been baking again, then?' she asked.

'Chocolate chip cookies,' said Patti. 'Delicious.'

'Yeah, that should just about do it. Who's with you?'

'Pete and Travis. They've gone on ahead, just to cordon the area off, but I've instructed them to stay at the edge of the woodland and not go in for a nosy; figured it was best to leave that to you.'

'Lucky old me,' said Gordy.

'Yeah, you get all the plum jobs, don't you? Less of the old, though.'

'Comes with the rank.'

'Maybe I'll just stick with where I am, then.'

'Probably for the best.'

Patti led Gordy over to a small, wooden gate in the wall running down the side of the layby. Seeing where they were heading, Gordy popped back to her car and changed out of her shoes and into a more practical pair of wellington boots. Then she joined Patti and followed her through the gate. On the other side, they walked through the trees covering the layby with their branches and were then in a field of long grass. Wind tussled it like hair.

'Silage,' Gordy said, as they followed a thin line across the field, a path cut across it by numerous pairs of feet out exploring the countryside.

'What is?' asked Patti.

'The grass; you can tell.'

'You can? How?'

Gordy didn't really want to get into a discussion about what farmers grew in their fields, mainly because right then it reminded her a little too keenly of her previous life in the Dales.

'Where are we heading, then?' she asked, glancing around them at the countryside. Somerset was a beautiful place, she thought, momentarily forgetting why she was there and what she was soon going to be looking at.

Patti pointed ahead and to the right.

'We follow this path through a couple of fields, then take a right across another field and into those woods over there.'

Gordy looked to where Patti was pointing. The trees were thick, and from this distance looked almost impenetrable.

'At least the weather's holding,' she said.

The day had started grey, then for a while grown brighter, the sky clearing to show streaks of blue beneath. Gordy had been hopeful for sunshine when she had left the prison, only to find that the cloud had won the battle and grown thicker in the meantime.

'Rain's not forecast,' said Patti.

'Doesn't mean it won't, though, does it?'

Across the fields they tramped, the grass catching their feet as they went. As they pushed through another gate, this one metal and held in place by what Gordy thought was an overly complex latch mechanism, a flash of movement caught them both off guard.

Stumbling back into the gate, Gordy nearly tripped up, and only just managed to keep her footing in time to hold her hands up and stop Patti from tumbling into her.

'Deer!' she said, as she saw two of the beasts bound off across the field in front of them. 'Must've been sheltering on the other side of the hedge when we came through the gate.'

Watching the deer as they made their way across the field, Gordy was struck by their grace. They moved with an ethereal smoothness, she thought, and right then, they seemed almost too beautiful, too perfect, to exist in the real world. They were of another place, another time, and yet here they were, gallivanting across a farmer's crop, heading for the safety of trees far off. She envied them their freedom, though the running she would probably give a miss.

For a moment that stretched on forever, Gordy was back home, and the deer were bounding away in that haunted glen. It was a place that wore its harrowing memories as just another jewel on its vast necklace of legends and mountains, tales and crags. She hadn't been back in years, but the Highlands of Scotland still called her. Probably always will, she thought.

'Beautiful, aren't they?' said Patti, breaking Gordy from her thoughts as the deer finally disappeared into the trees.

They are, indeed, Gordy thought, and thinking of where they were heading, and what they would soon see, she was grateful that the beasts had granted them a glimpse of something considerably less horrifying.

Gordy turned away from where the deer had run. The woods they had been making for were off to the side of them, at the far edge of the field. She could see two small figures standing just away from its edge, patiently waiting beside the broken bones of an old tree.

'Best you lead the way, then,' she said, and with that, Patti turned off the path and towards the trees, Gordy following on behind.

FOURTEEN

The sight of PCSO Travis Waring's enormous beard against the backdrop of thick trees and even thicker bramble and bush, put Gordy in mind of a warrior of ancient times protecting his land. All he needed, really, was to swap his current police garb for something more appropriate, a sword and shield perhaps, maybe even a helmet, and some chain mail over a leather tunic and breeches. Throw in a battle axe and he really would look the part. Sensibly, though, she kept this observation to herself and simply acknowledged him with a polite nod.

'Travis,' she said.

'Boss,' he replied.

Gordy then looked to Detective Constable Peter Knight. Younger than Travis, and considerably more wiry and cleaner-shaven, his usually ferociously spiked black hair was gone completely, bar a thin covering of fuzz on his scalp. It looked more like Velcro than hair, Gordy thought.

'What happened, then, Pete?' she asked, deciding for

now that there was little, if any, need to talk about his and Helen's visit to Simon's wife the day before. She'd learned enough about it from Patti, and she had no urge at all to revisit any discussion about ghosts.

The question drew a baffled look from the DC.

'We've no idea, not yet,' he answered. 'Stayed out here to wait for you, as Patti directed.'

'No, not what's in the wood,' Gordy said, and pointed at her own head to emphasise what she actually meant. 'That! What did you do to your poor, wee head? And more to the point, why? I thought Jack was the only one on the team daft enough to walk around with a haircut only a gooseberry would be proud of.'

'Got bored,' said Pete. 'And I was spending a lot of money on hair gel.'

'And that's possible, is it, to spend a lot of money on hair gel? So much, in fact, that you needed to get rid of your hair to save money? Really? I never knew.'

Pete rubbed a hand across his head.

'Feels a bit odd,' he said. 'But it's a lot less hassle.'

'You look like a bollock,' said Travis.

Gordy smiled when his eyes widened with the realisation of what he'd said.

'Sorry, Boss,' he said. 'Sort of forgot you were there.'

'Oh, so I'm forgettable, am I, Travis. Is that what you're saying?'

Gordy watched Travis try to work out if she was kidding around, or genuinely annoyed, then gave him a hint, courtesy of the smallest smile in the corner of her mouth.

Travis, clearly relieved, said, 'He does look odd, though, doesn't he?'

'Well, I rather like it,' said Patti, smiling at Pete.

'You do?'

'It's good to have a change. Suits him. You ever thought of getting rid of that huge beard, Travis?'

Travis shook his head vigorously.

'God, no,' he said, shock piercing the words as he reached up and stroked the thing like it was a family pet. 'It hides a multitude of sins, believe me.'

'Sins? Really?' asked Gordy, intrigued now, and taking full advantage of just a few minutes to allow herself to get into the right frame of mind for what she would soon be seeing.

'Weak chin,' said Pete, and Travis turned a slow, fierce gaze in his direction.

'I have not got a weak chin.'

'Then why hide it?'

'I am not hiding it.'

'It certainly looks like you're hiding it.'

'I am not hiding it!'

Gordy held up a hand.

'Interesting though this discussion is, and fascinated as I am to see how an argument about whether a chin is hidden or not would conclude, perhaps we should get on? Who knows the way?'

Patti said, 'There's not really a path through the trees to the pool as such. We only know that this is where the man with the dog entered because he mentioned that tree.' She pointed at the tree Gordy had spotted when they had deviated from the path across the field to head over to Travis and Pete. 'He referred to it as the blasted oak.'

'It's not an oak,' said Gordy.

'It is blasted, though,' said Patti. 'Looks like it was hit by lightning at some point in its life. Anyway, this is where he entered the woods. He said it's easy going to begin with, then you kind of have to just sort of navigate as best you can towards the middle of the wood.'

'But how do you know you're going in the right direction?' Pete asked.

'He said that the pool's quite large,' explained Patti. 'Plus, the woodland sits in a sort of small dip, so as long as you head down, you'll get to the pool. Can't miss it, apparently.'

'Then let's get cracking,' said Gordy, and headed straight off, pushing through the middle of Travis and Pete.

No sooner had she entered the woodland than she noticed a drop in the temperature as the light faded. The air, cool as it was, bore the sweet smell of damp earth, tree sap, and beneath that, decay. Gordy could almost feel the woods breathing as she pushed deeper into its embrace, and as eerie as the place was, she didn't feel threatened by it at all.

This was not a place where folklore nightmares hid within the grey half-light waiting to ambush any who walked past. Something about it made her feel peaceful, as though all the trees had ever witnessed over the centuries was the slow passing of time. There's wisdom here, she thought, though how she could ever tap into it, she had no idea. But the thought did cause her to pause for a moment and reach out to rest a hand against the rough bark of a horse chestnut tree. At the same time, though, she had to wonder why she was thinking any of this. But then life had changed dramatically, hadn't it? she thought. The impact of losing Anna was seismic. So much so, she'd had her cards read, for goodness' sake! Perhaps the harder, more pragmatic edges of her mind were feathering a little, and allowing other ideas, other thoughts and notions, to sneak in. No bad thing. Didn't make it any easier, though.

'You okay there, Boss?' Pete asked, clearly wondering why Gordy had stopped.

'I'm good,' Gordy replied, but she kept her hand against the tree just a moment longer, before continuing on her way.

A few steps later, the way through the woods became more problematic, the ground choked in places by bramble and bush fighting for dominance, their weapons thorn and twig. But there were a good number of ways through, no doubt put there by the wildlife that called this place their home, and Gordy found herself quietly thanking them as she wound her way to and fro, and continued to make slow, steady progress towards the still-hidden pool.

At last, when the brambles gave way to clear ground again, Gordy spotted a faint slick of silver between the trees just ahead; the pool was only a few steps away. Pressing on, she was soon at its edge, her eyes drawn to the thing floating in the water, pale as freshly risen dough.

Patti, Travis and Pete came to stand beside her. None of them said a word, and Gordy was sure that the trees leaned in closer, as though keen to know what was going to happen next.

Gordy saw that the body was, for all intents and purposes, naked, though whoever it was, they were wearing bright red shorts, so at least their modesty was protected. That the body was floating told Gordy about how long it had been in the water; a body doesn't float immediately, and can stay beneath the surface a good while, before decomposition really kicks in and gasses inside it cause it to become buoyant.

'Swimming shorts, by the looks of things,' said Patti, and Gordy caught her eye at that; they were both thinking the same thing, remembering what Simon's wife had told Helen and Pete, that he had been heading out to go swimming. Except this very much wasn't the River Avon, was it? In fact, this wood, this pool, wasn't even near it, so why was he here?

'If that's the case, then where's the rest of his gear?' asked Pete. 'No way whoever that is just walked across the fields half-naked and then lobbed themselves in the pool.'

'We need to spread out and have a good look around the edge of the water,' directed Gordy. 'Maybe we'll find a bag or something.'

'But why come swimming here in the first place?' asked Travis. 'There are plenty of other places you can go for a dip, aren't there? I mean, there's Farleigh Hungerford, and there's Warleigh Weir as well, right? And considering I don't really like swimming, especially out of doors, even I know where they are. Just seems a bit odd to me, really, to be here at all.'

'And to me as well, if I'm honest,' agreed Gordy, 'but we don't know what we're dealing with yet, do we? For all we know, this was just a tragic accident; whoever that is, they came here for a little private swim, slipped and fell, or maybe they had a heart attack. Both are plausible. Either way, there's nothing here, as yet, that's telling me this is anything we can class as suspicious.'

With that said, Gordy sent the rest of the team out into the woods to see if they could find clothes or anything else that may have belonged to the person in the pool. While they did that, she decided to go in for a closer look.

The pool was larger than Gordy had expected it to be, perhaps ten metres across at the middle, and maybe fifteen to twenty metres from its top end, which sat beneath a small, rocky outcrop, to the bottom end, where it seemed to pinch itself into a little stream making its way off through the roots of the trees.

Shuffling to the pool's edge, Gordy found herself oddly drawn to the water, even with the body floating there just a few metres away. She couldn't quite put her finger on why, but there was definitely something about where they now were. The place felt unspoiled, she thought, as though the world had simply passed it by. Centuries of lives had crafted the landscape around it, and yet here it lay, undisturbed, an oasis hidden beneath green leaves.

With one eye on the body, Gordy walked up to the top end of the pool. As she did so, she noticed something odd about the dirt and leaf litter about halfway up. It had been disturbed, quite violently, she thought, and dropping to her heels, she had a closer look. At first, she could make little of what she was seeing, but then odd shapes started to reveal themselves as her eyes adjusted to the various shades of brown at her feet.

Here and there, she caught sight of the marks of bare feet, and with them the marks of some sort of footwear. In places, the footprints had been smudged out or cut in half by the other prints, and Gordy traced a line with her eyes from the pool's edge and back up into the trees. She also saw longer marks in the dirt, like something had been dragged into the pool. As she looked again from the pool, and back up into the woods, a head appeared from behind a tree, directly in her line of sight, and perhaps ten metres from where she now was.

'I've found something,' Pete called down, and pointed behind the tree he had just emerged from.

Gordy, careful not to step on any of the prints she had just discovered, marched up to where Pete was standing.

'What is it?' she asked, but Pete didn't need to answer as she saw what it was herself; a tough-looking waterproof holdall. It was unzipped, and inside she could see folded clothes, a towel, and what looked like a large, black, waterproof jacket, with a bright green fleece lining. A pair of trainers sat beside the bag.

Gordy stared at the bag, and saw that the ground around it was disturbed, and considerably more so than down by the side of the pool. She also saw the same drag marks as she had at the water's edge.

'What are you thinking?' Pete asked.

Gordy was about to say that all of this was beginning to look rather suspicious, when a shout cut through the soft peace of the dell. She glanced down at the pool and saw Patti standing on the other side, pointing at the body. Travis was up on the rocky outcrop, and he was pointing at the pool now as well.

'What have they spotted?' Pete asked.

'Beats me,' said Gordy, and together they walked down to the pool, Gordy instructing Pete to go carefully and not disturb the markings she had spotted on the ground.

'What is it?' Gordy called to Patti, once she and Pete were close to the water. 'What have you found?'

'There's something around the neck,' said Patti. 'Can't quite make it out. It's green. Might be weeds, I suppose, something from the pool that's got caught somehow?'

Gordy narrowed her eyes, couldn't make anything out, then decided it would make sense to go and see things from where Patti was standing. So, she jogged down to the bottom end of the pool, jumped over the stream to which it had given birth, nearly fell on her face as her boots got stuck in some deep mud, and eventually came around to stand beside Patti.

Pete was not so fortunate.

'I'm stuck ...'

Gordy looked back the way she had come and saw Pete was stationary, with his legs buried in mud halfway up his calf muscles.

'How on earth did you manage that?'

'Not a clue,' said Pete. 'Can you give me a pull?'

Before Gordy could reply, Travis was there, having come off the rocky outcrop and made his way behind Gordy to approach Pete from the same side. Reaching out for the detective constable, he grabbed his arms and gave him a heave. Pete shot out of the mud with a plop.

'Well, at least you've managed to not lose your shoes,' said Gordy, as Pete and Travis came to stand with her and Patti.

'Mistletoe,' said Patti then, and Gordy turned her eyes from Pete's muddy legs to the milk-pale body in the water.

'What was that?'

'It's mistletoe,' said Patti. 'Around the neck. No white berries, because it's the wrong time of year for that, isn't it? That's why I didn't recognise it immediately. But it's definitely mistletoe. And I don't think it's there by accident,' she added. 'From here, it looks like it's looped around the neck, like a necklace. Reminds me of when I used to do the same with daisies as a kid, make little chains of them and wear them like I was some kind of fairy princess.'

Gordy narrowed her eyes at the body, at the green thing wrapped around its neck.

'And there's something else,' said Travis, as they were

now all gathered together. 'I only spotted it because I was up on the cliffs.'

'And what's that?' asked Gordy.

'The side of his head.'

'What about it?'

'There's an area about the size of a tennis ball, looks like it's been struck by something. It's all black and matted.'

'Could've happened because of a fall,' Patti suggested, and to emphasise what she was saying, she pointed at the small crag Travis had recently come down from.

Gordy was considering this when the body released both an appalling smell and a decidedly amusing sound, though no one laughed.

'God in Heaven,' said Gordy, and went for a pocket to retrieve some vapour rub to dab under her nose, only to realise she didn't have any on her because she wasn't wearing her work clothes.

'Here,' said Patti, and Gordy looked over to see the kind hands of the DS hold out her own tub.

'Bought some for myself,' she said.

Gordy took the pot, and Patti said to hand it around, and as she did so, the body in the pool moved.

With ghoulish fascination, Gordy edged closer to the water, noticed the others do the same.

'What's happening?' Travis asked. 'Is there something in the water trying to, well, you know …'

Gordy guessed that he just hadn't fancied putting words to the thought of something eating whoever this was in front of them.

The body rolled over, slowly, deliberately, then came to rest on its back.

'Bloody hell!'

Pete's exclamation said it for all of them, thought Gordy, as they all stared at the body. Yet her shock wasn't just down to what was now in front of her. After all, she had seen numerous bodies over the years, and a good many of them in a considerably worse state than this one. No, it wasn't that at all. Instead, it was the fact that she was remembering what Patti had told her Maria claimed to have seen in her lounge; the vision of her husband, and that he had been soaking wet.

FIFTEEN

Tony Mills was enjoying a much-needed day off. He was between jobs, and exhausted, really, from the last one, mainly because of the client's inability to stick to an agreed plan. The money that had been, to his mind, needlessly wasted due to delays, indecision about the colour of tiles, and baseless complaints about his team's standard of work was ridiculous, but it wasn't his money. He'd been paid, so in the end, all was good.

The temptation to let the day just drift by was strong, and Tony really did fancy heading out into the countryside to wander a few paths and just soak up what mother nature had to offer, which was plenty. Trouble was, he liked to be busy, and relaxing often meant doing something. Which was why today he'd decided to do one of the few things that would ease the stresses of his everyday life; he was heading to his local shooting range. He'd not been in a good while, so with his rather expensive air rifle packed in the back of his van, he'd headed off straight after a most excellent breakfast of bacon, eggs, mushrooms, and toast, all washed down with a large mug of tea.

Having arrived at the range, and somehow managing to avoid popping into the shop to tempt himself with a new toy, Tony had settled down to what he felt sure was going to be a great day. His rifle, which was pre-charged from a diving bottle, rested on a carbon-fibre bipod, and he took the gunstock to his shoulder and stared through his scope and at the various targets presented. They were all different designs, from crows to pigeons to simple spinning discs, though his favourite were the bells; they gave a very satisfying ding when struck by a pellet. Hitting one of those as far out as ninety yards was no small achievement, not least because at that range they were smaller than an aspirin.

Tony had never gone further with his shooting than just turning up at the range now and again to spend a few hours plinking away. He had no urge to take it seriously, to enter competitions, or to even join a club. He did it because it gave him a way to focus that wasn't work-based, to the point where the act of sending those tiny pellets down the barrel was akin to meditating. He had to focus not just on the target, but on his breathing, and in those moments, that was all his mind contained. It was bliss. No wonder, then, that having spent only half an hour shooting, he was less than happy to have his day ruined by the arrival of a vision of such violent, helpless horror that he almost fell off his chair.

With his right eye resting close to his scope, he had placed the crosshair exactly where he felt sure it needed to be to ensure that the pellet, at that distance, would drop perfectly onto the bell and let out that satisfying note. He'd inhaled nice and slow, then exhaled, and in that natural pause, with his body statue still, he'd gone to take the shot, squeezing the trigger with barely a flex of his finger.

The thing that came at him right then, right at the moment his finger eased the trigger back to send the tiny, lead pellet down range, swept in from nowhere. Its panicked howl was of such raw terror that it caused Tony to instinctively jump back, the action jolting his rifle. The pellet disappeared harmlessly into the high-grassed bank at the end of the range, missing the bell completely. Not that Tony cared right then, because it was happening again, another godawful vision smashing its way into his life like a shotgun blast.

His calm repose now replaced by adrenaline and a spiked heart rate, Tony was forced to brace himself against the bench his rifle rested on, as the thing came at him repeatedly, as though it firmly believed once was simply not enough.

Wide-eyed, with the telltale sign of the hairs on his neck and arms standing to attention, Tony stared down the range at what had decided to interrupt his day in the most appalling manner. He started to make out familiar shapes, an arm perhaps, and was that a leg? And there was a head, yet all of it was ruined somehow, caught up in a twisting, swirling mist, a violent vortex of the deepest purples and blacks, all shot through with star-like sparks bursting bright and hot as they burned out.

Tony was only slightly aware of the eyes of the other shooters now on him, all of them undoubtedly baffled by what they were seeing, which was a man, his hands clamped to the bench, and teetering on the rear legs of his chair. He knew that none of them could see what he was witnessing. They were lucky.

'You alright there, mate?'

The voice of concern managed to slip into the gaps of Tony's sudden, shocking vision, but he couldn't yet respond, as the horrifying thing, a creation born of nightmares, just kept coming at him, again, and again, and again.

It had been well over a year since he'd last experienced anything like this, but what he was seeing right then was different. The visions weren't usually this desperate, this violent and confused, and Tony wasn't quite sure why. What the hell was going on?

'Hey, watch yourself, now ...'

Tony felt firm hands on his shoulders as he was eased forward to have his chair back on four legs, and away from the risk of slamming the back of his head into the ground behind him.

Still the vision came, and with it a full-on sensory overload.

'Is he having a stroke?'

'Do we need to call an ambulance?'

'I've a first aid kit in the car.'

'Give him a bit of air. That's all he needs, I think.'

'Shot of brandy might do him good.'

The voices swirled around Tony's head, and although he could hear them, he wasn't really listening. His mind was too taken up with what it was being forced to experience, the smells, the sounds, the sensations, all of it rushing into him like water into a balloon, and he felt sure he would soon burst.

Tony screamed, or at least he thought he did, but something told him that the sound came out like the pathetic cry of a man trapped in a nightmare, a whimper he desperately needed someone to hear, trapped as he was in a paralysing dream.

Shaking ... Someone was shaking him by the shoulder.

Tony managed to get some words out in a feeble reply.

'I'm ... I'm alright ...' he lied, because he really wasn't, but the last thing he wanted or needed was for those watching what was happening to start pestering him with weird and awkward questions that he simply wouldn't be able to answer.

More shaking.

'Please,' he said, 'I'm ... I'm good. Honestly, I'm fine.'

The shaking stopped.

The vision was gone.

Tony breathed deep, exhaled. He was okay. He could relax, take stock, try and work out just what the hell—

His ears popped.

'Help me!'

The voice, which was somehow both a whisper and a scream, came from all around him, from inside his head, threatening to shatter it.

'Help me!'

Tony jumped to his feet, sending his chair skittering across the floor.

'Help me!'

He grabbed his head, clamped his hands over his ears, scrunched his eyes shut.

'Help me!'

Turning away from his rifle, and only just managing to keep himself on his feet, Tony marched himself away from the shooting range, out into the car park, then across to a small patch of grass.

The voice was still there, begging for him to help, and Tony knew he just needed a moment, away from other people, so that he could do something about it. As to what that was, he wasn't quite sure yet, because he was a little out of practice, but he'd have a go, at least.

'Help me!'

Tony forced himself to calm down, to be still, to be fully in the moment. It was the only way he would have any chance of doing anything, of reaching out, of making contact.

'Who are you?'

The voice cut itself off, as though shocked at having been heard.

Tony repeated the question, and added, 'What do you want me to do? How can I help you?'

The voice became a panicked rasp; no words, just a wet, gurgling thing, like the sound of someone trying to call out over the sound of a huge tin bath being drained.

Tony waited, then asked, 'Where are you?'

Before he knew where he was, Tony's world dissolved, and all he could see was darkness swirling around him. Then something pressed hard into his back, his lungs filled with water, and, in those final moments, he felt the burning, blind panic of death.

SIXTEEN

By the time Keith 'Cowboy' Brown arrived, and with his usual posse in tow, the sun was low, and cotton wool clouds had gently gathered to paint a Monet in the sky. All thoughts of Charlie had gone from Gordy's mind, and her focus was now on the body in the pool. But then, how could it not? When it had rolled over and filled the air with an eye-watering stink of death and decay, the wound on its head had provided a vivid and lurid answer to the question of what had happened.

It was the how that bothered Gordy, though, because right now, they had no idea at all if what had happened was by design, or by accident. People fell, death came when least expected, and sometimes it could be horribly violent. This body, its injuries, where it had been found, the pool, the trees and the small, rocky outcrop? Gordy knew she could easily come up with half a dozen scenarios to explain it all, and not one of them would have to be anything other than a mix of bad luck and awful chance. But it was still suspicious, and that was what held her now, reaching deep inside to give her gut a twist.

It was these thoughts that burned hot and hard in Gordy's mind as Cowboy walked over to greet her. Behind him, the thin trail of the Scene of Crime team followed on.

'You really do like that hat, don't you?' she asked, as Cowboy came to stand in front of her.

She was standing a few metres away from the edge of the woodland, along which a thin line of cordon tape had been placed by Patti, Travis, and Pete. She had sent Travis back to the road to make sure that was all organised and things didn't get out of hand with traffic passing and people wanting to goose-neck. He could also direct as and when needed.

Patti was set as the Scene Guard, having collected a clipboard from the rear of the vehicle she had turned up in. Pete had, just a moment ago, headed back into the woodland with the photographer to guide him to the pool, and to make sure he didn't do himself a mischief on the numerous branches and brambles on the way.

The massive, and wildly inappropriate Stetson, from which Cowboy had secured his nickname, was perched on top of the man's head with undeniable pride. And he wore it well, Gordy thought, not that she would ever tell him, of course. If she did, she doubted the hat would ever fit him again.

When she'd first met him, over at Nunney Castle a good few months ago now, his whole cowboy schtick had struck her as not just unnecessary, but ludicrous. Thankfully, this time, he had refrained from arriving with the cacophonous sound of appalling country music vomiting itself out of a portable music system.

Gordy did not like country music. Never had, never would, considered it to be an abomination. That it had arrived at a crime scene when she had first found herself in Somerset still made her shudder a little. She'd warmed to Cowboy himself, though, because beneath all the theatre, she'd discovered a deeply professional, and surprisingly sensible and sensitive man. And one that she could work with, even with the ridiculous hat.

With a finger, Cowboy tipped the peak of his hat at Gordy, a playful wink flashing at her with just enough mischief to try to make her smile. She didn't, though, managing to keep it in; his ridiculousness didn't need any encouragement from her.

'I sure do,' he said, laying it on thick with a drawl John Wayne would've been proud of. Then the accent dropped, and was replaced by his soft, natural accent all the way from the black country. 'A body in a pool, then.'

'Pool, pond, never been sure what the difference is.'

Cowboy gave his chin a thoughtful scratch.

'My guess, is that a pond is basically a large puddle, and a pool is not only larger, but fed continuously by a stream or a spring, that kind of thing.'

Gordy gave a nod of appreciation at that description.

'Makes sense,' she said. 'I like it. Never knew you were so clever.'

'I'm full of surprises.'

'I don't like surprises.'

'What about sherbet lemons?'

On that, Cowboy slipped a small, white paper bag from a pocket, unravelled the scrunched-up opening, and offered it to Gordy.

'Shouldn't be too much paper stuck to them quite yet,' he

said. 'Not been in my pocket long enough for them to start going gooey.'

Gordy smiled at the little bag in Cowboy's hand and was immediately taken back to The Old Sweet Shop in Hawes, up in Wensleydale. She'd popped into that place probably a few too many times, but then it was just over the road from the office the team had worked from, so how could she not? The tiny, Wonka-esque space was stacked with shelves of multicoloured jars, all of them filled with tastes that took her straight back to her childhood. Every trip through its doors was an exercise in nostalgia.

'Thanks,' she said, taking a sweet and popping it into her mouth. 'So, have you done many water-based crime scenes?'

Cowboy shook his head.

'Can't actually remember the last one I worked on,' he said, then corrected himself. 'No, that's not correct at all. Five years ago, or thereabouts, I think, husband drowned his wife in the bathroom sink. Some argument about the price of hair product, if I recall.'

Gordy rolled her eyes, being reminded of Pete and his hair gel.

'And that memory just popped in there, did it?'

Cowboy gave a little shudder, like a chill breeze had just swept past only him, bypassing Gordy completely.

'Sadly, yes. This job kind of stays with you, no matter what you do, doesn't it? It's not like we can just delete our memories, more's the pity.'

'We can shut them away though, can't we?' said Gordy. 'Lock them up deep, deep down inside.'

At that, Cowboy narrowed his eyes at Gordy.

'Not sure what a therapist would have to say about that kind of approach.'

'Oh, I do,' said Gordy, and decided to not follow that line of inquiry any deeper. So, she swiftly moved on with a run-through of what they'd found and what Cowboy would be dealing with.

'Ambulance should be along soon,' he said, once Gordy had finished. 'Sounds like the body's easy enough to recover.'

'The pool's not too deep, I don't think,' said Gordy. 'Not that I went wading in myself. It certainly doesn't look it. But they'll still get wet feet fishing him out.'

'It's a him, then?'

'And so is that MISPER I mentioned, but whether the body belongs to the name, that's yet to be confirmed. Hopefully, your team will find some ID in his gear or his car.'

'The Porsche?'

'That'll be the one.'

'For a moment I wondered if you'd splashed out.'

Gordy laughed.

'One day, if I win the lottery or something. Not sure a Porsche is me, though. I'm more an Aston Martin girl, I think.'

'I can see that,' agreed Cowboy. 'So, whoever it is, they drove over here to go swimming in a pool in a woodland, only to end up dead?'

'It's an odd one, isn't it?'

'Certainly sounds like it to me,' Cowboy agreed.

Gordy glanced around where they were standing, taking in the trees, the quiet, the atmosphere.

'You'd only come here if you wanted to come here, wouldn't you?' she said. 'I know that sounds clumsy, but you know what I mean. This is someone who's turned up to a pool I shouldn't think most people even know about. He's brought with him all his swimming kit. What happens after that, we've obviously got no idea about, but somehow, he ends up in the pool, in his swimming shorts, mistletoe wrapped around his neck, and with his head half bashed in. Been there a few days as well, I think, but not too many. That all ties in with the MISPER and when they went missing, but like I've already said, that needs to be confirmed before we go pinning names to corpses.'

'Is that anything like pinning the tail on the donkey? And what makes you say that, about the days the body has been in the pool tying in with the time this person's been missing?'

'He's floating. And though the body is swollen, decomposition isn't too advanced yet. There's a stink to it, because there always is after a day or two, isn't there? But we're no' talking about them being unrecognisable by any stretch. If it is the MISPER, then I think someone who knows them would still be able to identify them.'

'And if it is who you think it is, do they have a family?'

'There's a wife. She called in yesterday about him being missing. The body was found by a dog that ran off from its owner, into the wood. He chased after it and found a wee bit more than he bargained for.'

A sound of rustling caught Gordy's attention, and she turned around to see the crime scene photographer being accompanied back out of the woodland by Pete.

'All good?'

The photographer tapped his camera.

'I know this will sound weird, but in a strange way, that was actually all rather beautiful, wasn't it? The light was really quite something in there, coming in through the trees to shimmer on the water. And the body, it was almost peaceful. I mean, you have to ignore the fact that it's a dead body, but you can't help but ...'

Gordy could feel the frown on her forehead growing tighter and tighter with every word the photographer was saying.

'I've said too much, haven't I?' said the photographer, then he pointed across the fields, back towards the road. 'I'll ... I'll just get going, shall I? Then I can get this all processed and back to you sooner rather than later.'

'I think that would be for the best, yes,' said Gordy, and could see the faintest of smirks curling Cowboy's lips.

The photographer said nothing more and headed off.

'He's an odd one.'

'Good at his job, though,' agreed Cowboy. 'And I think we're all a little odd, really, aren't we, those of us who do this kind of work?'

'I'm not,' said Pete.

At that, both Cowboy and Gordy turned to stare at him.

'Says the man whose head looks like a kiwi fruit,' said Cowboy.

Even Pete laughed at that.

'We'll leave you to get on with things, then,' Gordy said.

'You going to hang around, see what we find?' Cowboy asked.

Gordy had been thinking about that while they'd been talking.

'No,' she said. 'I want to see if I can find out a little more about this pool.'

Pete asked, 'You think the location could be important?'

'I think,' said Gordy, 'that coming here is a conscious decision. I also think that there are numerous ways for them to end up dead in a pool in a woodland in the middle of the countryside. The injuries we've seen could be deliberate, could be from a fall. There's a little craggy outcrop above the pool; could've fallen off that or been stupid enough to dive in without checking the water. If someone else is involved in what happened, once again, it could still be an accident, couldn't it? Doesn't take much of an imagination to have two people in a pool, getting a bit frisky, and then someone slips. If it's deliberate, premeditated or not, then why do it there in the first place? Is it an argument that got out of hand? Is it more sinister than that, and if it is, why kill them here, and not somewhere more accessible?'

'That's a lot of questions,' said Cowboy.

'Then let's all get on with trying to answer them, shall we?' Gordy replied.

'What are you going to do first?'

'See a man about a dog.'

With a nod at Pete and Cowboy, and an instruction for Pete to keep her up to date with everything at the crime scene, and that he was now to be Scene Guard, she left them both at the edge of the wood and, with Patti at her side, made her way back to the road to head back to Frome.

SEVENTEEN

The runner, a man called Mr Gregory Barnes, and his dog, were sitting in one of the interview rooms at the station. Vivek had provided good coffee, and his chocolate chip cookies really did look delicious. Smelled it, too, and that was a good thing, Gordy thought, because sometimes the station's history as a Pizza Hut would leak from its walls. Trying to get on with much-needed paperwork, or interview a witness or a suspect, wasn't exactly made easier if the walls decided that what you really needed was the sudden waft of a meat feast with a stuffed crust.

Having introduced herself and Patti to Mr Barnes, Gordy had then had a quick chat outside the room with Helen and Jack.

'How does he no' trip up, then, when he's out running?'

The question, though hardly pertinent to the investigation, had been on Gordy's mind from the moment she had been told the body in the pool had been found by someone out running with their dog.

'How do you mean?' replied Jack.

'The dog, it must get in the way,' said Gordy. 'That's what they do, isn't it? Dogs, I mean. Imagine trying to run with a dog dashing all over the place in front of you, getting between your legs.'

'It's on a leash,' explained Helen.

'How does that make it better? Isn't a leash just another trip hazard?'

'It's attached to a belt around his waist,' said Jack, miming a belt around his own waist, and a leash leading from it to an invisible dog, which he then leaned over to pat. 'He's really into it as a sport.'

Gordy stared at Jack, unsure whether she was impressed by what he'd done and how convincing it had been, or mildly disturbed. Probably a bit of both, she thought, and said, 'It's a sport? Running with a dog is something people do competitively? How?'

'It's called canicross.'

Gordy sighed.

'Sometimes,' she said, 'I half wonder if humanity isn't just really bored, and we're collectively dreaming up new and even more ludicrous ways to make our lives more interesting while at the same time reducing the population with increasingly elaborate ways to die.'

'That's an interesting theory,' said Patti.

Gordy asked, 'Has he said much about what happened?'

'He's talked mainly about canicross, to be honest,' said Helen, rolling her eyes a little.

'Like I said, he's really into it,' added Jack.

Sending Jack and Helen off to get in touch with Pete for an update on what was happening at the wood, and to see if they could find anything out about the pool, Gordy walked into the interview room with Patti and sat down in front of the man.

He was small, wiry, and she put him in his mid- to late-fifties. Dressed in a fleece jacket and lightweight trousers, he looked at her over the nibbled edge of a cookie.

'Tasty, aren't they?' said Gordy, reaching for one of Vivek's creations herself.

'Can't say good catering was on my list of things to expect from my local police station,' Barnes replied, his accent just West Country enough to show he'd lived in the area for a good part of his life.

'We're full of surprises.'

That got an unexpectedly wide-eyed response. Gordy decided to ignore it.

'So, Mr Barnes,' she began, and was immediately interrupted.

'Greg,' Barnes said. 'I know you have to be all official, but I'd prefer it if you just used my first name.'

Gordy smiled.

'Greg it is, then.'

'What do you want to know?'

'Just take me through what happened,' Gordy said.

'This daft dog of mine ran off, that's what happened,' Greg said.

Gordy had momentarily forgotten about the dog, mainly because she had expected the animal to be all over her with hair and slobber. Instead, however, she'd neither seen nor heard it. She scanned the room, then looked under the table. There, on its back and fast asleep, was a terrier-sized dog, with one white paw set against its black body. She reached down and gave the bare tummy a tickle. The dog wriggled and let out a satisfied huff.

'And you followed it into the woods.'

'I'd whistled for her to come back, and most of the time she does. But all I could hear was this yap and bark, so I followed. She doesn't yap and bark, you see, so that got me thinking there was something wrong, like maybe she'd got stuck somewhere or hurt herself, that kind of thing.'

'Where is it you'd come from?' Gordy asked.

'Little place called Downhead,' the man said. 'Sits just south of the wood. Old Bugger Lugs here sodded off into it.'

Gordy smiled, looked down at the dog again, then said, 'I'm assuming that's not her actual name, Bugger Lugs?'

'She's called Sock,' said Greg. 'On account of that one white paw making her look like she's wearing one.'

Hearing her name, Sock wagged her tail. Gordy found herself once again reaching down to give the dog a scratch.

'Did you see anything out of the ordinary?' Gordy asked, sitting back up.

'What, other than a body floating in that pool?' asked Greg, then shook his head. 'No, not that I can recall. How do you reckon he ended up there, then? I've been running out that way for years, and the only people I've ever seen are the occasional tree-hugger type, if you know what I mean.'

'Not sure that I do.'

'You must do,' continued Greg. 'Colourful clothes, assuming they're wearing any, covered in jewellery, probably vegan, too, most likely. The people, not the jewellery, though I bet you can get vegan jewellery, can't you? Not sure how that works. Love a bit of yoga as well, don't they? I've tried that, fell asleep within minutes. Not for me. Yoga, I mean, not sleeping. Love me a good nap when I can get one.'

Greg, Gordy thought, was a man who was possibly a little set in his ways, and could no doubt ramble on a little once he got going, and probably with very little encouragement.

'And what were they doing in the woods when you saw them?' she asked. 'These tree huggers you've seen?'

'Swimming, chanting, that kind of thing,' said Greg, then he leaned forward conspiratorially and added with a wink, 'I've even seen them, well, you know ...'

'Not sure I understand,' said Gordy.

'You know,' Greg repeated. 'In the pool, and ...' He winked again, then added, 'Naked and stuff.'

'Having sex, you mean?'

'Well, if you want to come straight out with it, yes,' said Greg, a faint note of shock in his voice at Gordy's apparent bluntness. 'I was just trying to be tactful.'

'This is a police station,' said Gordy. 'We don't always have time for tact.'

'Why do you think they'd want to be doing that, having sex, I mean, in a pool in a woodland?' Greg said. 'I certainly wouldn't. Far too cold for any of that sort of business to be going on with, if you ask me.'

'Back to the body,' said Gordy, attempting to return the conversation to the subject they were supposed to be discussing.

'Not much more to say, really,' said Greg. 'It was floating in the pool and that's what Sock here was barking at. I think she was trying to get whoever it was to get themselves out of the water, like she was worried or something.'

'Was the body on its front or back?'

'Definitely arse up. Fancy going for a swim there all on your own! Ridiculous. That's how accidents happen, isn't it? My guess is, whoever it is, they slipped, knocked themselves out, and drowned. Sad, really, isn't it? But like I just said, accidents do happen, don't they?'

'That they do,' Gordy agreed. 'You said you'd been running out that way for years; lived in the area long?'

'Too long,' said Greg. 'I don't mean that in a bad way, though, more like the place has got under my skin. Can't see me leaving anytime soon, if ever.'

'And do you know much about the woods, the pool?'

Greg shook his head.

'Not really,' he said. 'It's fed by a spring, that much I do know. I've never gone swimming there myself, and neither will I, either. It's a pretty place though, isn't it? Nice place to go and have a sit and a think.'

'Or to have sex.'

Gordy knew she shouldn't have said it, but she just couldn't help herself. Sometimes, it was impossible to ignore that hot little flame of mischief that burned deep down inside her.

'Each to their own,' said Greg.

Something tapped against Gordy's leg, and she looked down to see Sock staring up at her from beneath the table. She reached down and gave the animal a pat on its head. It nuzzled in, asking for more.

A sharp knock sounded at the door.

'Shall I get that?' Greg asked, making to stand.

Gordy smiled. She liked Greg, couldn't help herself really. There was a down-to-earth honesty and openness that she appreciated. How she wished more folk could be the same.

'No, that's for me to do,' she said. 'But I think we're done here for now, Greg, thank you.'

To Gordy's surprise, Sock, who had slinked out from under the table, jumped up onto her lap.

'She likes you,' smiled Greg.

Gordy stared at the little dog as it gazed at her, face-to-face, its small tail thumping gently on top of her legs. She gave it a scratch behind an ear, then it jumped back down to the floor.

'Lovely to meet you, too, Sock,' she said.

Though she wasn't quite sure how much of what Greg had said was useful, she had found what he'd said about the people he'd seen down in the pool a little odd; it struck her as a strange enough place to go for a swim as it was, but to have sex? Each to their own, for sure, and outdoor shenanigans had never really been her thing, but Greg had clearly seen enough of it happening to make her think there was something else going on. What, though, she had no idea, and she couldn't rightly think there would be any link to the body. Unless, of course, it was a little sex thing that went terribly wrong. That was entirely possible. That, or some kind of lover's tiff that had turned violent. And they did, because love and hate were just two sides of the same coin, weren't they?

With that bleak thought in her mind, Gordy watched as Greg rose to his feet and Sock padded over to sit in front of him, wagging her tail. He clipped a lead to the collar around the dog's neck.

Gordy opened the door to find Patti in front of her, worry in her eyes.

'Got a minute, Boss?'

'We're finished here,' Gordy said. 'You mind seeing Greg here out of the building?'

'I'll have Helen do that, if that's okay,' said Patti.

Gordy caught the serious tone in Patti's voice, which only confirmed that something was up.

'Of course,' she said, then she thanked Greg for his time, saying that if they needed to be in touch, they'd just give him a call.

With Greg gone, Gordy said, 'Is it about the pool?'

'We've a visitor in reception,' said Patti.

'Who?'

'He's a builder.'

'That's a what, not a who.'

'I know.'

'How's that relevant, then, Patti?' Gordy asked. 'What does a builder have to do with anything we're dealing with right now?'

'It doesn't. It's just that he didn't give me a name, just said that he was a builder and that he needed to speak to whoever was running things here.'

'Which is me.'

'Exactly.'

'And what does our builder want to talk to me about? I don't think we've any building work that needs to be done, have we? And I doubt I'm in any position to go asking for quotes on having a nice patio laid outside as a lovely little sun trap for our lunch breaks. Can't see Firbank signing that off, can you?'

Patti said, 'You're not going to like it.'

'Let me be the judge of that, Patti,' Gordy replied. 'Come on, out with it. What is it he wants to discuss?'

When Patti spoke again, her voice was quieter, hesitant, as though she wasn't entirely sure she wanted Gordy to actually hear what she had to say.

And when she'd finished speaking, Gordy knew why,

because everything the detective sergeant had just said was impossible.

EIGHTEEN

After what Patti had told her, Gordy decided she needed a few minutes to gather her thoughts. So, she excused herself for a short break to go and grab some fresh air, leaving the detective sergeant to get their next visitor, the so far nameless builder, nice and comfortable in the interview room.

She headed out into the car park. There wasn't really all that much to see, as the police station was surrounded by an edge-of-town retail park, and a seemingly ever-growing new-build estate. The air was rich with the aroma of car fumes and fast food, and she found herself yearning for the fresh air of the Yorkshire Dales. But then, how could she not? When she got home to her little flat over in Evercreech, she would take a quick walk across the fields, maybe even pop to The Bell Inn for a pint and that natty little snack she'd never seen anywhere else in her whole life, a mousetrap. Actually, that sounded like a fantastic idea, because cider, served with a packet of crisps inside which had been dropped a huge slab of mature cheddar cheese, and an enormous, pickled onion, would make everything better, she was sure.

Somerset air, she had found, was different to the air she had grown so used to up in North Yorkshire. The Dales' air was cut through with the tang of the moors, of peat and heather and bracken. When the cold winds rushed in, swooping down the fell sides with the raging ferocity of a cavalry charge, they would gather those scents and serve them on ice, enough to chill each breath. In Somerset, the air was rich as well, but here she caught more of the scent of crops and grass. Sometimes, in Wensleydale, she would notice the sharp tang of sheep dip. In Somerset, especially in autumn and when the sun had a chance to sit high and bright, there would be something like toasted corn hanging just at the edge of the breeze, as it did its best to coax leaves into a whirling dance across the fields.

These thoughts made Gordy think of Jameson. He could wax lyrical about Somerset given the chance, and he took little persuading to meet up for a natter, so she sent him a quick text to see if he was around that evening. No sooner had she sent the message, than her phone rang.

'You didn't need to call back so soon,' she said, answering Jameson's call. 'I was just seeing if you were around later. It's nothing urgent.'

'A pint is always urgent,' said Jameson. 'Especially if it's at a certain pub we both know and love, combined with good company and that most perfect of snacks, the Mousetrap.'

That made Gordy smile, especially as she'd only minutes ago been thinking exactly the same thing. Jameson reminded her a little of Matt Dinsdale, the detective sergeant she'd worked with closely up in the Dales. Matt was softer around the edges, she thought, whereas Jameson had an edge to him, which though well hidden, she suspected could cut fast and deep. It was no doubt born of the cases he'd been involved with. That wasn't to say at all that what Matt had dealt with up north had been easy, because it most certainly hadn't been and wasn't. Jameson was older, though, and he, like her former DCI, Harry Grimm, had no doubt done more than they would ever tell of, and some of it dangerously undercover. As to the Mousetrap? Well, he certainly had a point. She smiled.

'So, how's work?' Jameson asked, his voice light and jovial, which was quite the tonic after what Patti had told her. 'Any requirement for an aged police officer who's kicking his heels a bit?'

'You need a hobby,' said Gordy.

'I do. But I'm not sure what best suits.'

'What've you tried?'

Jameson didn't answer.

'So, nothing, then. Not the best approach, but then you know that, I'm sure.'

'Like I said, I don't know what would suit me, what I'd find interesting. It's hard to settle on any one thing.'

'You don't know until you try, do you? I mean, you can't make a decision on one thing, if you've not actually tried anything.'

'I'm not good at doing something for the sake of doing it, Gordy. If I'm filling my time doing something, then it needs to have a purpose. By which I mean, I need to have a purpose.'

Gordy couldn't miss the emphasis on that *I*.

'Doing something different, learning something, that's a purpose, isn't it?'

Jameson replied by not answering the question at all, and instead asked, 'So, what've you been up to lately?'

Gordy decided she didn't want to mention anything

about Charlie, because that was her business for now, and said, 'Oh, you know, the usual.'

She had no idea what *the usual* was, but that was by the by.

'I'm hoping you don't mean weird cults intent on human sacrifice,' Jameson said, in reference to a case he'd helped Gordy and the team on. 'That kind of thing should never become the norm.'

Gordy laughed, even though the memory wasn't exactly funny.

'You'd be surprised.'

As soon as the words were out of her mouth, Gordy knew she had already said too much and wanted to kick herself.

'Would I, really?' said Jameson, already caught on the hook Gordy hadn't intentionally dangled. 'Out with it, then, Gordy; what's going on?'

'Oh, it's probably nothing.'

'Which means it's something, doesn't it? Come on ...'

'Honestly, it really isn't. And I can't just go sharing any and every case with you, can I? That's not how you being a freelance consultant works.'

For a moment, neither Gordy nor Jameson said anything, then the retired DCI broke the silence with, 'Well, you don't have to tell me everything, do you? Just give me something to work on, to look into, that kind of thing. I don't need to know the ins and outs, but at least you'd be making use of someone with a little bit of experience, wouldn't you? By which I mean me.'

'You're like a dog with a bone,' laughed Gordy, then added, 'Now there's an idea; get yourself a dog.'

'Too much of a commitment.'

'You're a retired widower trying to pester a detective

inspector into giving you a job because you've nothing to do,' sighed Gordy. 'How can commitment to a dog be an issue when you're so desperate for something to fill up your days?'

Gordy heard a sigh down the line to match her own, then her mentioning of a dog gave her another idea.

'Pools,' she said.

'As in betting or the game? Or is it both?' Jameson replied. 'The pub pool leagues can get quite serious. Not as much as the skittles leagues, but that's not really a surprise, is it? Is there something going on, then? Threats maybe? Illegal bets?'

'Nothing of the sort,' said Gordy, now wondering if Jameson knew something about pool and skittles leagues that he should probably tell her but wasn't. She was pretty sure that he was currently rubbing his hands together, excited at the prospect of something to get his teeth into. 'I mean the watery kind.'

'Well, I'm not going swimming, if that's what you're suggesting. Never seen the attraction.'

Gordy's idea for what Jameson could do was developing quickly as she thought about it.

'What do you know about outdoor swimming?'

'I've just told you, I'm not—'

'I need to find out about an outdoor swimming group called The Ebb,' Gordy continued, not giving Jameson time to object; if he wanted something to do, then that's what he was going to get, and he'd best like it or just hush. 'It might have nothing to do with a case we're on with, but I'm going to have my team chatting to the members, anyway.'

'So, why do you need me to get involved if that's what your team are doing? Aren't you just doubling up?'

'Because you're not police, are you?' Gordy replied.

'Well, you are, but you're not, not anymore, seeing as you're retired. You know as well as I that if you're in a uniform, you get a certain response, don't you? However, if you're just Mr Joe Public who's enquiring about membership, someone who's maybe asking about joining, about what the group gets up to, that kind of thing, you might get a different response, right?'

'You're not asking me to join, though.'

'No, I'm most definitely not. But if duty calls, Jameson, then ...' Gordy laughed at that, but Jameson, she noticed, did not. 'Also ...'

'What, there's an also?'

'See if you can find out why people would meet to have sex in pools fed by freshwater springs.'

There was a faint gasp of disbelief down the line.

'What? Can you repeat that, just so I'm clear?'

'What do you mean, can I repeat that? I can't be any more specific, really, can I? I think what I said was very clear.'

'Well, you could try.'

He had a point there, Gordy thought, and thinking back to Greg and what she guessed he had been trying to say, realised she was both clutching at straws and potentially being rather judgemental, which was the last thing she wanted to do. Trouble was, Greg hadn't given her much to work on, but she really needed to direct Jameson as best she could.

'What I'm thinking is people into alternative lifestyle stuff. I know hippies aren't really a thing anymore, but there's still a subculture, I'm sure, the fringe stuff at Glastonbury, that kind of thing.'

'That covers a hell of a lot, Gordy,' said Jameson. 'As you well know.'

'Well, I don't really want to direct you too much,' said Gordy. 'And I don't want to go suggesting things that are way off the mark, even out of order, because that's not my intention.'

'Sex in freshwater pools, then ...'

Gordy was sure she could hear Jameson shaking his head.

'Yes, if you could find out anything at all, that would be great. Not just the people, as that might be difficult, but maybe locations, reasons, history, that kind of thing. Cast a wide net, see what you can catch.'

'This isn't for personal reasons, is it?' Jameson asked. 'You're not getting any funny ideas yourself now? Somerset, the West Country, it can have that effect on people.'

'Oh, I don't know,' Gordy smiled. 'Might be a bit of fun. Don't knock it till you try it, right?'

'Each to their own.'

Gordy decided it was time to head back inside to talk to the mysterious builder with no name.

'See you this evening, then?' she said, checking her watch. 'It'll be late-ish, seeing as the afternoon's almost gone itself.'

'Of course,' Jameson replied. 'Who knows? I might even have something for you by then.'

And with that, the conversation was over, and Gordy headed back into the station, up the stairs, and through to the interview room.

NINETEEN

As Gordy placed her hand on the door handle to the interview room, a message came through on her phone. It was from Charlie: *We escaped! Didn't want to message too soon, as I know you're busy. Call me when you're free. It was lovely to see you again. C x*

Gordy stared at that little *x* at the end of the message and to her surprise felt the faintest of stomach flips. Yes, she knew that it was little more than a bit of teenage-like excitement, but still. It meant that she then entered the interview room with a somewhat larger smile on her face than she would typically have.

Patti was sitting at the table, and she looked up with a rather bemused expression. No doubt due to the grin, Gordy thought, and quickly swept it away. Sitting in front of Patti was a man with short hair, a day's worth of stubble, and skin that told of a life spent outdoors. He was dressed casually in denims and a fleece jacket over a T-shirt. The jacket, like the denims, was decorated almost artistically with flecks of paint and the occasional small rip. He carried the look well, as though such things were just a part of his everyday life, and he had considerably more important things to worry about.

Gordy sat down beside Patti, holding out a hand as she introduced herself.

'Tony Mills,' the man said, reaching out and shaking Gordy's hand.

His hands were rough and calloused, she noted, and she struggled to square a circle—being the kind of person who did the work his job entailed, and also the kind of person who would turn up at a police station with the story he'd told Patti. The two things just didn't fit together well at all, not in her mind, anyway.

Gordy knew she was making assumptions, and she was more than happy to have those challenged, but that didn't mean it was easy. She understood, though, that an open mind was considerably more useful than a closed one, so she shoved a metaphorical foot in the door, and decided to see what Tony had to say. If he turned out to be a joker, though, someone wasting police time with a prank, a hoax, some mad story that would then end up on social media, or even just a story to laugh about with mates down the pub on a Friday night, she'd make him think twice about ever doing something similar again, that was for sure.

With that in mind, Gordy realised that the grin she had walked into the room with had not so much vanished as taken on a considerably more knowing, even threatening tone, so she softened it.

'Thank you for popping in,' she said. 'DS Matondo has told me some of what you spoke with her about.'

'I know it sounds strange, and I know you probably think I'm a loon, some idiot just making stuff up, but I'm not, I promise. It's not like I want to be here, believe me.'

'Maybe we should just start at the beginning?' Gordy suggested. 'Would it be okay if we took a few notes? I don't think we need to have a recording of this, because it's not an interview as such, is it?'

Gordy knew that she had every right to record what was said, but part of her wasn't entirely sure she would want to listen to it again if it turned out to be nonsense. A few notes by Patti would be fine, though, for now.

'Of course, no, it's fine, I completely understand,' nodded Tony, and Gordy noted how genuine he sounded. Whatever it was he'd come here to say, he fully believed every word of it. Or, if he didn't, he was doing a damned good job of making it seem that way.

Patti took out her small, black notebook, and a pen.

'Over to you, then, Mr Mills,' Gordy said.

'Tony, please.'

'Of course, Tony. In your own time.'

Gordy leaned back in her chair, watching Tony do the same. He held his hands up in front of him, palms forward, fingers splayed. A display of apology almost, Gordy thought.

'Please, I want you to understand,' he began, 'I've never done this before. Come to the police, I mean, about the things that I see sometimes. It's been happening to me for a few years now, and I usually deal with it in private, contacting those I need to because of what I've seen, or having people come to me to see if I can help. But this? It seemed like I needed to come here. I don't think I had any choice, really.'

'And here you are,' said Gordy, trying to sound both encouraging and to let Tony know that she was taking him seriously.

Tony sat forward with enough urgency to show that he

wasn't finding any of this easy and was most certainly not comfortable. He was here, Gordy thought, not because he wanted to be, but because he clearly felt he had to be, like he'd said.

'I just want you to know that I'm not making this up. I wouldn't, truly. There's nothing in this for me at all. In fact, if any of my mates knew that I was here, I'd never hear the end of it.'

'They don't know?'

'Oh, they know,' Tony said. 'But I've always kept it very quiet, never made a big deal out of it. This isn't that, really, is it? I mean, you're the police, and I'm here because of what I saw, and you've every right to think I'm on something. Which I'm not,' he added rather quickly.

'Well, that's a relief,' said Gordy. 'But please, Tony, just take us through what happened, and we'll go from there, shall we?'

Tony gave a nod, sunk back in his chair, sucked in a deep, slow breath through his nose, then exhaled as he readied himself to talk. It reminded Gordy of an athlete at the Olympics in those last few seconds before they threw themselves into those mad, life-changing seconds of their event.

'Like I said, this has been happening to me for a few years. Everything was fine, by which I mean, everything was normal. I was just Tony, the builder. Then I knocked myself out after a night at the pub and smashed a mirror in the process. Didn't think anything of it at the time, but now? Well, it's pretty much all I can think about some days. And that's not easy, believe me.'

Not a good start, Gordy thought, but she held her tongue and waited for Tony to continue.

'The first time, it was all tied up with the house I was

living in. I don't live there now, moved a couple of years ago, but I managed to put a few things to rest before I left.'

'Like what?' Patti asked, though Gordy silently wished that she hadn't.

'There'd been a house fire,' said Tony. 'Didn't know it at the time. Same site, different house, though, because the original one was pulled down after it happened, and that was decades ago; structurally unsound and all that. Young couple died in it, and they'd copped the blame, but it was started by rats, would you believe?'

Gordy raised a finger to interrupt.

'I'm sure this is relevant, Tony,' she said, 'but we are pushed for time, as I'm sure you understand.'

Secretly, she was thinking about meeting Jameson later on, but she also didn't want to spend her time listening to stories about ... Well, no, she couldn't bring herself to admit what this was really about, not at all.

'Yes, sorry,' said Tony. 'I get so used to having to explain why it is that I see these things in the first place that I just do it automatically.'

'That's fine, I understand,' said Gordy, attempting a little bit of reassurance.

'You do? That's a relief.'

'So, on to why you're here?'

'I was at the range,' Tony said. 'Target-shooting. Just a day off between jobs, really, you know how it is? Anyway, there I was, thinking about nothing other than what I was doing right then, just hitting the target, which is why I do it, really; it's kind of like meditating, or it is to me. Does that make sense? I'm not sure.'

'Tony ...'

'Sorry, I'll get to the point.'

'Fantastic news,' said Gordy, unable to disguise the sarcasm.

'Like I was saying, I was at the range, and I was about to take a shot, when it happened, when … Well, when he came at me.'

'Who came at you?'

'I've no idea, and I really wish that I knew. But that's kind of why I'm here.'

Gordy stalled a little on hearing that and wasn't sure what to ask or to say next.

Patti came to the rescue with, 'Can you describe this … person?'

Tony was quiet for a moment or two before he spoke again, a deep frown ploughing great furrows across his brow.

'I know there's water involved,' he said. 'Whoever it is, whoever it was, they're in water and there's a lot of shock and a lot of pain, and that's how they died. They don't know what's actually happened or why. I think they were swimming though, not just because there's water, but because I saw a white towel.'

'But you saw this person at the shooting range,' said Gordy, having trouble keeping up with the tsunami of crazy she was now witness to.

'I did.'

'How?'

Tony's eyes flicked rapidly between Gordy and Patti and she could see a little bit of panic in them.

'I see … Well, I don't call them ghosts, because that's not what they are, and also, it makes people think a certain thing, doesn't it? You know, movies, that kind of thing. Horror.'

Gordy leaned forward, resting her elbows on the table.

'I'm not sure I understand.'

'What I see—they're people,' said Tony.

Gordy could tell that he was clearly struggling with how to explain things. 'But also, they're not. It's like they're in this transitioning place, a between-places-place. They're not here, they're not there, and they don't know what to do, or they're trapped, or something's stopping them going where they need to. I don't really understand it myself, but that's how I've come to see it, or explain it.'

'And they come to you?' said Patti.

'They do. The way I think of it is that I'm a bit like a lighthouse.'

Now there was an image, thought Gordy, and asked, 'How do you mean?' while doing her best to try not to imagine Tony with a massive light stapled to his forehead.

'Well, where they find themselves, it's a bit like being in a storm in a boat, and you need to get to shore, and the only way to do that, the only chance you have, is to follow the light. Lighthouses can warn of rocks, reefs, shallow waters, but they also guide vessels safely into the harbour, don't they? I think that's what I do.' He gave a shrug. 'Well, that's the best explanation I can come up with. They need help, that's why they come to me. That's why they all come to me.'

That got Gordy's attention.

'All?'

'Every time I see something, it's because they want help. I've a connection, you see? I can't explain it. I just know that after I banged my head—and I know how mad this sounds, believe me—that's when I could see them. I didn't ask for this, trust me. But that's what happened. I actually think it's more like they can see me now rather than the other way around, which goes back to my lighthouse thing; it's like they're drawn to the light.'

Gordy was struggling with what Tony was saying, but she was still doing her best to give him the benefit of the doubt, as hard as it was.

'So, we have this person you saw, but they're not a ghost, and we have water,' she said. 'You also mentioned pain and shock and them wanting your help.'

'Yes. That's why they come to me. Usually, it's because there's some misunderstanding or some unfinished business, but this was, this *is*, more than that. It has to be. I've never experienced anything like it. Don't ask me why I've experienced it now, because I don't know.'

'What about a name?' Gordy asked, jumping in.

Tony shook his head.

'I didn't get one. I just got all this pain and terror and they were screaming for help. A name might come through later, it's hard to say. That's something that's fairly hit or miss. This person, whoever it is, they're still in shock, and I think they were as surprised to see me, as I was at seeing them. They're confused, I think. Angry, too. And terrified. Fair enough, really, if you think about it.'

Makes two of us, thought Gordy, who'd had enough. Tony seemed genuine, that was true, and she'd thought that from the moment he had walked into the room. He probably even believed everything that he was saying he had seen, but it was time now to draw a line. She sat back in her chair.

'I hope it's okay to ask this,' she began, 'and I really can see that this has been very traumatic for you, both the experience, and I think, coming here, but to what end, Tony? Why is it you're here? What is it you expect us to do?'

'Help them,' said Tony. 'You have to help them. That's what you do, isn't it?'

'Help who, exactly? We have no name, no idea who this

is, which leads me to then ask the obvious question: how do we help them?'

Gordy could see that there were commonalities between the body in the pool, and what Tony had just told them, but they were gossamer thin; her overriding thought right then was that somehow there was a leak, that information had got out about what had been found in the pool, perhaps even that Greg hadn't been the first person to find the body at all, that he'd maybe told someone else.

'I don't know, not yet,' Tony replied, his voice a little frantic now. 'But something tells me this was no accident, that there's more to come.'

Gordy didn't like that at all, and she held up a hand to make it clear she didn't want Tony to say anything else.

'Tony,' she began, working to keep her voice measured and calm. 'You're a builder, yes? Your company, I'm sure does work all round the county. You've lots of contacts.'

'Yes, but—'

'You seem genuine, and maybe you are, but right now I'm erring towards thinking somehow information about some incident somewhere, not necessarily even local, has got to you, and maybe you're impressionable, maybe someone's trying to make you look a fool by telling you things that you've then brought to me, I don't know. But I do know that we need to bring this chat to an end.'

'I'm not lying.'

'I'm not suggesting that you are. But there's no' a thing I can do with what you've told me. Nothing, Tony, you do understand that, yes? Not only because you've not given me anything to go on, but also because I can't exactly go acting on a vision or whatever it was that you had. I need something real, something concrete, actual evidence, and this isn't that, is it, not by a country mile?'

Tony's mouth fell open, and he just stared at Gordy for a moment.

'But ... but he came to me! There's water, so that's something, isn't it? Whoever he is, someone did this to him, I know they did, you have to believe me!'

'Tony, what I believe is that you truly believe what you saw was real. And you know what? Maybe it was. But it doesn't detract from the fact that I can't do anything with any of it because there's no hard evidence. I mean, where did this even happen, can you tell me that?' She held up a hand to stop him from replying before he had a chance to. 'Don't answer, because we both know that you can't. You worry about what your mates would say down the pub if they found out you were here, yes? Well, imagine if I started taking this seriously, acting on what you've told me, and the press got a hold of it? Detective listens to Ghostbuster! I need facts, Tony, not visions!'

'Ghostbuster? I'm not—'

Gordy wasn't listening and rose to her feet.

'I really appreciate you coming in,' she said. 'And I admire you for doing so, Tony, I really do. Took guts, if I'm honest. But please understand that this can't go any further. So, go home, rest, get some sleep, and maybe you'll have no more terrifying visions.'

Tony stood up.

'It's not a lack of sleep that causes any of this.'

'That bang on the head then,' said Gordy. 'Did you ever get it checked out? Maybe something happened and you need help?'

Gordy saw Tony's eyes grow wide with indignation.

'Help? I don't need it! I'm fine! It's him that needs it. Whoever that was that roared at me out of nowhere! And you, Detective Inspector, you need help, too, or you're going to, believe you me.'

Gordy pursed her lips.

'Tony, I hope that's not a threat.'

'The truth can feel like that to people who aren't ready to hear it.'

Yeah, that's enough now, Gordy thought.

'Out,' she said, and pointed at the door. 'Please, Tony, just go. Now.' She looked at Patti. 'Can you escort Mr Mills from the building, please, Detective Sergeant?'

Patti stood up to do as Gordy ordered, but Tony was already at the door.

'I know you don't believe me,' he said. 'I know that you think I'm making it all up, but I'm not. I've no reason to. There's nothing in it for me, is there? This is real!'

Gordy nodded at the door.

'Goodbye, Tony. And thank you. Have a nice evening, not that there's much left of it.'

Tony opened the door, hesitated, turned his head and looked directly at Gordy.

'There's something else. I wasn't going to mention it, because I don't like to spring things on people.'

Gordy wasn't interested in the slightest.

'Perhaps you could tell it to the detective sergeant here,' she said, looking at Patti.

Tony shook his head.

'It's for you,' he said. 'What I need to say. I don't really know what it means, and as I've just said, I wasn't going to mention it, because I don't want you to think I'm prying or sticking my nose in.'

Gordy stared at Tony.

'Well, what is it, then?' she asked.

Tony ran a hand down over his face, then said, 'Just so you know, she's fine with it.'

'Who's fine with what?' Gordy asked, her frustration close to turning into anger now. Tony was pushing his luck. 'What are you talking about, Tony? Or are you just here to waste police time?'

'No, I'm not. But this isn't to do with anything police, it's to do with you, and with her.'

Gordy looked at Patti.

'Her? Do you mean Patti? And if you do, why don't you just say so? Get to the sodding point!'

'I am!' Tony replied. 'It's not an exact science any of this, and I didn't ask for it, either, you know that, right? I just get these visions, hear voices, and I have to live with it, because I've no choice in the matter! And that's how I know that she's happy for you, that she wants you to be happy. She also thinks that the ring is beautiful and that what you did with it after she was gone was perfect.'

A chill swept through Gordy, and she felt her skin goosebump.

'What?'

'You know exactly what,' Tony replied, 'because I certainly don't! It's a message for you, not for me, so make of it what you will. It came to me when I arrived here. I wasn't going to say anything, because I didn't know who it was for, anything like that at all. But it's for you, and I knew that as soon as I saw you. Make of it what you will. I'm done.'

And with that, he was gone.

For a moment, neither Gordy nor Patti said a word.

Patti broke the silence.

'Look, I'm sorry,' she said. 'I should've sent him on his way, not entertained him at all, but what he told me, I couldn't ...'

Gordy rested a hand on Patti's shoulder and smiled.

'It's fine,' she said, still shaking a little from what Tony had said before leaving. 'Honestly, it is. I'd have done the same.'

Visibly relieved, Patti turned off the light, then stood at the door to let Gordy through first.

'Takes all sorts to make a world, doesn't it?'

'It does,' Gordy agreed, and made to leave the room.

'What do you think he was on about?' Patti asked. 'When he was leaving, and he said something about someone wanting you to be happy? And what was that about a ring?'

Gordy gave the slightest of shrugs.

'I think he was clutching at straws, that's what,' she said. 'Doesn't take much to do a bit of research, find something out about someone, and use that as leverage. That's all it was, Patti, that's all it was.'

And with that, Gordy said her goodbyes and headed off, leaving the office to drive herself home to Evercreech. And the whole way back, she couldn't shift the niggling feeling deep down that there was more to what Tony had said than she dared to admit, even to herself. After all, how could he know anything about the ring?

TWENTY

The following day, Gordy was back at The Hut, her head just fuzzy enough to remind her that, against her better judgement, she'd had three pints of cider at The Bell with Jameson, instead of two. Jameson, as he was driving, had stuck with one. It wouldn't impact her work in the slightest, but it was enough to make her feel thankful she'd not met Jameson at the weekend and decided to have more. She found now that drinking too much one day meant borrowing time from the next. She was no longer the sprightly young woman who could survive on just a few hours' sleep, while chasing away a hangover with tea and a fry-up.

The evening at The Bell had been both pleasant and useful, though. Chatting with Jameson was always fun, and this time they'd also covered a bit more about what she wanted him to try and find out about, with the retired DCI probing her with questions. He'd not come up with anything since their chat on the phone but was going to be on with it the following day, which meant that he was probably busy right then. Gordy had no doubt that he would be, either, and had enjoyed teasing him about how he'd soon be throwing himself into a river or lake as part of his consultancy role. They'd also chatted about Tony Mills, and that had been rather cathartic, with Jameson at first interested, and then rather angry that the man had decided to turn up with such a story. He'd dismissed it and advised Gordy to as well.

At the station, Vivek had provided the team with coffee and an especially moist lardy cake. Gordy felt sure she could feel her arteries complaining as she bit into her second slice, but that wasn't about to stop her from demolishing it. Maybe she should see if Vivek couldn't bring something a little healthier now and again? She somehow doubted it.

The team was gathered, and the board had been wrestled across the floor by Jack, its wayward wheels having proved sufficiently taxing to have him rap his knuckles against the door to her office, where the board had been residing. His swearing had been matched only by the look in his eye, which told Gordy that given the chance, he'd have kicked and stamped the thing to pieces.

'Seriously, we need to get a replacement,' she said, as she stood in front of it, ready to guide the team through the investigation so far, and to divvy up jobs. 'Patti? Can we not order one?'

'I have,' Patti replied.

'Then where is it, if it's not here?'

'I'll chase it up.'

'Thank you.'

Gordy took a pen. She had already stuck a few things up on the board, including various photos of the crime scene. An initial report had been sent through from Cowboy, and she'd had a quick read of that. She would mention a few things she'd learned from it once the meeting got started. The body had not yet been examined by the pathologist, but that was no surprise, and she'd been informed that this was being done that very morning. She was visiting the mortuary once the meeting was over, and would learn more then, though they had enough to be going on with, that was for sure.

After quickly running through the Action Book, to make sure there was nothing too pressing in that to be dealing with, she ran through the usual details about the crime scene, before getting on with the specifics.

'First, we've a confirmed identity, as you all know,' she said. 'The body is that of Mr Simon Miller, age sixty-three, a retired accountant. He was discovered by a runner, Mr Gregory Barnes. To be more accurate, it was his dog, Sock, who found Miller, but I'm not sure a dog is a reliable witness.'

'Cute, though,' said Patti, and added, 'I'm meeting with Maria later today to do the official identification at the mortuary.'

'Injuries to the body comprise mainly a wound to the head,' continued Gordy. 'Though cause of death has yet to be confirmed, we should have something later today. I'm heading there myself as soon as we are done here, and I'm sure Charming will have something for me. We do know that the estimated time of death coincides with what we've learned from Miller's wife, Maria, about where he was Wednesday last week, which was when she last saw him. In addition to the vehicle belonging to Miller, a bag containing various items was found close to the pool. These are now with the SOC team for further analysis and include a phone and a wallet.'

'So, what are we on with today?' asked Pete.

'A few things, actually,' said Gordy. 'First, we need

confirmation of where Miller's wife, Maria, was from the time she last saw her husband to when she called to report him missing.'

'Wasn't she away with an old university friend for a reunion?' said Travis.

'She's not yet provided us with the details of whoever she was with,' said Patti. 'Helen, seeing as you were round there yesterday, can you check up on that with her? Give her a call, go round for another chat, perhaps?'

'It's best we check up on her anyway,' said Helen.

'Agreed,' nodded Patti, 'but maybe do that after I've met with her? Get the difficult bit of confirming the body is her husband over with, and perhaps go round after? She'll need checking up on anyway and I might not be the person she wants to speak to after being with me at the mortuary.'

With that arranged, Gordy moved the meeting on.

'There was something from the SOC team about the crime scene; at least two sets of footprints by the pool, in addition to what are clearly Miller's.'

'From the dog walker?' asked Jack.

Gordy shook her head.

'Those have already been identified and checked off. And it's not like the place has a lot of traffic, as it's a little off the beaten track. Whoever it was, they were there before Miller, as the other prints and the drag mark, cross over those prints. Obviously, this might be nothing at all, but it's something we need to be aware of.'

'I'm meeting with someone from The Ebb, the swimming group he was a member of,' said Pete. 'Once we're done here, I'll be on with that.'

'That's good,' said Gordy. 'We know that he was swimming that morning in the river at Bradford-on-Avon, so we do need to check in with those he met up with while there. Also, and as a point of note, I've got Jameson doing the same, but from a different angle, just in case you bump into him.'

'How do you mean?'

'Pete, you'll be approaching them from the perspective of wearing a uniform, and that gets a certain response, doesn't it?' Gordy explained. 'People may not realise they're being guarded or not telling us everything they know, but that's what happens. So, I've asked Jameson to get in touch with the group and find out more from the perspective of being a member of the public keen to join.' She laughed and added, 'Which, I have to say, he really isn't.'

'Not a swimmer, then?' said Jack.

'Apparently not, no. I've also asked him to see what he can find out about that pool, if anything.'

'Isn't it just a pool?' said Travis. 'Just a bit of water in a woodland?'

'Yes, and also no,' said Gordy. 'The dog walker, Gregory, mentioned that he'd seen people up there before, described them as tree huggers.'

That description got a titter of laughter.

'And what does he mean by that, exactly?' asked Jack.

'Said they were wearing colourful clothes and that in addition to swimming in the pool, he'd heard them chanting and seen them having sex.'

The laughter changed immediately to looks of disbelief.

'Who'd have sex up there?' Helen asked. 'And why?'

'Well, that's what I'd like to find out,' continued Gordy. 'Perhaps the pool has some special significance or something? Maybe the other members of this swimming group will know something about it; they're more likely to, aren't they?' She looked at Jack, remembering someone over in Frome she'd met with during a previous investigation, which to everyone's shock, had ended up in the arrest of their previous DCI. 'Jack, can you pop in and have a chat with Lily Twelvetrees? She's a counsellor over in Frome.'

'Is she the one who thinks there's wisdom in a stick?'

Gordy laughed at that.

'That's her. Lily's great fun, you'll love her, I'm sure. She might know something about what happens at pools like the one we're dealing with, so she's definitely worth having a chat with.'

Gordy then turned her attention back to the team as a whole. 'We've also got that mistletoe wrapped around our victim's neck.'

'It's worth mentioning, then, that no mistletoe was found in the woodland,' said Pete. 'I chatted with one of the SOC team who mentioned it. It must've been brought in from elsewhere.'

'Mistletoe strikes me as a very clear choice,' said Gordy. 'It's not a random plant grabbed at the last minute I don't think. Hopefully Jameson will be able to tell us more soon.'

Gordy, who'd been taking notes on the board as they'd been speaking, then said, 'I think that's enough to be going on with for now. It's not like we haven't got anything to do, is it? Patti?'

Patti, who Gordy noticed looked hesitant, said, 'There's also, you know, the builder, Tony Mills?'

The mention of Tony gave Gordy an immediate headache, but she forced it away as quickly as it had burst painfully inside her skull.

'Yes, I suppose I should mention him,' she agreed, though she really didn't want to, and had hoped to get on with the day without touching on that particular interview. Casting her eyes around the team, she had a feeling they all knew about it anyway. 'We had a visit from a builder, a Mr Tony Mills. As ridiculous as this sounds, he popped in to tell us about a ghost he saw. Not something I've had to deal with before in my career, if I'm honest, but I suppose it's worth you all knowing we've someone like that playing around on the periphery of the case.'

Helen raised a hand.

'What was it he said, exactly? Patti mentioned it, but didn't say much about the specifics.'

'Exactly, not much,' Gordy said. 'He'd been at a shooting range and supposedly had a vision of something he thought we needed to know about. I begged to differ. And I still do.'

Gordy saw Helen glance over at Pete.

'We had something similar with Maria.'

'I know,' Gordy nodded. 'I've already spoken with Patti about that and given her my thoughts on what that was.' She paused for a second, thinking quickly, then looked to Patti. 'It is an odd coincidence, though, isn't it? I'm not saying we start taking visions of ghosts seriously, but the people behind them, well, that I'm interested in.'

'How do you mean?'

'We need to check up on Tony. I'd like to have his story confirmed by the shooting range. And no, I'm not suggesting we see if someone saw what he did or anything like that. However, if it was as traumatic as he clearly implied, then my guess is he caused quite the scene. And if he didn't, well, we can make of that what we will, can't we?'

'Travis can get on with that,' said Patti, turning to look at the PCSO. 'I'll give you Tony's details, then you can give him a call, and the shooting range as well.'

'If he questions why you're asking for them, then that's

probably answer enough, isn't it, about what his true motivations are? Also, is there a connection between Tony and the Millers? I don't like having random people turn up with weird stories during an investigation, and this one is certainly that. I don't trust them when they do, and even less so when it's not a lone event, but two in quick succession.'

'We can check that when we go to see Maria,' said Helen. 'Maybe they had some work done or something and Tony was the builder?'

Pete asked, 'Are you thinking that they're both making it up?'

'Maria, I don't think so,' said Gordy. 'From what I've been told, I think she fully believes she saw something; however, I also believe that it was brought on by stress and other factors; the brain can play tricks. As for Tony, I'm going to go with attention seeker until I'm proved otherwise.'

'Why would someone just make stuff up though?' asked Travis. 'What's the point?'

'Attention, notoriety, five minutes of fame, or just to make the police look stupid,' said Gordy. 'Take your pick.'

'Like Patti said, I'll see what I can find out about him. Maybe he's done this before with customers of his? Maybe he's not even a builder at all; could be a con artist, couldn't he?'

'Quite easily, yes,' said Gordy, then turned her attention to the rest of the team. 'Just be aware of this, okay? We're going to be speaking to the members of the swimming group, so maybe there's something there as well. Maybe Tony knows one of them, or used to be a member? Just keep your ears open. I don't want anyone or anything becoming a distraction, or getting in the way of us doing our job.'

The team's silence was confirmation enough for Gordy

that they'd taken on board what she had said. She put the lid back on the pen she had been using, then clapped her hands.

'Right, then,' she said. 'Let's get cracking. I want everyone to stay in touch, and to keep me informed. Patti, I'll leave the organising to you, if that's okay? Now, let's see if we can't get this sorted nice and quickly, yes? Wishful thinking, I know, but let's do everything we can to find who's responsible.'

TWENTY-ONE

Shortly after arriving at the hospital, Gordy donned a long white lab coat, white rubber boots, and a disposable face mask. Standing opposite her was Doctor James Charming, the pathologist, though everyone referred to him as Prince. Gordy had no idea if he ever called himself that, but the ever-present glint in his eye gave her the impression that he did, and with enough tongue in his cheek to let everyone know he found the sobriquet amusing. She also wondered if, at any point in their working relationship, she would get to see what he actually looked like. To date, all she had ever seen of his face were those piercing eyes, the rest of his face covered with a face mask identical to the one she was wearing herself.

Keith 'Cowboy' Brown was standing to Charming's side, and between where they were standing and herself, and lying beneath a white sheet, was the body of a man who had once been the living, breathing, Porsche-driving Simon Miller. As she had reported earlier to the team, the man's identity had been confirmed, both by items found by the SOC team at the site of the pool and in his vehicle. Patti was meeting Maria at the mortuary later that day to provide support as the team's family liaison officer during the identification process.

'Ready?' asked Charming.

'I don't think I'm ever ready as such for this bit,' Gordy said. 'Postmortems aren't something I have in my little book of fun.'

'You have a little book of fun?' asked Cowboy.

'You don't?'

'No, but I'm suddenly keen to adopt the idea.'

The pathologist reached for the white sheet and carefully eased it down to reveal the body beneath.

'Bloody hell,' sighed Gordy, her eyes taking in the awful sight of the bloated and mottled body of Simon Miller.

Charming continued with the sheet until Simon's body was fully revealed, but Gordy's attention was focused on Simon's head. Though she couldn't see the wound completely, she could make out just enough of it.

'So, cause of death?' she asked, pointing to what was visible of the wound.

'The impact was hard enough to fracture his skull,' said Charming. 'He would have died from that wound alone, had he not ended up drowning in the pool as well. I've found little in the wound other than Simon's hair and some small slivers of wood.'

'He was hit with a stick, then?' said Cowboy. 'Makes sense, seeing as the pool he was found in is in a woodland. The killer would've been rather spoiled for choice when it comes to finding something to twat the poor bloke on the bonce with.'

Gordy smiled beneath her facemask.

'You have such a way with words.'

'Thank you.'

'You should write poetry.'

Gordy saw laughter lines crease the skin at the corner of Cowboy's eyes.

'I don't think I should.'

'No, neither do I,' she agreed, then thought back over what he had actually said. Something about it didn't sit right. But what?

'This all looks very planned, doesn't it?' she said, thinking out loud. 'Whoever did this to him knew it was what they were going to do, didn't they?'

Both Cowboy and Charming frowned.

'How do you mean?' Charming asked.

Gordy wasn't quite sure, so kept talking, to try and tease it out a bit.

'Well, considering where that wound is on Simon's head, he wouldn't have seen it coming, would he? And from what I can see right now, there appear to be no defensive wounds or bruising to his body; it doesn't look like he was trying to fend someone off, which makes me want to discount the idea that there was a fight or a struggle or an argument. Simon was taken unawares. Whoever the killer is, they didn't just turn up in a woodland and randomly decide to just kill our friend here on a whim, did they? Like I just said, I can't help but think there's an element of planning to this. But if that's the case, then why cosh him on the head with nothing more than a stick?'

'It's like I just said,' said Cowboy, 'they were in a woodland, so it was easy to just grab something to knock him senseless with before they went ahead and finished the job by filling his lungs with pond water.'

Gordy wasn't convinced and shook her head.

'No, that's not what I mean; if you've planned to kill someone like this, and part of that plan involves rendering them sufficiently out of action by way of a hefty thwack to the skull, so that you can then drown them nice and easily, why would you then risk all of that on hopefully finding a stick capable enough of doing the damage?'

For a moment neither Cowboy nor Charming spoke.

The pathologist was the first to break the silence. 'You mean you think they took the murder weapon with them?'

'I'm saying,' said Gordy, 'that this was done by someone who wasn't leaving anything to chance. We don't know what the motive is, not yet, but everything was done for a reason, wasn't it? I think that the location is important, and I say that because if they'd just wanted to kill Simon, then why go to the trouble of dragging him further into the pool to drown him?'

'Maybe they just went with it.'

Gordy disagreed.

'Look, I'm no' saying I committed to memory every single deadfall I saw in that woodland, of course I'm not, because that's impossible. What I am saying, though, is that it's no' easy to find something with enough clout to do that kind of damage. The human skull is a tough shell to crack. You'd want to know that what you were going to use wasn't going to break on impact.'

As if to support what Gordy was saying, Charming rolled the body over towards him to reveal the wound to Simon's skull in all its gory glory.

'I see what you mean,' said Cowboy, peering at the area of smashed bone. 'Even so, surely a stick big and hard enough could do that?'

'Remember being a kid, and whacking random sticks

against trees?' Gordy said, quickly following her thoughts as they pulled her forward. She mimed whipping an invisible stick through the air. 'They snap, don't they, sometimes explosively, sending bits off all over the place?' She pointed at the wound. 'To do that, and to know that you're going to do that, you need to be damned sure that the thing you're wielding isn't going to bugger it all up and leave you with a very confused and very angry Simon nursing a bruised head as he comes at you with a stick of his own. Plus, there's the other thing, isn't there?'

Charming and Cowboy glanced at each other.

Cowboy asked, 'The other thing? What other thing?'

'The mistletoe. It was placed around Simon's neck, like a necklace, almost.'

'That's a jump,' said Cowboy.

'Is it?'

Gordy paused for a moment. On the drive over, following the meeting, Jameson had given her a call, and they'd had a good chat while she was at the wheel. He'd been a busy bee from the moment he'd got out of bed, and because of that, he'd given her a good amount of information about the pool. He'd not been in touch with the swimming group yet, but was on with that now, having once again reiterated that at no point was he going to be joining them and throwing himself into freezing cold water, all in the name of doing his duty.

'I've had someone looking into the location,' she said, 'and we've a few interesting things to consider.'

'Really?' said Cowboy. 'I'm intrigued.'

'We've got a pool, but not just any pool, because where Simon was, well, it isn't just some stagnant puddle of water acting as a reservoir for the woodland around it, full of all kinds of mouldering leaf litter and whatever else a woodland drops to its floor from its myriad branches. This is a pool fed by a freshwater spring, yes? I can't see that being entirely random. If it is, then so be it, but I'm not convinced, not knowing what I know now.'

'So, it's a freshwater spring,' said Cowboy. 'There's plenty enough of those about, for sure.'

'True,' Gordy agreed. 'The thing is, we've now got one with a body in it, wearing a mistletoe necklace. And do you know why mistletoe is significant?'

'You're going to tell us, aren't you?'

'Yes, I am,' smiled Gordy. 'Mistletoe is linked to male fertility. The Celts, would you believe, saw those white berries as the semen of the god of thunder. The Romans had one of their heroes using mistletoe to reach the underworld. And then there's the druids.'

Gordy was quietly impressed with the amount of detail she was now recalling from her chat with Jameson. He had promised to send notes through, but that would be later in the day, so for now it was her memory or nothing.

'Something told me you were going to mention druids,' said Charming, and Gordy guessed from the crinkle in the corners of his eyes that he was smiling as well.

'The druids had this ritual where they would climb a sacred tree, cut down the mistletoe, sacrifice a couple of white bulls, then use the mistletoe to make some kind of potion or whatever to cure infertility.'

'I'm fairly sure, given the chance, there's a few people would be up for that even now,' said Cowboy.

'I don't doubt it,' agreed Gordy. 'The thing is, though, that there are suggestions this ritual may have originally included human sacrifice, and that it was because the Romans banned it, that bulls were then used instead.'

Cowboy tutted.

'Spoil all the fun, don't they, those Romans?'

'So, what are you saying, exactly?' Charming asked. 'That what we've got in front of us now was a ritual sacrifice? I mean, it's tragic and horrible, for sure, but to go all the way into that kind of thing based on so little seems a bit tenuous.'

Gordy stepped back from Simon's body and folded her arms.

'If I'm honest, I don't know what I'm saying,' she admitted. 'I'm thinking aloud, just getting my thoughts out, giving them some air. But you can see what I mean, can't you? How all of this seems a little too organised? It could be random. It could also be a coincidence. But at the same time, I'm not going to stand here and discount everything else. There's too much going on, too many damned ingredients for me to ignore that this is potentially one properly messed up recipe.'

Gordy stopped talking, almost out of breath. The mortuary fell silent, and she felt terribly aware of not just death, but of the as-yet-unknown reasons why Simon had been killed. Why had this man, a retired accountant who had seemingly just gone for a swim on his own in the Somerset countryside, ended up having his skull stoved in before being drowned and then decorated with mistletoe? Throw in the hotel, the fact that his wife was away, and it was all very strange indeed. Tony Mills' ghost story briefly threatened to push its way into her thoughts, but she ignored it.

Cowboy broke the silence.

'Recipe?' he said. 'If that's what it is, then I'd dread to think what whoever's responsible is cooking up.'

'One more thing,' said Charming, and rolled the body

over a little further to reveal Simon's back. 'See those marks? The bruising? He drowned, yes, but not just because he was unconscious in the pool. Something heavy was on top of him. From the shape of those marks, I can quite confidently surmise that the something was a someone; the marks aren't at first glance obviously those made by feet, but closer examination reveals them to be exactly that.'

'Someone stood on him to keep him on the bottom of the pool?' said Gordy.

Charming gave a nod as he covered the body.

For a moment or two, no one spoke, until Gordy's thoughts tumbled out once again.

'I feel like I've got lots of information, but that none of it is pointing me in the direction I need to go.'

'Understandable,' said Charming.

'What's the motive?' Gordy asked, not expecting or wanting an answer. 'Why was Simon killed, and in this way? Is it smoke and mirrors, or is there a method in the madness?'

'Easy to see how it's both and neither,' said Cowboy. 'Who'd be a detective, eh?'

Tony Mills once again knocked at a small, well-locked door in Gordy's mind.

'We've even had someone turn up to tell us about a ghost he'd seen,' she said.

'That's a new one.'

'Isn't it just?'

Gordy wanted to check in with the rest of the team, see if anyone had found out anything important, though she doubted it, not this early on.

'I'm going to head off,' she said. 'I'd like to say it's been a pleasure, but ...'

'I'll check in with my team,' said Cowboy. 'Might be something else, you never know.'

'I've not had results back on stomach contents, blood work, that kind of thing,' said Charming, 'but I'll let you know as soon as I do.'

Gordy thanked Cowboy and Charming, then made her way out of the mortuary, removing the jacket, the boots, and disposing of the face mask. Outside, and heading back to her vehicle, she really wanted to focus on the investigation, and she was, but annoyingly, she found that despite all of that, her mind kept drifting back to what Tony had said to her. She had no time for charlatans, for people who preyed on the grief and vulnerability of others, and her grief, despite the excitement of meeting Charlie, was still raw. That she felt like she was now on the receiving end of exactly that didn't just irritate her, it set a fire in her belly that she needed to either control or find some way to extinguish. For now, though, she would do her best to ignore what he had said and to focus on the facts. She had a murder to solve, and messages from the other side weren't going to help—of that she was damned sure.

TWENTY-TWO

Having spoken with Gordy on her way to the hospital, Jameson was on his way to meet with a member of the outdoor swimming group, The Ebb. Having carried out some research into strange little pools of water, and satisfied Gordy enough with it to be able to move onto something else, he'd done a little bit of investigating into The Ebb.

Unfortunately, what he'd first typed into Google was The Egg instead of The Ebb, and that had been rather confusing, presenting him with information about a short story, a theatre, a rock band, and various other things, which clearly had nothing to do with outdoor swimming. He had come across a good recipe for pickled eggs, though, so that was something. And it had been years since he'd made his own.

The thought of laying down a couple of large jars for the winter months had got him thinking about what else he could pickle and preserve for winter, and that had sent him down a rabbit hole of home preserves, salting meat, brewing beer and running a small holding. Though he wasn't about to sell up and buy a little place with a couple of acres, it had got him back to thinking about what Gordy had said about him needing an interest. Were pickled eggs the doorway to a new hobby? It was certainly something to think about.

Forcing himself to get back to what Gordy had tasked him with, Jameson had eventually found a link to a Facebook group and what he guessed was one of the most basic websites in existence. As he wasn't on Facebook, and had no urge to ever be, either, it had been the website or nothing. The page itself comprised the name of the group, an out-of-focus photograph of waves washing up onto a beach, a contact email address, and a short paragraph explaining what the group was all about. On reading it, Jameson was only more convinced than ever that he would not, under any circumstances, be joining the group for real and ending up in the water.

Having sent a brief message to the provided email address, Jameson hadn't expected to get a response right away and had thought, after having spoken with Gordy, that he would have the rest of the day free. What he would do with it, he hadn't been sure, so he had been somewhat relieved to receive a message on his phone from someone called Gail Carpenter. Gail had introduced herself as a member of the group and had said she would be happy to meet that same day. So, that was what Jameson was on with now, driving over to Vobster Quay, where he would do his best to sound interested in outdoor swimming, while making sure he didn't make the fatal error of signing up for a trial session and end up having to throw himself in. Following Gordy's instructions, he would maintain his cover story as someone who wanted to join the group and would not mention anything about his connection to the police.

Arriving at the quay, Jameson parked up, then headed on down a concrete lane towards the lake. The quay itself was actually an old quarry, now flooded thanks to being fed by a very enthusiastic freshwater spring, and according to the website he'd had a brief look at, was terrifyingly deep. As to the temperature of the water, which was taken throughout the day? Well, that was just ridiculous, wasn't it? Another good reason for him to have nothing to do with jumping in, even in a wetsuit. He didn't own one, and he certainly wouldn't be buying one either.

It wasn't so much that Jameson couldn't swim, or that he didn't enjoy it, more that he wasn't a fan of getting cold. Why anyone would want to get cold on purpose, in water, baffled him utterly, and no amount of being told it was good for his mental health was going to convince him otherwise. As to diving, and exploring the deep, dark depths, that was an activity he'd never seen the sense in. Yes, it looked very impressive and beautiful on television, but that had never made it any more attractive to him. Why people would come to a place like this and throw themselves into a man-made lake to go have a look at the sunken remains of a transit van or a caravan baffled him completely.

Down by the lake, Jameson spotted a woman waving at him from a picnic bench by the water's edge and headed over. He weaved through various groups of people, all of them wearing everything from dry robes and wetsuits to swimsuits and beach towels that had seen better days. Far too many of them, he noted, were wearing bobble hats.

'Afternoon,' Jameson said, as he sat down opposite the woman. 'Gail Carpenter, I assume? Unless you just like waving at random people who've arrived here.'

'A bit of both,' said Gail. 'Tea?'

Gail removed a flask from a bag at her side and presented two small mugs.

'Why not?' replied Jameson.

Gail poured out the drinks and handed one of the mugs to Jameson.

'I'm going to assume Jameson isn't your first name,' she said.

'It's Peter,' Jameson replied. 'I'm just used to going by my surname, that's all. So much so that I've almost forgotten I have a first name.'

'Why's that, then?'

Jameson sipped his tea as he tried to come up with a reason that didn't involve him mentioning his life in the police.

'It's just always been that way,' he said. 'Probably from school. Guess I thought it sounded cooler.' He looked over at the lake. 'So, this is where The Ebb meets, is it?'

'We don't just swim here, though,' Gail explained, clasping her mug with both hands. 'This is our regular spot. Saturdays and Tuesdays are mostly here, but we go to various rivers and coastal spots as well.'

Gail, Jameson observed, was a small woman, who spoke with a soft, quiet voice. Dressed in a blue fleece jacket, with a pair of unremarkable glasses perched on her face, he put her at around his age, give or take a year or two. She was doing well so far with the conversation, he thought, but there was a flatness to her voice, like she wasn't really into it, or was distracted by something. He wondered if news of the death of one of their members had already spread through the group. There was no reason to suspect that it hadn't.

'You're interested in joining our group, then?' Gail asked.

Jameson wanted to say no.

'Yes,' he lied as convincingly as he could.

'Done any outdoor swimming before?'

'Oh, you know, probably no more than most people. A dip in the sea, that kind of thing.'

'Strong swimmer?'

'Strong enough.'

'Swimming somewhere like this, it can be intimidating. How are you with deep water?'

Jameson remembered what he'd read on the website about the depth of the lake.

'It's a little unnerving, but I think it would do me good to try and overcome that.'

'I still find it difficult,' Gail admitted, which rather surprised Jameson. 'It's part of the reason I keep coming back, to try and make myself a little stronger, improve my resilience.'

Jameson sipped his tea.

'What's the group like, then?' he asked.

'In what sense?'

Jameson gave a shrug.

'I'm not big on clubs,' he said, and that was the truth of it right there as to why, perhaps, he found hobbies and interests so difficult. He'd never got on well with hanging out with people whose only reason for knowing each other and socialising was because they shared an interest. Soon enough he'd find it all a little cliquey. He'd always been that way, though, and he remembered how his wife had teased him about it. A memory of her laugh cut him sharp, and he realised he wasn't listening to Gail.

'Really?' he said, hoping that response to whatever she'd said was enough to cover up the fact that he'd drifted off.

'Well, we're not a club, for a start,' Gail said, thankfully oblivious to Jameson's wandering attention. 'We're not official or anything; there's no committee, nothing like that.'

'That's a relief,' said Jameson.

'There's no competitiveness to what we do. We just meet up, natter, go for a dip, natter some more, drink far too much hot chocolate, and hopefully get something out of it.'

'Like what?'

Gail smiled.

'I could give you all the usual about how good cold water is for your mental health, for circulation, for all kinds of things, but I think there's more to it than that.' She went to say something else but something caught her eye, and she said, 'Here's someone who can give you a better answer than me.'

Jameson turned around as a man approached them. He was barefoot, dressed in shorts and a pale blue cotton shirt.

'Hi, Gail,' he said, coming to sit beside her, before turning to Jameson with a smile. 'Mike Small,' he said, and held out a hand, which Jameson shook. 'New member?'

'Peter,' said Jameson. 'And yes, potentially. Gail was doing very well at persuading me with the benefits of throwing myself in cold water.'

'Best way to find out is to come along and have a go. We accept everyone and anyone pretty much. So long as you're a confident enough swimmer, you're in.'

'And if you're not,' Mike added, 'we'll help you anyway, provide a bit of coaching, either one-to-one or in small groups, that kind of thing. For that, we've a few members who are qualified, including me, so it's all safe. And we can advise on what kit you'll need as well. You don't need much, and neither do you need to spend a lot, either.'

Jameson laughed.

'Me in a wetsuit? What a terrifying thought.'

'Most of us don't actually wear one.'

'You don't? What about in winter? You must do then, surely.'

'We just don't stay in the water as long, that's all,' said Gail, as though swimming in freezing-cold water was entirely normal. 'And we're really careful and safety aware. It's all part of the buzz.' She picked up her flask. 'Top up?'

'Why not?' Jameson nodded.

'You'll have to budge up in a minute,' Gail said, once Jameson's mug was full. 'I've someone else coming along for a chat. Though I don't know if they'll want you to be a part of it.'

'Really? Why's that?'

Gail sipped her tea.

'Not sure I should say, really, seeing as you're keen to join us. I don't want to give you the wrong impression.'

'That sounds ominous.'

Jameson gave her a moment, rather than pester her to explain, but before she did, Mike spoke.

'I'm afraid to say that one of our group drowned last week,' he said. 'We're none of us too sure about the ins and outs of what happened, where he was, anything like that, but the police are involved.'

Gail said, 'They've been in touch and want to speak to a few of us.'

'They do? Why?'

Jameson was quietly impressed with how he was maintaining his cover story.

'I think we might have been the last ones to see him alive,' she said at last, her voice quiet. 'I'd gone to the river for a swim, but a few others had obviously had the same idea. Then Simon, he turned up, as did a couple of his friends from his golf club, which isn't really how we do things, because we need to make sure that people are actually okay in the water. Open-water swimming isn't like jumping into the pool at the local leisure centre; cold water shock can kill. Anyway, regardless of all that, it's terrible what happened. No idea where he died, though. And no one's told us, either.'

'My guess is that he did something stupid,' said Mike. 'Just like how he brought those friends of his to the river without checking with anyone first.'

'You know, I thought I recognised one of them for a moment,' said Gail. 'No idea why, though; I've never played golf in my life!'

Mike stared hard at Jameson.

'Water's dangerous; you can't afford to not take it seriously.'

Gail punched Mike gently on the arm.

'Don't be like that. You'll put him off!'

Mike held up his hands in mock defence.

'I'm just saying that if someone had been there with him, then he probably wouldn't have ended up dead. That sounds quite harsh, I know, but there we are.'

'Can you be showy with swimming?' Jameson asked.

Gail gave a nod.

'Simon had all the gear pretty much as soon as he joined the group. He liked to go on and on about everything he knew about swimming, how to improve technique, the best places to go, even what plans he had to go swimming abroad. It was too much for me, really, but the group is for everyone, and it does take all sorts to make a world, doesn't it?'

'It does.'

Gail looked down at her hands for a moment before saying, 'I hope that's not put you off.'

'Of course it hasn't,' said Mike, smiling at Jameson. 'You don't need to worry about that, Gail.'

Jameson went to say something non-committal, when Gail lifted a hand to wave at someone behind him. He turned around once again, this time to see the familiar figure of Detective Constable Peter Knight approaching.

'This your other visitor, then?'

'Looks that way,' said Gail.

Jameson stood up.

'I'll leave you to it,' he said. 'Thanks for your time, Gail, much appreciated. And good to meet you, too, Mike.'

Pete introduced himself, then said to Jameson, 'You a member of The Ebb as well, then?'

Jameson shook his head.

'No, not yet.'

'I'll see you tomorrow, though, yes?' asked Gail.

Jameson did a double-take.

'Tomorrow? What's happening tomorrow?'

'We meet up every Tuesday for an early morning swim. You're more than welcome. You don't have to swim, but we might get you to dip your toe in the water, right? We also meet Saturdays, but why wait?'

Jameson was about to say that he was busy when Pete rested a hand on his shoulder and said, 'Sounds like a great idea! No point putting things off, is there?'

Jameson narrowed his eyes at the detective constable, noticing the faintest of smirks at the corner of his mouth.

'No, I suppose there isn't,' he said.

'Excellent,' said Gail, and stood up to shake Jameson's hand. 'If you've not got a wetsuit, you can hire one here.

Bring plenty of warm clothes as well, so that you can get changed and shrug off the cold quickly. I'll message you with the time later on.'

'Fantastic,' Jameson replied, and knew very well how unconvincing he sounded.

He left Gail and Mike to have their chat with Pete and headed off. On the way back to his car, he heard his wife's laugh again, and before he knew what he was doing, he was joining in.

TWENTY-THREE

Gordy woke to the sound of her phone drilling its way into her head. Her first thought was that she really needed to change her ring tone to something considerably softer and more calming, so that when someone called, there was less chance of her having a heart attack. Her second thought was to just ignore it, especially considering she had been so tired after her day at work that she'd fallen asleep on her sofa watching reruns of Murder She Wrote. She wasn't even that much of a fan of the programme, but she'd put it on anyway while she'd tucked into her dinner that evening.

The day had been a long one, and after the morning meeting and the trip over to see Charming and Cowboy, Gordy had spent the rest of it keeping on top of what the rest of the team was doing and meeting up with them as and when she could.

Maria had confirmed that the body found at the pond, and now lying in the chiller at the mortuary, was indeed her husband, Simon, and Patti had been on hand to support her through that truly awful moment. She had gone home with her as well, cancelling Helen's visit to see Maria later that day; it had made more sense to stay with Maria herself, and to have Helen as the main point of contact back at the station. Patti had managed to get a few more details about where Maria had been for those few days. Helen now had the contact details for the friend that Maria had been away with, a woman called Amy Stanton, but as yet, had been unable to contact her, though messages had been left, requesting a return call, as well as letting her know further tries would be made to call her.

Travis had paid a visit to the shooting range and heard about what had happened while Tony was there. All he'd gathered from a member of staff who had been there at the time was that Tony had had a bit of a funny turn. He'd also been in touch with Tony Mills himself, but so far, the builder was being less than accommodating, claiming he was too busy with work to just drop everything and meet up. Gordy would have to see about that, if he continued to be evasive.

Pete had met with a couple of members from the swimming group; Gail, who had seen Simon at the river the morning of his murder, but beyond that had nothing else to tell him, and Mike, who had been working at his allotment all day and into the evening. Gail had, however, provided him with the contact details of the rest of the group who had been with Simon at the river that morning, which was useful, and he was now checking through those as well.

Gordy had laughed out loud when Pete had told her about bumping into Jameson and his imminent first dip in the water. She'd then had a chat with the former DCI, though most of that had been overshadowed by Jameson's lack of enthusiasm for going swimming, and Gordy's own hilarity at the situation. He'd also told her Gail mentioned

Simon having two golfing friends turn up at the river. That had been the first Gordy had heard about them, so tomorrow she would find out where Simon played golf, which club he belonged to, and get in touch with them.

Picking up her phone from the coffee table, Gordy didn't recognise the number at first, then realised that it was Charlie. Before she knew what she was doing, she'd answered, her excitement at receiving the surprise call overcoming her initial shock of being so rudely awakened.

'Well, this is a pleasant surprise,' she said, only to have her joy at realising who had called her crushed by the sound of sobbing. 'Charlie? What's wrong?'

Charlie didn't answer right away, though Gordy could tell she was trying to get words out between the tears.

'Gordy, I'm sorry ... I didn't know who else to call.'

'You can always call me,' Gordy said, the words out before she'd really thought about the implication of what she'd said. 'What's happened?'

Charlie sobbed again, then said, 'I ... I need your help. I think ... I think someone just tried to kill me.'

Gordy went from half asleep to wide awake in a beat.

'What? Charlie, where are you? What happened? Are you safe? Is there someone with you?'

More questions wanted to tumble out, but she held them back to give Charlie a chance to reply. For a few seconds, all Gordy could hear was sobbing, and the sound of it made no sense on so many levels. Why was Charlie crying? And why had she called her? They hardly knew each other, certainly not enough to be calling each other in times of crisis. So, just what the hell had happened? What was going on? Had she really just said that someone had tried to kill her?

At last, Charlie's crying subsided enough for her to speak through the sobs.

'They ... they came out of nowhere, just attacked me.'

'How? Where are you, Charlie? I need to know. I can send help. I'll come myself, for that matter.'

Charlie sniffed.

'I'm in West Lydford. There's a bridge by the church. I'm ... I'm there. In my car.'

Gordy had never heard of West Lydford. No surprise really, she thought; you only had to take a random left or right off any of the major roads in Somerset, and you'd end up in a village or hamlet tucked away from the rest of the world as though playing a game of hide and seek.

'You need to tell me exactly what happened.'

'I don't really know exactly what happened. I was ... No, I can't, Gordy ... It's ...'

Charlie broke down again.

'Charlie, is anyone with you?'

'No.'

'You said someone tried to—'

'They just attacked me. I don't know why! Something went over my head. I couldn't breathe, Gordy! Then ...'

'Then what?'

No response.

Gordy quickly looked up West Lydford on her phone.

'Charlie?'

'Yes?'

'West Lydford's only fifteen minutes from me. I'm on my way.'

Charlie's response was to break down once again. Gordy was already on her feet and out of her front door, running down to her vehicle, keys in hand.

'Are you safe? Have you locked your car? Are you sure you're alone now?'

'I think so, yes,' Charlie replied.

'Stay on the phone,' Gordy instructed, jumping behind the steering wheel and starting the engine.

Wheel-spinning out of the parking area in front of where she lived, Gordy was soon on the road and speeding through the dusky hours of late evening. Whatever had happened to Charlie, she needed to be there fast, and she focused on the road ahead, her senses all online now, adrenaline coursing through her body.

For now, the case she and the team were dealing with took a back seat, and Gordy tried to throw her mind over to where Charlie was, to see if she could make any sense at all of what was going on, what had happened, to prepare herself for every eventuality, no matter how impossible that actually was.

'You still with me, Charlie?'

'Yes.'

'That's good. I'm nine minutes away now, okay? Not long. Keep talking to me if you can. If you can't, just listen.'

'Thank you.'

Gordy was no longer on narrow lanes but zipping down a main road. The moon was high in a clear sky, and stars sat pinned to the dark like sequins.

'Seven minutes now.'

'I'm okay.'

'Charlie, when you're ready, try and tell me what happened, okay? Did you get a look at the person who attacked you?'

'No, I didn't,' Charlie replied. Her voice was calmer now, Gordy noticed, which was a good sign. 'They came at me from behind. I didn't know they were there until they grabbed me.'

'You said something was pulled over your head.'

'It was a plastic bag. They pulled it tight round my neck, then ...'

'Then what?'

Silence.

'Charlie?'

'I'm ... I'm still ... here.'

'Four minutes now.'

Gordy took a right, off the main road, onto a narrow lane, realised something about Charlie's voice, that she sounded more than just scared and upset.

'You sound like you're shivering.'

'I'm freezing. I've the engine on, though, and the heating.'

'That's good. Two minutes.'

Gordy saw houses and slowed down as much as she dared. Ahead, she saw a parking area, a church, and then a car.

'I'm here.'

Gordy pulled into the parking area too fast, slammed on her brakes, and came to a sudden stop. She turned the engine off and was out of her car, leaving the door open, as she ran to Charlie's car where she yanked open the driver's door.

Charlie stared up at her from the driver's seat. Then, before Gordy had a chance to say anything, to find out what had happened, check if she was okay, and ask just why the hell she was wrapped in a beach towel, Charlie was out of her car and shivering in her arms, wearing nothing more than a swimsuit.

TWENTY-FOUR

Gordy held Charlie close, her arms wrapped around the woman's shivering body, aware that her own clothes were already getting damp.

'You're freezing,' she said. 'What on earth have you been doing? Where are your clothes?'

The answer to that question was obvious, Gordy thought, but she asked it anyway, because she couldn't quite wrap her head around it.

'By the river,' Charlie said. 'Other side. Over the bridge.'

'And what the hell are they doing there?'

'I ... I left them there. I didn't think about grabbing them. I just wanted to get back to my car after it happened.'

Gordy led Charlie back to her own vehicle, helped her into the passenger seat, then started the engine and whacked the heat up to full. Then she jogged back over to Charlie's car and retrieved her towel.

'Here,' she said, handing over the towel. 'Wrap yourself in this while I go fetch your clothes. Where are they exactly? Over the bridge isn't much to go on.'

Charlie gave Gordy a stuttered answer.

'You've some explaining to do when I get back,' Gordy said, then shut the passenger door, ran back to the road and over the bridge, then down a lane until she found Charlie's bag spilled over on the bank of the river. Stuffing everything back inside and trying to avoid any thoughts linking Charlie to the investigation she was dealing with, Gordy ran back to her vehicle and jumped in behind the steering wheel.

'Here,' she said, pulling clothes out of the bag in no particular order. 'Get out of that swimsuit and get your clothes on. And don't go worrying about modesty either. You need to be warm, so I won't be doing with any of that shy nonsense.'

'I'm not shy.'

'But you are cold, so stop talking and get dressed.'

The car fell into silence as Charlie did as she had been instructed and Gordy tried to wrap her head around what had happened.

'Any better?'

Charlie had managed to shiver her way out of her swimsuit, all while somehow keeping herself fully covered by the damp towel. That had impressed Gordy no end, but she kept any praise she wanted to offer to herself for now.

'Yes,' Charlie said. 'Thank you. For coming out to help me. You didn't have to.'

'You rang me,' Gordy said. 'You woke me up from a very satisfying evening nap to tell me someone had tried to kill you. I was hardly going to stay at home with my feet up, was I?'

'No, I know, but still,' said Charlie. 'And I didn't mean to panic you.'

Gordy sighed and stared across her car at Charlie.

'I refer you, once again, to your mentioning that someone tried to kill you. So, how's about we start there? Because, so far, you've still given me little if anything about what actually happened. Oh, and while you're on with that, I'll be expecting an explanation as to why you're here in the first place, and for some reason dressed for a swimming gala.'

Charlie smiled.

'Swimming gala? My butterfly stroke is quite something.'

'I'm sure it is,' Gordy replied. 'But if you're going to practise it, can I suggest that perhaps a murky river in the Somerset countryside, in the middle of the night, is not the best of locations?'

'You'd be surprised.'

'Oh, you can colour me that and a bit more. And while you're there, throw in baffled, confused, stunned, shocked, worried ...'

'I get your point.'

'Good,' nodded Gordy. 'Now back to why I'm here, the reason you called me; you said someone tried to kill you.'

Charlie's response was to drop her head into her hands.

'I just needed a swim, that's all,' she said. 'This place is a favourite spot of mine. No one really comes here, certainly not at this time of the day, anyway.'

'It's night-time.'

'That's what I mean. There are other places to go. I just like it here, swimming under the bridge, heading upstream a bit. It's dark and a bit spooky, I know, but I like that.'

'You do? Why?'

Charlie shrugged.

'Gives me a bit of a thrill, I suppose.'

'There are safer ways to get a thrill, I assure you,' said Gordy. 'And warmer ones, too. But ignoring that for the moment; tell me what happened, everything you can remember.'

'There's not much to tell,' said Charlie. 'You saw where my bag was; that's where I got into the river, and I was just about to get out after my swim, when—'

'What? You were in the river when you were attacked?'

Gordy couldn't believe what she was hearing.

'Yes, I thought I said that?'

Gordy shook her head.

'No, you didn't, Charlie. All you've told me is that you were attacked. I then turn up and find you sopping wet and half hyperthermic in your car. There's been no mention of you actually being in the water when you were attacked.'

'Well, I was,' said Charlie. 'Like I just said, I'd already done my swim, up the river a bit, under the bridge and then on just far enough to make it worth it, then back again. As I was trying to get out of the river—it's not easy because the bank's quite slippery and muddy and it's a bit of a scramble—a bag was pulled over my head.'

Gordy was unable to hide her shock.

'Good God, Charlie ...'

'Whoever it was, they dragged me backwards into the river. Then we were under some of the trees that hang off the bank over the water. I tried to fight back, but it was hard to know where I was, what was going on, what to do. It's not something you really prepare for, is it, being attacked in a river?'

'No, not really,' Gordy agreed.

'I think I must've been too much of a struggle to hold,' Charlie continued. 'Next thing I know, I'm free of the bag, and whoever it was, they're gone. I headed to the bank as quickly as I could and ran back to my car. I've probably cut my feet to pieces as well, running back barefoot.'

'And you didn't see who it was?'

Charlie shook her head.

'They weren't on the shore when I climbed out. They didn't try and swim after me. I didn't care, I just wanted to be back in my car. I tried to drive, but I couldn't. I was shaking too much. Then I called you. And now you're here.'

'But you hardly know me,' said Gordy. 'We've met twice, that's it! You must have friends you can call, relatives? Why me?'

'Isn't it obvious?'

'I know I'm with the police, and that's fine, I get that, especially considering what you've said happened, but why me directly?'

Charlie gave a shudder.

'There's the other thing,' she said.

'There is? What other thing?'

'Simon.'

At the mention of that name, things fell into place and Gordy felt her whole world shift around her.

'You knew him?'

'Yes,' said Charlie. 'I belong to the same swimming group. I'm a member of The Ebb.'

TWENTY-FIVE

Back at the station was not where Gordy wanted to be, especially considering the hour. With the investigation that the team was now involved with, a couple of uniforms had been roped in to help staff the place, and they were certainly making short work of what Vivek had left in the snack cupboard.

With everything that Charlie had told her, Gordy had no choice but to take her to Frome to chat through it all again and get a statement put down. Within a few minutes of her arrival at the station with Charlie, the two uniformed officers had headed out to deal with a disturbance at a local pub, and she was rather happy they'd gone. That Charlie was somehow connected to Simon had unsettled her more than she'd dare admit, and she preferred a bit of space to deal with it.

Having talked through the traumatic experience of what had happened to her at the river, and in as much detail as Charlie was able to provide, Gordy was struggling with two things; one, that the information about Charlie's alleged attacker was scant at best, non-existent at worst, and two, Gordy simply couldn't see how this was coincidental, that there was no connection between Simon's death and Charlie being attacked. Charlie, to Gordy's surprise, belonged to The Ebb, and so did Simon. Simon had been attacked while out for a swim, and that was the same for Charlie. And they had both been swimming alone, something she couldn't quite get her head around, especially considering both had done so at night.

As yet, Gordy had no idea whether the river, like the pool, was significant in some way. Not that the pool itself held any actual importance, but the fact that it was fed by a freshwater spring, that the dog walker, Gregory, had seen others there, and not just for a dip, either, had seemed important. Still did, too. The river ran alongside a church though, Gordy remembered, so perhaps that was significant, too? The only difference really between the two places, the two events, was that Charlie had somehow managed to get away, and was relatively unharmed, if she discounted the trauma that would haunt her for a while yet.

As for the crime scene, Gordy had the pleasure of not only calling some of her own, but also the SOC team. Cowboy was unavailable, so it had fallen to another to respond, and she and Charlie had waited for them to arrive. While there, Gordy had cordoned the place off, then Pete had arrived, along with Travis. Both had done their level best to not look tired, but for most of the time Gordy had spent with them, before driving with Charlie over to Frome, they'd played ping-pong with a yawn and been generous enough to include her in the game as well. To Gordy's surprise, she had been rather disappointed not to see Cowboy's ridiculous hat that evening, or to hear his preposterous Western drawl.

With the statement taken about what had happened at the river, Gordy would've liked to have taken Charlie through to her office, simply because it was a little more comfortable. But that wasn't about to happen. Not only was it bang against procedure and pretty much every single police rule she both could and couldn't remember, there was also the issue of conflict of interest.

She had that covered, thankfully. First, the interview was informal, and Charlie wasn't suspected of having committed any crime. Instead, she was a victim of an attack by a person or persons as yet unknown. She had volunteered willingly to come along and chat things through. Also, Gordy had asked Patti to meet them at the station. The detective sergeant had sat in with them for the interview and was now away to get another hot drink provided, and to see if the two uniforms had left anything of Vivek's for them to snack on. Gordy had doubted it, but to her surprise been proved wrong, with Patti returning not just with drinks, but a little Tupperware box of ginger biscuits.

'So, it's Charlotte, not Charlie,' Gordy said, as they all reached for a biscuit to dunk in their drinks, and she searched for a way to push the conversation away from what had happened to Charlie and into finding out more about The Ebb, and Simon.

A shiver rippled through Charlie's body.

'I go by Charlie,' she explained, 'but not everyone calls me that.'

She was still cold, Gordy thought, guessing that the chill of the river had seeped through to her bones.

'I know you're tired,' continued Gordy, 'but we could do with just a bit more of your time, if that's okay? Unless you'd rather leave it to tomorrow? I'd prefer if we didn't, but—'

'What about my car?' Charlie asked, interrupting Gordy with a yawn. 'We left it in the car park in front of the church.'

'We'll arrange to get it back for you as soon as we can,' said Gordy.

'But I need it tomorrow to get to work.'

'What is it that you do?' Patti asked.

'I work at the library,' Charlie replied.

'The SOC team will be busy with it for a while,' Gordy explained. 'Is there any other way you can get to work?'

'The SOC team?'

'Scene of Crime,' said Patti.

Gordy saw shock register in Charlie's eyes.

'What? I'm the victim here, I was attacked! Why is my car being looked at? That makes no sense at all!'

For the first time since meeting her, Gordy heard anger in Charlie's voice.

'Do you have anyone who can give you a lift to work?'

Charlie shook her head.

'It's okay, I've a bike, I'll use that.' she said, then rubbed her eyes, clearly weary. 'I'm just making a fuss. Sorry. It's not like I live far away. Beckington's no distance. I'll be fine.'

That sorted, Gordy pushed on.

'As you know, we're investigating the death of one of the members of the swimming group, which you belong to.'

'There's no real official membership as such, though,' said Charlie. 'It's just a bunch of people who've gathered together with a shared interest in swimming outdoors, the benefits of cold water, and hanging out together.'

Gordy thought back now to what Jameson had told her about what he'd learned from Gail and Mike about Simon, how it sounded like he didn't quite fit in.

'What was Simon like?' she asked.

'Simon? Keen,' answered Charlie. 'He joined the group about three months ago, I think. Very good at ruffling feathers, but he's harmless.'

'Ruffling feathers?' said Patti, the words question enough on their own without further elaboration.

Charlie leaned back in her chair.

'We're a group for everyone,' she said. 'That's the way it's always been, always will be. It's not an elite thing, or anything like that, just a group of people hanging out together, like I've said, and we're from all walks of life. That's its strength, though at times, also its weakness.'

'In what way?'

'If you want to let everyone in, you can't then start inventing rules to keep people out, can you?' said Charlie. 'When we started, there were only a few of us. I was the youngest, bumped into the others at various swimming spots, and it sort of evolved from there, really. I pushed the idea that we should meet regularly rather than ad hoc, and that's how The Ebb was born.'

'So how do you mean about its strength being its weakness?' Gordy asked. 'You said something about inventing rules, but what you've said doesn't explain that.'

'It was a gentle thing to begin with,' said Charlie. 'I started cold water swimming because of past trauma, though I'm not about to go into that here. Gail, she had her own reasons, as did the other three.'

'Gail,' Gordy repeated, thinking back to her chat with Jameson. 'Carpenter?'

Charlie gave a nod.

'We call ourselves The Originals. There's five of us.

Myself, Gail, Margaret Ascott, Mike Small, and Terry Finch.'

'So, is it not gentle now?' Patti asked. 'And what do you actually mean by that?'

'We're mutually supportive,' said Charlie. 'No matter what you're going through, how you're feeling, what secrets you've got, what you've done in your life, your background, you can turn up. You don't have to talk to anyone, you can just be. That's what I mean. Some of the newer members, though, they don't quite get it. But that's what happens when a group grows, isn't it? It changes. Not everyone likes it, but you just have to get on with it, don't you?'

Gordy wondered what trauma Charlie had dealt with that had sent her into the world of cold-water swimming. She knew of the benefits herself, and though she had thrown herself into the occasional lake and river with Anna, she'd not ventured into the water for a good while now, not since they'd spread Anna's ashes. And no amount of clinically backed research as to its benefits was going to persuade her to rush into its embrace, either.

'And the group's changed, then, is that what you're saying?' asked Gordy.

'Yes.'

'How did Simon fit into all this?' Patti asked.

Charlie smiled, and there it was again, Gordy thought, that little light behind the woman's eyes that she really, really liked.

'As well as any of us,' Charlie said. 'We all do and don't fit in, depending on the day. That's the point, really. Maybe not for all of us, I guess, but it is for me. Gail's not a fan of the changes, I know, mainly because she's told me plenty of times. She's not alone in thinking that, though, that's for sure.' A sudden look of shock killed the brightness behind her eyes like a light switch being flicked. 'You think that's why Simon was killed, because someone in the group didn't like change? You can't be serious! I mean, that's ridiculous!'

Gordy leaned forward to try and give some air of reassurance.

'All we're doing is trying to work out what happened and why. We have to ask questions if we're to get answers.'

'I don't want you thinking I'm suggesting Gail's responsible though,' said Charlie. 'She can't be! I'm not throwing her under the bus! Have you met her?' Charlie held up the little finger on her right hand. 'That's how big she is!'

'You haven't suggested that at all,' said Patti. 'My guess is, from what you've said, that there are plenty of members who aren't big fans of how the group has changed.'

'Yes, but there's not being a fan of change, and then there's killing someone because of it. They're completely different things!'

'Do you have a list of the members?' Gordy asked.

'No,' Charlie said. 'We're not an official club or anything, like I've already told you. If we were, the group wouldn't work; I think a lot of the people who come along would leave immediately, myself included.'

'Why?'

'You can be as into it as you want or as anonymous as you want, it just doesn't matter. We have a private Facebook group, but not everyone's on that. Then there are little chat groups here and there, and I don't know of anyone who's a member of every one of those, either. I mean, I don't know every member myself. Some people turn up once a week, others once a month. There are those who come along if someone arranges a trip to the coast, and there are others who disappear for months, only to turn up unannounced as if they've been there all the time. That's just the way it is. That's its charm.'

Gordy yawned, only just managing to cover her mouth with her hand in time.

'Same here,' said Charlie, and joined in.

Patti was last to fall but soon succumbed.

'I think we should call it a day,' Gordy said, then looked at Charlie. 'Do you have anywhere you can stay tonight, somewhere you'll not be alone? Family, friends, that kind of thing?'

Charlie, Gordy noticed, looked at her with just enough mischief to show that she had one idea, but there was no way Gordy was going to follow up on that, and waited for her to speak.

'I can call Mike,' she said. 'He doesn't sleep anyway and is probably out picking slugs off his cabbages or something. He'll be happy to come sleep on my sofa. Probably do my garden for me in the morning as well.'

'He's a good friend, then?'

'Known him years,' said Charlie. 'He's helped me a lot. He's very kind, likes to look after people, I think, a bit of a mother hen. But don't tell him I said that.'

Gordy glanced at Patti.

'Would you be okay to take Charlie home?'

She saw a look of disappointment etch itself on Charlie's face as Patti said yes, so she sent a smile her way, then rose to her feet.

'Let's catch up tomorrow,' she said. 'You have my number, so don't hesitate to call or message if you remember something, no matter how small. Though if you can wait 'til the morning, that would be appreciated.'

Patti and Charlie stood up, and Patti opened the door, gesturing for Charlie to follow. Charlie walked to the door, then paused, and turned to look at Gordy.

'Thanks,' she said. 'For coming out tonight. I know I shouldn't have called you directly. I just panicked. Sorry.'

That said, she turned to leave.

Gordy went to say goodbye, then realised there was one other question she'd not asked Charlie and called her back.

'The night Simon was killed,' she said, 'can you remember where you were and what you were doing?'

Charlie's mouth dropped open, and Gordy saw a bright light of shock in her now wide eyes.

'What?'

'We need to know,' Gordy explained, sensing Charlie becoming prickly. 'We'll be checking the same with everyone who was with him that morning at the river.'

'Which I wasn't.'

'But you are a member of The Ebb.'

'Yes, but what's that got to do with anything?'

Gordy hated herself for this. She liked Charlie, but right now, she couldn't let her feelings get in the way.

'Please, Charlie,' she said. 'It's just so we can narrow things down, that's all. We have to be thorough in our work. I know it can make people feel like they're being picked on or accused, but it's really not that at all. We just need to know where you—'

'Swimming, okay?' Charlie snapped back. 'I was swimming!'

For a moment, Gordy was stunned by Charlie's reply, and not just from what she'd said, either, but how she'd said it.

'Can you remember what time, exactly?'

'It was the evening,' Charlie said. 'After work. I headed out straight after. It's a ritual I have. I do it on the same day every year.'

'A ritual? How do you mean? What kind of ritual?'

That word worried Gordy.

'I went through a tough time a good few years ago, and that's my business, but it's why The Ebb has become so important to me, because it healed, me, Gordy. I can't explain how, it just did.'

Gordy wanted to ask *from what*, but instead said, 'Is there anyone who can confirm where you were?'

'An alibi, you mean? What is this, some cop show on TV? Of course I can't! I live on my own, Gordy. I went out on my own. I came back on my own.'

It was Gordy's turn to have her mouth drop open.

'But you were on your own tonight as well.'

'I swim a lot on my own. Tonight, well, that's my regular thing. I do it in the same spot every week. Last week, that was different, like I've said. That's once a year, and only ever once a year, regardless of the weather. I plan my time around it, it's important.'

'I didn't realise solo swims were such a thing,' said Patti.

'Sometimes, swimming can feel like it's doing you more good if there are no distractions, no chitchat,' said Charlie. 'There's a peace to it, in the solitude of being in the water all by yourself.'

'Were you swimming in the same place, then?' Gordy asked. 'The river by the church?'

Charlie shook her head.

'For my yearly dip, I go somewhere really special. Means more there for some reason, more cleansing. Probably the fact that it's a spring, all that fresh water, it's properly cold, too. And private. Well, it usually is, anyway. I think I disturbed someone else going there for a dip as well, but they'd buggered off by the time I got to the pool.'

A chill raced through Gordy. Glancing at Patti, she saw a look of concern in the detective sergeant's eyes that told her she was thinking the same thing.

'Did you see who it was?'

'What?'

'This other person you saw.'

'No, not really, anyway. I saw them through the trees, but like I just said, when I got to the pool, they were gone. Wait, why are you asking me this. Why does it matter? It's got nothing to do with what just happened, has it?'

Gordy took a deep breath, in and out.

'Charlie,' she asked, working hard to keep her voice steady and calm, 'this place where you swam last week, where you might have seen someone, it wouldn't happen to be anywhere near a little place called Downhead, would it?'

'Yes, that's it,' Charlie answered. 'It's a lovely little pool in some woods out that way. A smashing little spot.' Then her face fell. 'Wait, Gordy, how did you know?'

Gordy was glad that she was still sitting down.

'You've just described the place where Simon was found,' she said. 'And it sounds to me like you might have seen his killer.'

TWENTY-SIX

Alone in her office, Gordy slumped back down into her chair and closed her eyes, her mind a jumbled mess of thoughts and questions. And now, having found out that Charlie had gone swimming at the same spot as Simon, on the very same night, and possibly even had seen the person responsible for Simon's death, had sent her mind into a spin. Because of that revelation, and also the attack at the river, Gordy had immediately arranged for an officer in an unmarked vehicle to keep an eye on Charlie. Glad as she was that Charlie had this old friend, Mike, who she could call on, Gordy felt safer knowing that a police presence would be nearby.

Yawning, Gordy let her mind wander through everything that had happened, to see if there was any link between Charlie and Simon's murder, beyond them belonging to the same swimming group, and the possibility of Charlie having seen the murderer. Arguably, she didn't have much information to go on yet, but even so, it was hard to imagine why the person who had killed Simon would then go after Charlie for any reason other than having been seen. Simon's death struck Gordy as planned and brutal, but the attack on Charlie wasn't just more risky, it had, thankfully, failed, because Charlie was still very much alive.

Sitting up and stretching, Gordy allowed her thoughts to grow darker. It wasn't that she wanted to, but exploring all avenues, all reasons for something so awful happening, required her to do exactly that. That meant pondering, even for the briefest of moments, that Charlie knew more than she was letting on, and was involved in what had happened in some way. Try as she might, however, Gordy just couldn't work out how or why. There was that unclaimed room over at the hotel in Wells; had Simon been heading there to meet with Charlie? Gordy laughed at that, couldn't help it. The mere suggestion utterly preposterous! But even so ...

As to the idea that Charlie herself might have something to do with Simon's death, well, how was that even possible? Why would Charlie be so open about being in the same place at the same time? And hadn't she looked genuinely shocked when she'd realised Gordy knew about the pool, and why? Then there was the attack while she was swimming; she was a victim in this as well, wasn't she? The only reason that made sense was her having seen someone, and that someone being Simon's killer.

Gordy suddenly felt like her little flat in Evercreech was a very long way away. She half wished that she had a sleeping bag and a camping bed stowed in a cupboard somewhere. She didn't though, so she forced her eyes back open, and her body to take her from the station to her car. The journey home was a blur, her mind exhausted but refusing to shut down its constant whirring about the case.

Arriving back in Evercreech, the flat welcomed Gordy with cool, quiet darkness. She didn't even bother to turn the lights on as she navigated her way to her bedroom by touch alone, feeling her way along the walls. Once undressed, she fell into bed and crisp, cold sheets welcomed her. She closed her eyes and a dreamless sleep came for her. Gordy embraced it gladly.

COME THE MORNING, still exhausted and still very disturbed by the previous evening and everything that had happened with Charlie, Gordy was once again back at the station. A team meeting, fuelled by Vivek's coffee and cake, had been held, with Patti leading it. Gordy was still waiting on a report about the crime scene from the SOC team but wasn't holding up much hope of there being anything of use in it. It would be another day or so before that came in, anyway. And there were still the findings from the pool in the woods, Simon's car, further analysis of his body, and the labs. Thanks to Pete's meeting with the two members of The Ebb the previous day, they had been able to contact all of those who had been on the river with Simon that morning. Interviews had been set up with each of them throughout the day.

Gordy had spoken briefly with Jameson first thing before heading to work, though that conversation had descended into laughter when he'd told her that he was rushing off to once again meet with Gail and some other members of The Ebb, not just to chat, but to join in. The thought of him pulling on a wetsuit, then throwing himself into some very cold water had put quite the smile on Gordy's face, but not half as much as listening to the old DCI rant and rave about it.

'What am I doing, Gordy? What? I don't even know why I agreed to it!'

'You'll love it.'

'I won't.'

'Positive mental attitude, Jameson, that's what this needs. Have an open mind.'

'My mind is plenty open enough.'

'This might be the new hobby you've been looking for.'

'Can't be, because that's pickled eggs.'

Gordy had hesitated at that, wondering why Jameson had suddenly shot off on such a bizarre tangent.

'Pickled eggs?'

'I'm going to make them, you see, Gordy? And beer. And piccalilli.'

'I'm lost.'

'I'd stay that way if I were you, because—and assuming I survive throwing myself in a quarry lake—once I've done with this swim, we're going to be having words.'

'You can't blame me for this.'

'Oh, I think I can ...'

As for Charlie, Gordy had hung back from messaging her. Conflict of interest was a serious issue, and she was concerned enough to hold back from checking in. Instead, she had messaged Patti and asked her to get in touch with the officer watching her house, and Charlie herself, to check in to see how she was doing. Patti had reported back that, just as Charlie had said, her friend, Mike, had stayed with her, and had indeed put himself to work doing a bit of gardening for her as soon as the birds had started chirping. Charlie had slept well but had woken stiff and bruised from what had happened the night before. Patti would be visiting her later that morning, and checking in with the officer outside again, though by that time, a new one would have taken over the shift.

Gordy had also tasked Patti with finding out who Simon's two friends who had turned up at the river were. She had planned to do it herself, but something else had come up.

Travis, having done a little bit of digging to find out more about the builder, Tony Mills, had uncovered something, and that was what she was looking into now; a connection had been found between Tony, and Simon and Maria Miller. Gordy hadn't been at all surprised by this, and having been told that Tony's company had built a modest extension on their house a few years ago, she had no choice but to speak with him again. The connection wasn't much, tenuous at best, but it worried her enough. It also angered her, because she remembered clearly what he'd said to her when their last chat had come to an end. She wasn't about to be made a fool of.

Taking DC Knight with her, Gordy dropped into her vehicle and waited for Pete to join her. When he did, he slumped down into the passenger seat.

'You've the directions?' Gordy asked.

Pete held up a sheet of notepaper.

'The address is in Witham Friary. Good little pub there, if you like something a bit different; the Seymour Arms.'

'Define a bit different,' said Gordy, starting the engine.

'Well, for a start, I don't think it's changed in like eighty years or something.'

'And that's a good thing?'

'Adds to the charm,' Pete smiled. 'There's no bar, just a glass-panelled hatch, and your choice is pretty much between a beer and a cider, both local. Good garden as well.'

Gordy wondered if Jameson had mentioned it to her at

some point over the past few months, because it certainly sounded like the kind of place he'd know about.

'Well, we won't be popping by today, I'm afraid,' she said. 'But thanks for the recommendation. Might have to check it out one evening.'

'Make sure of it,' said Pete. 'It's an experience you won't forget, I can promise you that.'

Leaving Frome and heading in the direction of Shepton Mallet, Gordy waited for Pete's directions.

'Left at the roundabout,' he said. 'We could go straight on, but I think this way is nicer.'

Gordy did as instructed.

'And you'll want the next right,' said Pete, pointing ahead, as Gordy turned them down a long hill.

Gordy took the right, cutting across the road, and soon enough was on country lanes, which, within minutes, shrunk to barely the width of the vehicle they were in.

'See?' said Pete. 'Nice, isn't it? I've biked from Frome to the Seymour Arms a few times and ended up in the bushes on the way back, as well.'

Gordy glanced at Pete, an eyebrow raised.

'Not sure you should be telling me that,' she said, smiling a little.

As they came up to a T-junction, Gordy's phone rang, so she pulled onto the verge, and just in time, too, as a huge tractor appeared in front of her, swinging in off the junction to rumble past them almost close enough to peel the paintwork off of the car.

'Bloody hell, that was close,' she said, reaching for her phone.

'Farmers know the road a little too well sometimes, I think,' said Pete.

Gordy answered the call.

'Haig,' she said.

'Gordy? It's Jameson.'

The retired DCI's voice was unexpected. Wasn't he supposed to be recovering from a cold-water dip?

'If you're calling me because you've chickened out of that swim, I'm not going to be very happy.'

'No, it's not that. In fact, I've already been in. Enjoyed it, too, but I'll tell you about that some other time.'

'Then why the call?' Gordy heard raised voices down the line. 'What's going on? Is everything okay?'

'Remember that builder you told me about, Tony Mills?' asked Jameson.

'What about him?'

'He's here.'

Gordy took a moment to process what Jameson had just said.

'What? But ... we're supposed to be meeting him now at a build he's on with! We were told by someone at his office he was over at a house in Witham Friary!'

'Good pub there,' said Jameson. 'The Seymour Arms. I'll have to take you some time.'

'The pub is irrelevant!' Gordy snapped back, not at Jameson, but at what he had just told her about Tony, though she really didn't want to be hearing about the pub again. 'What the hell is Mills doing there with you? If he's a member of The Ebb as well, I think I might bloody well scream!'

Gordy heard more raised voices, then the muffled bark of Jameson telling someone to quieten down.

'Jameson?'

More shouting came down the line, not all of it muffled.

'Peter!' Gordy yelled. 'What the hell's going on?'

In the car, and at hearing his name roared out so suddenly, DC Knight jumped high enough to bounce his skull off the roof of the car.

'What, ma'am?' he replied. 'What is it? What's happened? What—'

Gordy looked at the young officer and reassured him with a quick smile and shake of her head, then pointed at her phone. 'The other Peter,' she said.

'Right, that's all sorted,' Jameson said at last. 'Don't suppose you could head on over here, could you? Might be sensible. I've no powers to arrest anyone, have I? Not that there's anything to arrest him for.'

'Send me the location,' she said. 'We'll be there as soon as we can.'

Conversation over, Gordy waited for Jameson's message, then turned the car around.

'Change of plan,' she said, then added, 'Don't suppose you've packed your swimming shorts, have you, Pete?'

TWENTY-SEVEN

Gordy and Pete arrived at the lake about half an hour later. Driving down a narrow lane, Gordy turned off into the parking area and was immediately confused. To her, it seemed to have been designed by someone who had combined a few too many drinks and a surplus of wood to create a layout more akin to crazy paving.

With a parking space found between a luridly painted campervan and a silver-coloured car about the size of a shoe, Gordy turned off the engine, climbed out, and led Pete back out of the parking area and down a hill towards the lake.

The day was a bright one, with a soft, warm breeze, and to Gordy's surprise, as they approached the lake, she found herself wishing she wasn't there on business, but to have a dip herself. The last time she'd been open-water swimming had been Anna's little wake, down at the edge of the River Ure, in Wensleydale. With the weather such as it was, it really would've been nice to throw herself in. Another time, perhaps, she thought.

The lake was surrounded by high cliff edges, the home of

peregrine falcons. Gordy knew this only because she'd done a little bit of research on the place. She found herself peering across the water to see if she could spot one soaring through the air.

Where the edge of the lake was occupied by those there to enjoy it, the shoreline, if it could be called such, was a mix of scaffolding, wood shack, and brick-built building, all of which housed changing rooms, a shop, and a covered area at the water's edge. Gordy noticed a little trailer serving food, which by the smell of things, would taste great but would do you no good at all. Which, she guessed, was perfect for anyone recovering from time in the frigid water.

Gordy spotted Jameson, who was standing with a small group of people, most of whom were huddled together around a couple of picnic tables. She had never seen so many bobble hats.

'I tell you what,' said Pete, as they strolled over. 'I wish I had brought my swimming shorts now! Perfect day for a dip, isn't it?'

'It most certainly is,' agreed Gordy. 'When I was a kid, days like this, I'd be messing about in the loch. My uncle had this old two-person canvas canoe. Told us it was the type used by the commandos in World War Two to do raids. Made us feel even more adventurous and daring as we got bumped around by the waves.'

'Sounds brilliant.'

'Aye, it was a good childhood, mostly,' Gordy said, then came to a stop as Jameson walked over to meet them.

'You'll need a swimming cap,' he said. 'And even though the water looks inviting, it's bloody freezing, believe me.'

'Had fun, then?' Gordy asked, unable to hide her smile. 'Wish I'd been here to see you getting in.'

'Graceful it was not,' said Jameson. 'Thanks for coming over. I think my cover's blown now, though, what with me having a direct line to the local detective inspector, who also happens to be leading the investigation into the death of one of their own.'

Gordy looked over Jameson's shoulder at the collection of faces staring back at them, though she found it hard to not just stare at the ludicrously coloured knitting creations on their heads.

'Is that part of the uniform?' she asked.

Jameson turned to see what Gordy was referring to.

'The dry robes or the hats?'

'Both.'

'Knock it as much as you want,' Jameson said. 'That stuff is vital if you want to get changed and warm quick.'

That caused Gordy to raise an eyebrow.

'Sounds like you're eying up a purchase.'

Jameson winked.

'Who's to say I haven't already?'

Gordy spotted Mills, the builder. He was sitting at another table and looked like he was being kept from escaping by nothing more than the firm stare of a man and a woman sitting directly opposite him.

'So, what happened, then?' she asked.

'I'm not entirely sure,' said Jameson. 'I was in the water when he arrived. I somehow managed to get all the way round to that floating platform over there out near the other side of the lake.'

He pointed across the water and Gordy was surprised to see just how far away it was.

'When I climbed back out, with even less grace than when I'd got in, I hasten to add, it was all kicking off.'

'What was?' asked Pete. 'Can't say any of them look like the kicking-off kind.'

'You'd be surprised,' said Jameson.

'I wouldn't,' said Gordy. 'I once had to attend a domestic disturbance call out when a woman in her eighties had got so sick of her neighbour's loud music, she'd gone to the shops to purchase a very large hammer.'

Pete's eyes went wide.

'She didn't kill the neighbour, surely?'

'No, but she made a proper mess of his car. She was the mildest, meekest woman I'd ever met, yet she'd really gone to town; every window, every light smashed, and not a panel was untouched either.'

'No hammers here, thankfully,' said Jameson. 'The most any of them seem to be armed with is flasks of tea and hot chocolate. Some even have Tupperware filled with various homemade cakes and biscuits. Anyway, there was a lot of pushing and shoving, and a good deal of shouting.'

'Why? What did Tony do?'

'I've not got to the bottom of that, which is why I called you. As far as I've gathered, though, I don't think they were all that impressed with him turning up and acting like he was here with Simon Miller himself.'

'What?'

'Oh, I'm not kidding,' said Jameson. 'I don't know the details, but from what I've gathered, he said something about Simon being with him, and that he'd had no choice but to come along and do what Simon asked.'

'Which was what, exactly?'

'Find out who killed him, I think.'

Hearing that, Gordy was tempted to just turn around

and go home. She really didn't have the time or the patience to be dealing with this kind of idiocy.

'Best we go have a chat with him then, don't you think?' she said, looking at Pete. 'You did bring the Ouija board, didn't you?'

'Never leave home without it,' said Pete. 'I actually had a pocket one specially made, so that whenever I travel, I can just whip it out and get to communing with the dead.'

'I'm envious.'

'Of course you are.'

Gordy looked over at Tony. He was staring back at her, stoney-faced, arms folded.

'Doesn't look very happy, does he?'

'Would you be if you could talk to the dead?'

'Do you think he can, then?' Pete asked. 'Talk to the dead, I mean?'

Gordy rested a hand on Pete's shoulder.

'Pete,' she said. 'I think the man's an attention seeker talking a right load of old shite. So, no, I don't think he can talk to the dead. He can talk to us though, can't he? So, let's go over and see what he has to say, shall we?' She glanced at Jameson. 'After you?'

'My pleasure,' said Jameson, and turned on his heel, as Gordy and Pete followed after.

TWENTY-EIGHT

Gordy came to stand at the picnic bench Tony Mills was sitting at. The man and woman sitting with him stood up and introduced themselves as Margaret and Terry.

'We're not married, though,' said Margaret.

'Goodness, no,' said Terry. 'Can you imagine?'

'I can, so I don't,' Margaret replied with a laugh. 'Horrifying beyond all imagination.'

Gordy wasn't sure whether they were protesting too much, because something *was* going on, or if it was just the banter of an old friendship. It was disturbingly difficult to tell the difference.

Terry leaned in close.

'We've been keeping an eye on him,' he whispered. 'Well dodgy, if you ask me.'

'Of course he's dodgy,' agreed Margaret. 'All that rubbish about Simon being with him and telling him to come here. Ridiculous. And markedly inappropriate, too. I know we didn't know Simon that well, or like him that much, really, but even so, it's awful what happened, isn't it?

And he comes in here with that cock and bull story about Simon's spirit or ghost or whatever it is he's talking about, and—'

'Well, perhaps I could have a talk with him, if that's okay?' said Gordy, deciding it was better to cut Margaret off mid-flow, because she didn't want to be there for the rest of the day. She then stepped back to allow Terry and Margaret to pass.

As they shuffled away from the table, and the man sitting at it, Gordy remembered what Charlie had told her the night before about how the swimming group had started and who had been there at the very beginning.

'You're two of the founding members of The Ebb, aren't you?'

'We are indeed,' said Terry. 'Proud of it, too. The group's changed a bit since then, though, that's for sure.'

'Bigger,' said Margaret. 'It's nice having new people around, but sometimes it feels a bit too much, doesn't it?'

'You weren't at the river with Simon the day he was killed, were you?' Gordy asked.

They both shook their heads.

'Gail messaged us to see if we could go along, but we couldn't,' said Terry. 'Work commitments and all that. Otherwise, we'd have been over there to support her.'

'She needed supporting?'

'She finds the new people more difficult than the rest of us,' said Margaret. 'I think she threatens to leave the group at least once every couple of months.'

'She's not here today, though?'

Margaret pointed over to the food trailer.

'That's Gail, over there, grabbing something hideously unhealthy, no doubt. Rather tempted to join her, actually.

She arrived after all the ruckus and went straight over. No one's actually spoken to her yet.'

The smell from the food tickled Gordy's nose again, and she looked at Pete.

'Can you let her know I'd like a quick chat, once I'm done with Mr Mills here?'

With a nod, Pete turned and made his way over to Gail.

Gordy then looked at Jameson.

'You mind sitting in on this one with me? Might be worth having two heads rather than just one.'

'No problem,' agreed Jameson.

Gordy turned her attention to Tony Mills. He was sitting with his arms crossed and looking decidedly disgruntled; Gordy could see his jaw clenching, and for added effect, his nostrils were flaring as well.

'Hello, Tony,' she said, sitting down opposite the builder, as Jameson slid in beside her.

Tony's reply was little more than a cock of his head to the side and a huff through flared nostrils.

'You've met my friend here, Peter Jameson. You mind if he joins us? He's a retired detective chief inspector and works for me on a freelance consultancy basis now and again. Keeps him out of trouble more than anything, I think.'

Gordy waited for some kind of reply beyond another nostril flex, got nothing, and decided to just crack on regardless.

'So, Tony,' she said, 'perhaps you can tell me why you're here? I was informed by someone at your office that you were on-site at a house over in Witham Friary, which is where I was heading earlier, so that we could have a chat.'

'Why didn't you call?'

'I called your office.'

'They could've put you through to me.'

'Didn't see the need, seeing as I fully expected you to be where they told me you'd be. You can imagine my surprise, then, to find that you were here instead.'

'I didn't have a choice,' said Tony. 'I had to come. It's not like I want to be here, I can promise you that. Anyway, why were you coming out to see me? I'm guessing it's not because you've suddenly decided I might be of help.'

'I don't really recall you offering any help the last time we met,' said Gordy. 'As to why I was driving to Witham Friary, it was because one of my team uncovered a connection between you and Mr and Mrs Miller.'

'That I did their extension, you mean?'

'Yes.'

'What's that got to do with anything?'

'Quite a lot, actually,' said Gordy. 'You didn't provide that information when you came to the station, which makes me suspicious.'

Tony shook his head and rolled his eyes to the sky, his lips almost breaking into a smile.

'Suspicious? I didn't know it was Mr Miller, did I? I had no name back then, remember? All I knew was that someone had died in water. That's why I came to you. I'm not making any of this up. Why would I? There's nothing in this for me, I've explained that. How could there be?'

'Where were you Wednesday night?' Jameson asked.

Gordy wasn't so sure about the question coming in so abruptly, but she would've asked it soon enough anyway.

'I live on my own,' Tony said. 'I grabbed myself a takeaway, watched some rubbish on YouTube, then went to bed. I've the receipt for the food, which'll have the time on it, won't it? But for the rest of the night, I've got nothing. Sorry. May as well arrest me now, right?'

'You can understand my concern though, yes?' said Gordy. 'I have you turning up at the station telling us, or at least implying, things about which you really shouldn't know, and I then find out you know the victim and his wife.'

'That job was eight years ago, at least, maybe ten? I've not spoken to them or seen them since, except for, well, you know ...'

'The incident at the shooting range?'

'Yes.'

Gordy leaned back a little, and Jameson, taking the hint, took over.

'Do you have any friends or contacts in the police?' he asked. 'Is there any way at all that you might have been party to confidential information, without perhaps realising?'

'No, not at all,' said Tony. 'The only reason I know any of what I do is because—'

Tony stopped himself from saying anything further.

'Because of what?' asked Gordy.

Tony unfolded his arms, rested his elbows on the table, and dropped his head into his hands.

'I don't like this. You do know that, right?' he said. 'This is not something I want. It never has been. I didn't even believe it myself in the beginning, thought there was something wrong with my head after I knocked it. But it's real. I've tested it. And there's not a damned thing I can do about it.' He looked up, and eyeballed Gordy. 'I have to live with this. I don't know when it's going to hit, when I'm going to see or feel or hear something. It's not a happy way to live, I can promise you that, and it's not great for trying to have a relationship with someone, either, and believe me, I've tried! But it freaks people out if you're in the middle of a nice meal out, or just hanging out together, and suddenly there you are, yelling and pointing and telling them that someone's in the room with you that only you can see and hear.'

'Doesn't answer the question, though,' said Jameson. 'All of that does sound very traumatic for sure, but it doesn't explain why you're here now, does it?'

'I'm here because ... because Simon told me to come here, that's why! He's not with me all the time, you know? It's a bit like trying to tune the radio in, and you can't quite find the channel, and then you do, and the music is crystal clear, then a moment later it's gone and everything's fuzzy. That's why he's so upset and angry about last night.'

Gordy started at those words.

'Last night? What do you mean about last night?'

'You really want me to spell it out for you?'

'Yes, Tony, I do.'

Of course she did; she wasn't about to give him all the detail and then let him just regurgitate it for her disguised as a bad cabaret act.

Tony sighed.

'Look, I don't know all the details, because I just don't. And like I've said, I didn't have a name before, but now I do. That's come through, and it's Simon, right? Simon Miller. Don't ask me how or why it's come through now, either, because I can't explain any of this; I literally have to just live with it without any of it making any damned sense, and that's not easy.'

Gordy really didn't care.

'I'm waiting for you to continue what you were saying about last night,' she said. 'Are you here to tell me something happened, and if so, what?'

'Simon didn't know about it either, or he did, but not everything, and that's why he's forced me to come here now.'

'Get to the point. You're not making any sense.'

'I can't help that! It doesn't make sense to me either! Whoever killed Simon, and someone did, right? Well, I think Simon's connected to them somehow, because of what happened, but the connection is sketchy to say the least. As for last night, all I know—all Simon, knows—is that someone who knows something about the killer was attacked and that they survived. Simon's not happy that he was unable to prevent the attack, but he is relieved it wasn't successful. And that's why I'm here; Simon knows that whoever was attacked last night is now protected. My guess is by you, but it's someone else he's worried about now.

Gordy didn't like that what Tony was saying could be linked to what happened to Charlie. Instead, she focused on the here and now.

'Simon wants you to prevent someone else being attacked, is that what you're saying?'

Tony shook his head.

'It's more than that, more serious. He wants to prevent someone else being—' Tony's voice died like it had been sucked away in a vacuum. As Gordy waited for him to continue, she noticed something odd, the way he was staring, not at her, but past her. His eyes were wide to the point where they looked like they could just pop out at any moment.

'Tony?'

No response.

'It's an act,' said Jameson. 'Convincing, I'll give him that, but it's definitely nothing more. Give him a moment. When we don't respond, he'll have to do something else. It'll be fun to see what, won't it?'

Gordy understood where Jameson was coming from, but still, this seemed odd. There was something unnervingly sincere about what Tony had said, and it had been like that when she'd first met him as well. Whether she believed what he said didn't matter, because she felt sure that Tony really did. From where he was sitting, from his own experience, he wasn't lying.

'He looks terrified,' she said.

'He should be,' said Jameson. 'He's talking a right load of old bollocks, isn't he, and potentially wasting police time. We've every right to—'

Tony got to his feet.

'Wasn't expecting him to do that,' said Jameson. 'What do you think he's up to?'

'Tony?' Gordy said. 'You need to sit down, tell us what's going on, okay? Whatever it is, we'll try and help.'

She wasn't sure if they could or not, but it was worth a shot, just to get the man to listen and to calm down.

Tony didn't listen. Instead, he was moving away from the picnic table.

'Where's he going?' Jameson asked, staying where he was and watching Tony walk on by.

Gordy got up and stood in front of Tony, but he pushed past her, his eyes fixed on something else.

Jameson was out of his seat.

'Right, we're not having that,' he said, reaching out for Tony. 'You can't go getting physical with a police officer, now.'

Tony pulled himself out of Jameson's grip, then sped up.

Gordy could see that they were getting some strange

looks, not just from the members of The Ebb, but from others at the lake. Then, without any warning at all, Tony broke into a sprint.

Gordy, taken somewhat by surprise, was too slow to catch him. She saw that Pete was still with Gail, over at the food trailer, that Tony was heading directly towards him, and gave a shout, but didn't give up her own pursuit.

Pete looked over, saw Tony and stepped away from Gail, ready to intercept him, but as he did, and as Tony closed in, to Gordy it looked as though the detective constable was shoved to one side by something, but that was impossible, surely. Maybe he'd just tripped? As she tried to work out exactly what had happened, she noticed that Tony had stopped in front of Gail. He then grabbed her shoulders, and in a voice that was both his and also not, yelled loud enough to scatter birds from the trees around the lake.

Just one word: 'You!'

Then he dropped like liquid, unconscious, to the ground.

As Gordy stood there trying to work out what the hell had just happened, Jameson strolled over to stand beside her.

'Well, I'll give him something,' he said, 'he certainly knows how to put on a show, doesn't he? I'd pay good money to see that in a theatre.'

Gordy, though, having quickly checked to make sure Gail was okay, was already crouching down beside Tony and, despite herself, starting to wonder if it wasn't so much a show after all.

TWENTY-NINE

Though Gordy had a good amount of first aid training herself, she was more than happy to stand back and let the staff at the lake deal with Tony's apparent collapse. Two of them rushed over with first aid kits and got busy, their efficiency and knowledge clearly surpassing Gordy's own. Not that she was surprised, considering where they worked. A place like this, with not just swimmers, but divers, SUP enthusiasts, and the maddest of all in Gordy's eyes, free divers, needed their staff to be on it at all times.

Tony wasn't unconscious for long, though he was a little confused when he came to, wondering where he was, why he was there, what was going on. At this point, Gordy had offered a concise explanation, and followed Tony, along with the first aiders, to a little room inside the main building. There, he was sat on a comfortable seat, wrapped in a blanket, checked over once again, then given a glass of cold water, and left to recover.

Gordy, having decided it was best if she spoke to him alone, left Jameson and Pete to make sure that Gail was alright after what must have been quite the fright. They'd already established that she had never met Tony before in her life, had no idea who he was, and that the first time she'd met him had been when he'd marched right up to her and yelled in her face. As first impressions went, it hadn't been the best.

Alone with Tony, and sitting on another chair, Gordy gave him a bit of time to get comfortable, sip his water, and perhaps just think about what was going on, what had happened, and why he was a part of it.

'Sorry about that,' Tony said at last, resting his glass of water on a small table. 'That ... I didn't know it was going to happen, truly.'

'Is it a medical thing, do you think?' Gordy asked. 'These episodes you seem to have. I'm assuming you've been checked over, especially considering how you think it all started, with a knock to the head.'

'No, it's not a medical thing at all,' Tony replied. 'And believe me, I wondered the same myself for a good while.'

Gordy was surprised to hear how calm he sounded. She'd decided to ask the question after he'd collapsed and had expected Tony not to take it as well as he was.

'You've been checked over, then?'

Tony gave a firm nod.

'I've had numerous scans, and there's nothing wrong anywhere. I've been to see various specialists, not because I wanted to, but because the doctors thought it was for the best. So, it's not a fit or an episode or something wrong with my brain. I've not got a personality disorder. In fact, I'm fit as the proverbial fiddle. I just, well, you know ...'

'See things.'

'Exactly.'

'Can't imagine it's easy to live with, whatever it is.'

'It isn't. I really wish I didn't have to. Live with it, I mean. I'm still not used to it. And it's been five years now, give or take.'

Gordy had decided to try a different tack this time, and rather than dismissing what Tony said he was experiencing, simply accept it and go from there. So far, it was working, and Tony was considerably more relaxed.

'Are you able to explain what happened just now?'

Tony shook his head.

'Do you remember any of it?'

Tony stared into the middle distance for a moment.

'I remember driving to the job this morning, then just knowing that I had to come here. When I arrived, I didn't know why, didn't recognise anyone, just had this damned voice in my ear yelling at me to stay, stay, stay.'

'A voice?'

'Yes,' said Tony. 'Simon's. I mean, I can't say that it's definitely his, and I don't remember what it sounds like, because that job I did for them was so long ago now. Frankly, I wouldn't even recognise him if he walked in here right now. I just know it's Simon.'

'But you said you saw him, at the shooting range.'

'I did, but there's a massive difference between what this looks like, and a soul, isn't there?' Tony then prodded himself in the chest. 'I don't think our physical bodies are the same as our spiritual ones, not in the slightest.'

Gordy had nothing to say to that, so stayed quiet, and allowed Tony the space to continue.

'Don't worry,' he said, 'I feel as weird saying it as you do hearing it. Anyway, I tried to work out why I was there, spoke to people, obviously mentioned Simon, and that's when things got a little out of hand.'

Gordy had a question, one she wanted to ask, but also didn't.

'When this happens,' she said, 'how do you know? I mean, how do you know something is happening, that you're about to have a ghost or a soul or whatever it is communicate with you?'

Turned out, asking it only made her wish she hadn't, but it was out now, and best to know than not.

Tony tapped the back of his neck.

'The hairs go up,' he said. 'Here, and on my arms. Then my ears pop, like when you're going up in an airplane, that kind of pop? That's usually enough to tell me someone wants to come through.' He leaned forward, his shoulders sagging a little. 'As for what happened today, I didn't mean to upset anyone. I'm not here to do that. I'm really not. I'm just doing what I feel I have to, what Simon wants me to do.'

'And what is that, exactly, Tony? What is it that Simon wants you to do?'

'Help you find out who killed him, killed Simon,' Tony replied, as though stating the blatantly obvious.

'What's any of that got to do with the woman you shouted at?'

'I'm sorry, but it wasn't me who was shouting. I know that sounds nuts, but then all of it does, right? But it wasn't. I don't go up to people and shout at them. Simon obviously wanted to say something. What was it that I said?'

'You just grabbed her shoulders and shouted, *You!* And then you hit the deck, unconscious.'

'That's a first, I think.'

'The shouting or the hitting the deck?'

'Maybe both.'

'What you're telling me then, and if I'm to take what you say as the honest truth, is that Simon thinks Gail is somehow involved? You do realise that there's no way I can act on that information, don't you? Not if I want to keep my job. Also, I can't have you just turning up at places, talking about someone who's dead, shouting at people, and whatever else it is that you do. I'm not sure it's an arrestable offence as such, but it'll certainly piss people off.'

'I'm sure. Like I said, I don't want to be here. I don't want any of this. It's quite difficult to control, by which I mean, I can't.'

Gordy gave that thought a moment, then said, 'The woman you shouted at, have you met her before?'

Gordy already knew the answer from Gail's side of things but needed to check with Tony as well.

'No, I've never seen her before in my life. Who is she?'

'A member of the swimming group Simon belonged to.'

'So, I was right, water is involved, then, yes? That's what I told you when I came to the station.'

'You said a lot of things at the station,' said Gordy. 'But I'd rather not get into any of that right now. Let's deal with the here and now instead, shall we?'

'I don't know what else I can say.'

'I think an apology to who you shouted at might be in order, but I'd maybe leave that for now. You can't just go up to someone and accuse them of something, though.'

'I wasn't accusing her of anything,' said Tony. 'And neither was Simon.'

'Then what were you, Simon, whoever, doing then? Why did you go up to her and yell at her? Why were you talking about something that happened to someone last night, that they're now safe?'

Tony sat back, sighed.

'She's the reason I was brought here today. That's what Simon wanted to tell me, to tell you, to tell anyone who'd listen, I think. He knows!'

'Knows what?' asked Gordy. 'You're not making much sense, Tony. Help me out here, because I don't understand any of this. And I can't believe I'm even sitting here trying to, believe you me.'

For a moment, Tony was deathly still and stared off into the middle distance. Then he turned his eyes back to Gordy, and she saw that they were blank, unfocused, as though the man was suddenly, inexplicably, entirely absent from his own body.

'Whoever killed me,' he said, his voice hollow, not his own, 'will kill her next.'

Then he slumped forward onto the table, once again unconscious.

THIRTY

Gordy was sitting in the interview room back at the station. Beside her was Detective Constable Peter Knight. Opposite them, on the other side of the table, Tony Mills stared back with eyes that somehow managed to look both annoyed and calm. The table itself was held in place by a plate of Vivek's cookies, and they were all drinking coffee.

'Everyone ready?' asked Gordy.

Tony didn't move, just continued with that odd stare. Pete gave a nod and took out a notebook and pen.

Gordy focused on Tony, stated the date and the time, then said, 'The purpose of this interview is to further question Mr Tony Mills in relation to an incident at Vobster Quay earlier today. This is in connection with an ongoing investigation into the death of Mr Simon Miller.'

Gordy paused to allow those words to sink in, then gestured at the digital recording equipment in the room with them, making sure everything was switched on and working as it should. Gone were the days of a simple tape recorder, which she still kind of missed. That system was simple, easy to use. This new gear, with touch screens and a camera, was definitely more secure, but no matter how often she used it, she always felt as though it was the first time, and that she was learning something new and needlessly complicated.

'This interview is being recorded. You do not have to say anything, but it may harm your defence if you do not mention when questioned something which you later rely on in court. Anything you do say may be given in evidence. You have the right to free and independent legal advice but have declined this for now. Present for the interview are Detective Inspector Haig, Detective Constable Knight, and Mr Tony Mills. Is all of that understood?'

Tony gave a nod.

'I need to remind you that this is being recorded,' said Gordy. Then whispered, '*You need to speak, Tony ...*'

'What? Oh, right, yes,' said Tony. 'Understood.'

With the official stuff out of the way, Gordy pushed on with the interview.

'Tony, can you explain to me what happened earlier today?'

'You know what happened today.'

'And I need you to explain it to me so that I know you are clear.'

'Do you want me to mention Simon as well?'

'You can include as much or as little detail as you wish.'

Tony reached for a cookie, then took a deep, satisfying slurp of his coffee.

'I was heading to a job I'm working on over in Witham Friary. On the way, I received a message from Simon Miller telling me to go to the water sports centre. When I arrived, it was unclear as to why he had insisted on me going, and for a while, he seemed unable to get through to me. I tried to explain myself to some of the people at the centre, but this only served to cause friction. You were called out to come and talk to me. After you arrived, Simon came through again and directed me to speak to a woman. I did as he asked, then passed out. And now, after a chat with you at the centre, where I passed out once again, I've been brought here, even though I've committed no crime. That do?'

'Can you remember what you said to the woman?' Gordy asked.

Tony shook his head.

'No, but I've been informed that I shouted, "You!" before passing out for a few seconds.'

'What about after that, when I spoke to you about what you'd done?'

'Before I passed out again?'

'Exactly then.'

'I said that whoever killed Simon will kill her next.'

Gordy glanced at Pete, indicating for him to take over for a minute or two.

Pete leaned back in his chair and folded his arms.

'Can you tell us why you said that?'

'It wasn't actually me,' said Tony. 'It was Simon.'

'Simon Miller.'

'Yes.'

'And who, exactly, is Simon Miller?'

Tony gave a shrug.

'I don't know. Well, I do now, because it turns out that my company built an extension on his house around eight years ago, right? I don't remember him, though, or that job, or know him personally. I was managing a number of jobs at the time, and my records show that I had a team working on the job at his house.'

Pete glanced over at the notes he'd been writing down since the interview had begun.

'If you don't know Simon, then how did he send you a message? How did he direct you to speak to the woman at the water sports centre?'

'I don't know.'

'For the record,' said Pete, 'the body of Mr Simon Miller was found last week floating in a pool in a woodland near the village of Downhead.'

Tony said nothing, just leaned back in his chair, mirroring Pete's body language.

Gordy decided to take over. They weren't playing good cop, bad cop, not by any stretch of the imagination. However, having two people alternate at points through an interview often helped to keep things focused, and also stop the interviewee from getting too comfortable with one person; it kept them on their toes.

'You know how this sounds, don't you, Tony?' Gordy asked. 'You're telling us that a dead man told you to say what you said.'

'Of course I know how it sounds,' said Tony. 'I don't do any of this for fun, for money, for anything, other than the fact that I have to, because if I don't, it only gets worse. I've actually started thinking of it like a cut that gets infected; if you just leave it, it'll get worse and worse, right, and never heal. So, what you've got to do is clean it. And I think that's what this is like; I have to listen to the voices and do my best to understand what it is they want me to do. That way, I'm able to heal them, and help them go where they're supposed to. But if I ignore them, then the wound just gets worse and worse.'

'I wish I had the faintest idea what you were talking about,' Gordy sighed.

'You're not the only one. But I'm not lying, I'm not making any of this up.'

'Really.'

Tony leaned forward, rested an elbow on the table and leaned his head against his hand.

'The ring,' he said. 'I told you about that, didn't I?'

Gordy didn't move, didn't blink, didn't respond, just gave Tony the floor for a while longer.

'I've a name now; Anna, I think, yes? And I'm sure there's a way I could find that out, and I understand fully if you don't believe she told me that. But the ring? There's no way I could know about that, is there? Or that you gave it to ... Harry, I think, yes?'

Despite the ice now freezing her veins, Gordy ignored everything he had just said, and in as calm a voice as she could muster said, 'Let's stay on your connection to Simon Miller, shall we?'

'I built his extension, as you know, and that was way before any of this started, and clearly way before I even knew that the person who was coming through these past few days was actually Simon.'

Pete joined in with, 'By "any of this," you mean before you started seeing ghosts, yes?'

'Ghosts, spirits, souls, I don't know what they are, what you'd call them, but yes, before then.'

'What about since you built his extension?'

'It was just a job,' said Tony. 'We didn't stay in touch. I've not seen Simon since the last time I was on site, and I don't even remember that, because why the hell would I?'

'But you've said he told you to go to the lake and point someone out.'

'Not point out. It's more than that. She's in danger. Simon knows this. I don't know how he does, but he does. That's all I can say.'

'What about the swimming group?' Pete said. 'You're not a member.'

'No.'

'So why go there?'

'I've already said! Why aren't you listening? Simon told me to. I didn't know why, not even when I got there. Sometimes, I lose contact with those who come through. It's a bit like the Internet used to be in the nineties.'

'The woman you shouted at, Gail, you terrified her,' said Gordy, exaggerating just a little, because they'd checked on Gail, and she'd been surprised more than anything. She'd also decided not to press charges, stating that she was more worried about Tony than what he'd done. 'Was it your intention to do that? Were you threatening her?'

Tony sat up, shook his head.

'No. I ... I mean, Simon, was trying to protect her. She's the next target, and you need to know, don't you? Simon wasn't able to warn you about whatever it was that happened last night, but this time he can. So, that's what we've done.'

Gordy decided to skip over last night.

'Why would someone want Gail dead?'

'How the hell should I know? Maybe she knows something. Maybe she's in the way. Don't ask me what or how, I'm just trying to help. I don't control any of this at all. All I can do is just try and act on it. And that's not easy. Frankly, it's a bloody nightmare!'

Gordy changed tack a little.

'If Simon knows Gail is next, then how come he doesn't know who killed him? Seems a bit odd that, don't you think, Tony?'

Tony looked thoughtful for a moment before answering Gordy's question.

'I'm only saying this as a best guess based on what I've experienced since this all started, but the dead don't always remember how they died. It's fractured, like a smashed mirror. They catch small bits of it, shards of what happened, bits of memory, but that's it. That's why they come to me, I think, to help them put it all together again, see what the mirror shows once it's all back in one piece.'

'What did Simon tell you exactly?'

'That his death wasn't random, or an accident, or anything like that. Someone hit him with something, here ...' Tony lifted his hand to his head and, to Gordy's surprise, touched exactly where Simon had received the blow. 'Then he was held under water. He saw something as he went under, when he was being dragged into the water, something rolled up at the water's edge.'

Gordy jumped at this.

'What? You never mentioned this before.'

'You weren't listening before! And I did, actually.'

Gordy was finding it increasingly hard not to lose her temper, not just because it seemed to her that Tony was spinning them a yarn long enough to knit jumpers for every member of the lifeboat service, but that they were even giving him the time to do so. She had no choice, though, because when it came to stones unturned, she sometimes felt the need to not just see what they were hiding, but to smash them to pieces to make sure nothing could ever crawl under there again.

'What was it, then, this thing that was all rolled up?'

'It was a white towel, you know, those thick, soft fluffy things people use to dry themselves with?' Tony answered. 'I told you before, the first time we met, and I'm telling you again now because I think it's an important detail, isn't it? What with Simon and everyone else seemingly involved with swimming.'

'I don't appreciate the sarcasm, Tony,' said Gordy.

'And I don't appreciate constantly being thought of as someone who should be locked in a padded room with the key thrown away!' Tony snapped back.

Gordy reached out and rested a finger on the recorder, stated the time, ended the interview, then turned it off.

'Is that it?' Tony asked. 'I'm free to go?'

Gordy rested her eyes on the builder, ground her teeth loud enough for it to catch Pete's attention.

'What the hell am I supposed to do with you, Tony?' she asked, rubbing her temples to prevent even the suggestion of a headache from coming on. 'You've told me things you shouldn't, you can't know. You've somehow got yourself tied up in a murder investigation, and seemingly by your own volition. You're sitting here telling me you're getting cryptic messages from ghosts, from the victim of our murder investigation that my team is on with. So, now what? I can't arrest you because there's nothing to arrest you for. And I can't act on any of what you've said, because, well, ghosts, Tony, ghosts!'

Tony didn't turn away from the look Gordy was giving him, and instead held it willingly, comfortably.

'Check on Gail,' he said.

'Why shouldn't I be checking on you instead?'

'Feel free,' Tony sighed. 'I'm beyond caring. Have

someone follow me home if you want, stay with me, trail me, doesn't matter, makes no difference, because I'm not the problem.'

'And Gail is?'

'Keep an eye on her, that's all I'm saying. I don't know how you do that, or how you justify it, but please, that's what you need to do.'

'I'll see what I can do.'

Gordy looked at Pete and directed him to escort Tony from the building.

'We've your contact details,' she said. 'And we'll be keeping an eye on you as well.'

'Do what you need to do,' Tony said, standing up. 'Gail's the priority, though. Not me. And make sure you keep an eye on whoever it was who was attacked last night, just in case; this isn't over, not by a long shot. I know they're safe, but I'm just saying, that's all.'

And with that, Pete led Tony out of the interview room, and Gordy was left alone with more questions than answers.

THIRTY-ONE

A while later, Gordy was pleased to have some of those questions answered, thanks to the arrival of the forensics report on Simon Miller and the crime scene. The late lunch she'd then experienced had been a lacklustre affair of a tepid steak slice from a fast-food place nearby, washed down with a can of far-too-sweet iced latte. Having finished it, and only narrowly avoided throwing it all back up again, Patti had then showed up at her office with the report, and a decent mug of coffee from Vivek, which she placed in front of Gordy.

'Thought you might need this.'

'What I need is to plan my lunches a bit more.'

Patti glanced at the bin in the corner of the room, where Gordy had thrown the litter from her lunch.

'Nothing good can ever come of eating like that.'

Gordy's stomach rumbled.

'I hear you, and so does this,' she said, tapping her tummy. She then picked up the report with one hand, and the mug of coffee with the other, taking a sip. 'Have you read it, yet?'

'Printed it out and brought it straight here,' Patti said. 'It's fun to share.'

'That's one way to look at it.'

Focusing on Vivek's coffee, Gordy started with a quick scan through the report on the crime scene, and the accompanying photographs. First, there was mention of other footprints by the pool. They already knew that some of those could be attributed to Charlie. She had seen someone else at the pool, but according to the report, the prints were barely more than scuffs, so not much use. No murder weapon had been found, and there was nothing unusual from either Simon's own kit, which he'd taken with him to the pool, or in his vehicle.

Gordy then moved onto the forensics report. Most of it she already knew, however, the small slivers of wood Charming had found in the wound were polished, and traces of oil had been found on the wood as well. These details supported her notion that whatever had been used to hit Simon on the head with had been taken to the wood; the killer had not simply grabbed the nearest stick. Though there was no mention of the mysterious white towel Tony had mentioned, white threads had been found in the mud at the pool's edge. Coincidence or not, she wasn't sure, but still … There was one detail, though, that did jump out at her.

'Psilocybin?'

'I've just read that, too,' said Patti. 'Magic mushrooms?'

'Judging by the stomach contents, he ingested it with food, probably to disguise the taste.'

'You've tried them?'

Gordy raised an eyebrow at this question but saw the faint smile on Patti's face.

'No, I've never picked Liberty Cap mushrooms in my life,' she said, mysteriously enough to have Patti wonder what else she might have tried, information she would keep to herself. 'Doesn't make sense though, does it, to go for a solo swim and get high on mushrooms at the same time?'

'Not really, no,' Patti said. 'You're thinking something, aren't you?'

Gordy was always thinking something, and she was just about to explain what, when there was a knock at the door. She looked up to see PCSO Supervisor Jack Hill through the window, standing on the other side. She beckoned him in.

'Hello, Pete,' she said, 'I mean Jack.'

'Just because we have the same haircut now doesn't mean we look exactly the same.'

'I think it's cute,' said Patti. 'Pete obviously looks up to you.'

'I might grow mine again, then,' said Jack. 'Can't be having that, can we?'

'How can we help?' Gordy asked.

'Two things,' Jack said. 'First, remember you asked me to go have a chat with Lily Twelvetrees?'

Gordy had to think for a minute as to who Lily was, then remembered everything about her all at once, and smiled.

'How did you get on?'

'Only managed to catch up with her this morning,' Jack explained. 'She'd been away for a few days.'

'Doing what?'

Gordy watched as Jack pulled the kind of face that said whatever he was about to say, he really didn't understand at all.

'She said something about a cacao ceremony.'
'Chocolate?'
'That's what I said, and it was made very clear to me that no, that's not what it was about.'
'That's a shame,' said Patti. 'Rather like the idea of a ceremony that's all about chocolate.'
'I said that, too.'
'And?'
'I was told not to be so flippant and instead to give it a go myself.'

Gordy laughed.

'Did she book you in for a weekend retreat, then?'

Jack shook his head.

'She insisted we do a little cacao ceremony right there and then, or she wouldn't help me with my questions.'

Gordy looked over at Patti, who was struggling not to laugh.

'And how was it?'

Jack gave a shrug.

'Relaxing, I guess?' he said. 'Nothing wrong with trying new things, is there? And she was very helpful afterwards. She knew all about the pool Miller was found at, had been there herself a few times, too.'

Gordy thought about what she'd learned from both Greg, the dog walker, and Jameson.

'And?'

'It's a freshwater spring, and that's good for healing, apparently, both physical and spiritual.'

'I can't see Simon going to it for a reason like that though, can you?' said Patti, looking from Jack to Gordy.

'I mentioned the mistletoe.'

'And she told you it was linked to male fertility, yes?' Gordy said.

'She mentioned that, but also that herbalists use it for cardiovascular stuff, even cancer. She wasn't sure, though, that there was any ritual reason for it to be used with Miller.'

That got Gordy's attention.

'Why?'

'She just thought it was all a bit too dramatic,' said Jack. 'I didn't go into too much detail about what happened, obviously, but what I said was enough for her to think that it sounded more symbolic and personal than ritualistic.'

'There's a difference?' asked Patti.

'Don't ask me,' said Jack. 'I'm just telling you what Lily told me.'

Gordy turned to Patti, remembering something about Charlie, and a twist of worry caught her.

'That word, personal,' she said.

'What about it?'

'The Ebb, it was started by a small group,' she explained. 'Charlie was one of them, called them The Originals. The others were Gail, who we know about, Margaret and Terry, who I met at the lake this morning, and Mike.'

'Who was round at Charlie's last night.'

Gordy said, 'I want to talk to them all, sharpish. After what happened with Tony, and with him almost ordering me to watch Gail, I can kill two birds with one stone, can't I?'

'You think one of them is involved?'

'I think it's quite possible that someone knows something, even if they don't know that they know it, if that makes sense? And I'd like to bring them all in and see how they react as a group.'

'As a group? Why?'

'Ignoring that it's a more efficient use of our time, it'll be a more relaxed environment, and sometimes that makes people say things they don't mean to. It'll also give us an idea about the dynamics of the group and might even show us if there's any friction.'

'About what?'

'At a guess, new members,' said Gordy. 'People don't like change.'

Patti frowned. 'But to kill someone because of that?'

'You'd be surprised.'

Gordy turned her attention back to Jack.

'And the second thing?'

'We've heard from Amy Stanton.'

'Name doesn't ring a bell.'

'She's the old university friend Maria said she went away with for the reunion.'

'Oh, that Amy. And?'

'And something doesn't quite stack up.'

Gordy narrowed her eyes at Jack.

'What doesn't quite stack up, Jack?'

'Helen spoke with her, and Amy had all the details right,' Jack explained, counting things off on his fingers as he spoke. 'The address of the property they stayed at, the local pub, everything. Even described a few little walks in the area, and in great detail, too. Helen said it was almost like she was reading it.'

'I still don't know what you're getting at,' said Gordy.

'While Helen was talking with Amy, I was in touch with the owners of the cottage, just to confirm everything, really, and they said something a bit odd.'

'Odd how?'

'The cleaner found a pair of men's boxer shorts under the bed.'

'So what?' said Patti. 'They're surprisingly comfortable, actually. Or maybe one of them got lucky.'

Jack ignored that and went on.

'Well, the owner was adamant that there was no way they could have been left by a previous guest, because the previous guest was a woman and her young daughter; they were having a little holiday together after her divorce came through.'

'Maybe they were from another guest, then,' Gordy suggested.

Jack shook his head.

'Oh, she was very firm on that not being possible as well; not only is the cleaner very thorough, but the owner also goes round and checks everything after each visit. She would, and I quote, "swear on a nun's grave" that those boxers were left behind by Maria and whoever she was with for those three days she stayed at the cottage.'

Gordy looked from Jack to Patti, and then back to Jack again.

'Which means that either Amy or Maria is really into wearing men's boxers ...'

'Or they're lying,' said Patti.

Gordy thanked Jack and dismissed him, then stared at Patti.

'I'll call Maria as well,' Patti said, standing up. 'And I need to chase up those two friends of Simon's at the golf club. What about this Amy? Do you want to talk to her as well?'

'Let's see what Maria has to say first,' said Gordy.

Patti gave a nod, then asked, 'More coffee?'

Gordy lifted her mug and drained the tepid contents in one go.

'I think I'm going to need it,' she said.

THIRTY-TWO

An hour or so later, Gordy was back in the interview room, this time with Gail Carpenter, Margaret Ascott, Mike Small, and Terry Finch. Patti had provided a jug of water and plastic cups. Patti had also managed to get in touch with Maria, and she was going to be at the station in a couple of hours; plenty of time to see if anything at all could be gleaned from a chat with the original members of The Ebb. In the meantime, Gordy had given Patti a job to do.

'I don't drink from disposable plastic cups,' said Mike. 'Bad for the environment. I'm shocked you have them here.'

Gordy poured them all some water anyway, and everyone bar Mike took a sip or two.

'Thank you for all coming in at such short notice,' she said.

'Is this about what happened to Charlotte?' Margaret asked. 'Mike's told us all about it, as much as he knows, anyway, and we've heard from her as well, though she's not really given us too much in the way of detail.'

'She was advised to do that, because it's all part of a

police investigation,' said Gordy. 'And yes, it is about that, but not specifically. Really, I just wanted to get you all in to find out more about your swimming group.'

'You want to join as well, do you?' Gail asked. 'Like your friend, Peter?'

'How did Jameson do?' Gordy asked, ignoring how Gail had narrowed her eyes at her as she'd asked the question. She also remembered what Tony had said when she'd chatted to him earlier, voiced his concerns about Gail's safety. Acting on the warning of a supposed dead man was something she just couldn't do; that was career-ending.

'Surely the more important thing here is to do something about that mad bastard who turned up this morning?' said Mike, and Terry muttered his agreement. 'He can't go around attacking people, can he?' He looked across at Gail. 'You were terrified, weren't you?'

Judging by the look on Gail's face, Gordy wasn't so sure terrified was how she remembered the experience.

'It was a bit of a shock, that's all,' Gail said. 'Is he okay? You know, up here?'

She tapped her temple.

Terry said, 'And all that nonsense about seeing Simon's spirit or ghost or whatever he was saying. What rubbish.'

Gordy asked, 'Gail, have you ever met or seen the man from this morning before?'

'Never,' Gail replied. 'No idea who he is, except that he seems to know, or knew, Simon.'

'He's a builder,' Gordy explained. 'Could he have done any work on your house, perhaps?'

Gail laughed, bright and loud, and the sound seemed to bump around the room for a moment as though feeling a little awkward.

'Not a chance of it,' she said. 'My house is a bit tumbledown for sure, but it's not like I can afford to get a builder in to fix it for me. Anyway, I do a bit of DIY myself, and Mike helps me out if I need another pair of hands.'

Gordy saw Mike's chest expand a little at that comment, and a small smile slipped across his face.

'Can I just check where you all were yesterday evening?'

There was a moment of silence, then Mike said, 'What, you don't suspect ... I mean, you can't seriously ...'

Terry glanced at Mike.

'Suspect who of what?' he asked. Then realisation dawned, and he said, 'What, one of us attacking Charlotte? One of us? No!'

'This is just normal police procedure, that's all,' said Gordy.

'I was at the allotment, sorting out stuff in the shed,' said Mike. 'Then Charlotte called, and I was round there all night to keep an eye on her, as you well know.'

'And the rest of you?' asked Gordy.

'Pub quiz for us,' said Terry, looking over at Margaret. 'With our respective other halves as well, in case you were wondering.'

Gordy wasn't, but at least she now knew.

'Gail?' she asked.

'At home, on my own, if you don't class the bottle of red that I had for company,' Gail answered.

'Is that it, then?' asked Margaret. 'You can't seriously expect that any of us had anything to do with what happened to Charlotte.'

'Or, for that matter, with what happened to Simon,' said Mike. 'Because I bet that's what this is about as well, isn't it?

If you ask me, it's that Tony bloke you need to be investigating, not us.'

'Can I ask what you all thought about Simon?' said Gordy. 'I know you're the original members of the group, so I'm just wondering how things go when new people join.'

'Sometimes it's okay, sometimes it isn't,' said Margaret. 'Simon was more of an isn't, I think. Rubbed people up the wrong way, rather.'

'Not wishing to speak ill of the dead, but Marg's right,' agreed Mike. 'But I don't see why that should end up having us here with you asking these questions, though.'

Gordy said, 'I asked for you to give me details on where you were, that's all. No one is being accused of anything.'

'Unless you're Gail and being pointed and yelled at about goodness knows what by that Tony bloke, of course.'

'He didn't accuse me of anything, Mike,' said Gail. 'I'm fine. Really, I am. You don't need to make a fuss, honestly.'

Mike went to say something, but stayed quiet.

'Also,' said Gail, 'people don't really join The Ebb as such. We've always resisted becoming an official group, with rules and a committee and all of that.'

'Must be difficult to control, then,' said Gordy.

'When it began, with just the five of us, it was a relaxed thing for a group of friends. I've never wanted it to be anything other than that. And I certainly don't want anyone feeling like they're being controlled.'

'From what I gather, though,' said Gordy, 'Simon ruffled a few feathers and wanted the group to change. How do you deal with something like that?'

'It's difficult,' said Gail, 'and I'll be the first to admit to finding change hard. Doesn't mean I'm rude, though. I mean,

I had a barbecue a while back, and I invited Simon along, didn't I?'

Nods all around at that, though Gordy noticed that Mike's seemed to be done under duress.

'But no, I didn't like what Simon said about the group,' Gail continued, 'and I wasn't happy with him just turning up that morning with a couple of random new people. I had no idea at all if they were good swimmers, anything like that, did I? And sometimes, he was too forward, wasn't he? Especially with Charlotte.'

Now that is a new detail, Gordy thought.

'How do you mean?' she asked. 'In what way was he forward?'

'Fancied her,' said Terry. 'Kept on trying to impress her by being all chivalrous and giving her a dry robe to use. Obviously, she turned him down.'

'And with him being married, too,' said Margaret. 'Honestly, it really does make me think we need some rules for the group, and I know that none of you agree with me, but there, I've said it.'

'Again.' Mike sighed, then looked to Gail, and added, 'Rules aren't what the group is about, are they, Gail?'

Gordy had her eyes on Gail as well, as she thought of one of the tasks Patti was on with right then.

'The two friends of Simon's,' she said. 'Did you speak to them at all?'

Gail shook her head.

'Not on the day, no. I just wanted to get out of there, really, because by that point I'd had enough. My planned quiet swim had already been ruined.'

Something from what Gail had just said snagged in Gordy's mind, like wool on barbed wire.

'What do you mean by, 'not on the day'? You spoke to them after?'

'One of them, yes,' said Gail. 'Rupert Summerton. I thought I'd best check to see how they both got on with their swim, and also talk through how the group works, what it's about, that kind of thing. In case Simon hadn't done that, or if he had, then maybe not in as much detail as I would like.'

'But how did you know how to contact him?'

'Oh, that was easy. Simon said they were golfing friends, so the day after the swim, I popped round to Orchardleigh, the local club, and asked if there was a member there called Rupert.'

'But they wouldn't have been able to tell you if there was, surely?'

'I didn't expect them to. There were only two members called that, so I left my name and number and asked the receptionist to ask which of them had been swimming at the river with Simon, and to give them my contact details and ask them to call me back. Which Rupert did. He was very pleasant, actually. Quite the bag of plums in his mouth, if you know what I mean, but nice with it.'

'And what about the other friend?' Gordy asked.

'Rupert had no idea who he was. Said he just turned up at the river at the same time and was really friendly and chatty. One of those coincidences.'

Coincidence? Gordy thought. If there was one word that she really didn't like ...

'I remember thinking that I recognised him at the time.'

'And did you?'

'I just thought his was one of those faces I'd seen when doing my weekly shop at the supermarket, that kind of thing. You know how it is, when you go to the same place, and sometimes you see a face, and you think it's someone you know, but it isn't, is it? It's just someone you've seen a few times, that's all.'

Gordy really wanted Gail to get to the point.

'So, was he just a face from the supermarket, then?'

Gail shook her head and looked rather pleased with herself at what she was about to say.

'No! I was right, you see. I did recognise him!'

'How exactly?' Gordy asked, forcing any sense of urgency from her tone as Gail, she was sure, blushed a little, then laughed.

'Well, a few years ago, five or six I think at least, I gave myself a treat for my birthday,' she said. 'I know this will sound ridiculous, but I went and booked myself into this posh spa in Bath. Not the kind of thing I ever do, really, but I thought what the hell, why not? And it was wonderful! It had this Jacuzzi with mineral salts, I lazed around in a sauna and a steam room for ages, used an icy plunge pool, and even had a hot stone massage! I mean, get me, right?'

'What's any of that got to do with anything?' asked Margaret. 'Mind you, I've always wanted to try a hot stone massage. What was it like? And why did you never tell me? Why did you keep this a secret?'

'Felt a bit silly, really,' said Gail. 'Didn't want everyone thinking I was so sad that I bought myself treat days for my own birthday. Also, it's nice to do things on your own sometimes, isn't it?'

'That's not sad, that's brilliant,' said Mike. 'Well done you! Wish I'd have thought of it myself as a birthday present for you.'

'Oh, don't be silly,' said Gail. 'All those vegetables were a lovely thought.'

Gordy pushed her way back into the conversation.

'You were telling me how you recognised this other man,' she said.

Gail frowned at first, as though she had no idea what Gordy was talking about, then her face lit up.

'Oh, yes! Of course, sorry; he was the massage therapist who did the hot stone thing for me. Very fit for his age, very charming, really put me at ease. I was expecting someone younger, you know, in their twenties or thirties, but he was in his fifties! Looked ten years younger, though. Can't say I was complaining. I even went and booked in for a wood therapy massage with him, and that was amazing as well. Did that round at his house, because he's got a private therapy room there. Smelled lovely. Wished my house smelled like that, I can tell you.'

'Rather than damp swimming costumes and towels, you mean?' said Margaret. 'I hear you.'

Everyone bar Gordy laughed. She'd learned a few things from the conversation with the original Ebb members, most notably the view that Simon had had a bit of a thing for Charlie, and that one of the supposed two friends who had joined him at the river wasn't a friend at all, just some random stranger. As for hot stone and wood therapy massages, well, each to their own and all that.

Remembering something Tony had mentioned, Gordy then said, 'Just out of interest, and I know this sounds like a daft question, considering you're all into swimming, but what colour towel did Simon use?'

'I'm sorry, what?' said Mike. 'Colour towel?'

'Yes, what colour towel?' Gordy repeated.

'Simon didn't use a towel,' said Terry. 'Well, he did, but it was one of those microfibre ones that pack away really small.'

'Most of us use the same,' added Margaret. 'The robes we use do most of the drying, then it's just a quick rub down to make sure.'

'We don't all use robes, though,' said Gail. 'Charlotte doesn't, never has, either. And there's nothing much on her, either, so I've no idea how she doesn't catch her death.'

'So, not a normal towel, then? You know, a fluffy white one maybe?'

'White's not a very practical colour, is it?' said Mike. 'We swim outdoors so that's just going to end up all stained and horrible, isn't it?'

Gordy shook her head, and wished she'd kept her mouth shut. She also decided that it was probably time to draw the chat to a close. So, with a quick recap of what they'd discussed, a double-check that she had everyone's contact details and addresses, and also the name of the spa Gail had visited, the date, and Rupert Somerton's contact details, she sent everyone on their way.

As they all made their way out of the room, Gordy once again heard the nagging voice of Tony in her mind and stopped Gail for a moment.

'Just checking you're okay,' she said. 'After what happened this morning, it's good to be sure.'

'Oh, I'm fine,' said Gail. 'Though I have taken the chance to call into work and take the afternoon off. Seemed fair.'

'Good idea,' Gordy agreed. 'Any plans?'

'Gardening,' said Gail. 'Clearing things away, doing all those autumn jobs, and Mike's coming round to help as well.'

'Sounds perfect.'

'Doesn't it, just?'

Gordy let Gail go on her way and was happy that she

would be with someone, at least for the afternoon. Not that she held much truck with what Tony had said, but still, it made sense to be sure.

She called Patti in.

'I've a little more detail on those two friends of Simon's.'

'That's a relief,' said Patti, 'because I haven't.'

'Turns out one of them wasn't Simon's friend at all and apparently just turned up at the same time as his actual friend, a man called Rupert.'

'As in the bear?' Patti said.

'Maybe he even wears the same scarf,' said Gordy.

Patti smiled.

'A mysterious stranger; how exciting!'

Gordy gave Patti the name of the spa, the date of Gail's visit, and Rupert's details.

'He's a massage therapist,' she said. 'The description I have is that he's in his fifties but looks ten years younger. Gail recognised him because she had a massage from him at the spa on the date that I've just given you. I don't like loose ends, and he currently is.'

'I'll get right on it,' said Patti. 'And I'll give this Rupert a call as well.'

Gordy checked the time.

'Maria here yet?'

'Funny you should ask.'

'Why?'

'Rang to say her car's broken down. She's asked if she can come in tomorrow instead.'

'She's at home, then?'

'I believe so.'

Gordy stood up.

'Then you'd better call her back and tell her that she's about to receive a visit.'

'She is? Who from?'

'Me.'

THIRTY-THREE

Following the car crash of a morning at the lake, and then the considerably unenjoyable chat with the police at the station in Frome, Tony Mills had decided the rest of the day was his and his alone. Having called the office to let everyone know that he wasn't going to be around until the following day, he had headed home to hide. He'd even gone so far as to draw the curtains in his lounge, just to shut the world away good and proper. What was left of the day, he would give over to having a fire lit, sinking a few beers, munching his way through a takeaway pizza, and watching a spaghetti Western or two. And if Simon Miller decided to come through, tried to get him to do something utterly insane again, he would ignore him. Over the last few days, he'd made a fool of himself, upset more than enough people, and pissed off the police. Tony believed he deserved a break. And what could a ghost really do to persuade him otherwise? Wasn't Simon dependent on Tony being compliant? Well, not for the next few hours he wouldn't be, that was for damned sure.

The pizza was nothing special, but Tony didn't care;

pepperoni and a lot of cheese was never anything other than tasty, plus it was easy food and went well with the cold beer he was sipping. The movie he'd decided on, from a rather extensive pile of DVDs he refused to get rid of and replace with downloads, was Death Rides a Horse.

It had been running for nearly an hour and he hadn't really been watching any of it. He knew the film well enough to let it just play along in the background of his afternoon. When it eventually finished, he knew that there was a good chance he'd just put it on again, assuming of course that he hadn't fallen asleep by that point.

Tiredness, fatigue, was the one aspect of his bizarre condition that Tony had never really got used to or worked out a way to combat. Whatever happened when someone came through, it somehow drained him. The exhaustion felt nothing like the weariness of a long day at work, or the aftermath of exercise. No, it was deeper than that and seemed to go right to the very marrow of his bones. It was a weariness he could feel in every part of himself, as though his whole body just needed to shut down because something had been sucked out of every single one of his cells. What that something was, he had no idea really, but in private, the only way to describe it that made any sense to him was to call it his lifeforce. It was a phrase he knew sounded like it had come straight out of some dodgy seventies sci-fi or horror movie, but that was what it felt like; when someone came through and he ended up having to deal with whatever they wanted, they took some of that force, almost as though they were treating him like some kind of battery or charging device.

That was why Tony kept all of this to himself, because he knew that to utter any of it to a friend or a relative would make him very lonely, very quickly indeed, and surely a padded cell wasn't far behind. With Simon, though, it had been the worst yet. Sitting there in the gloom of his lounge, lit only by the glare from his television splashing a technicolour paintbrush across the walls, Tony felt like he could happily sleep for a year, and soon enough, his eyes were too heavy to keep open any longer.

When Tony woke up, he found that the movie had come to an end, he'd spilled just enough of his can of beer to make it look like he'd pissed himself, and he had no idea at all what the time was. He checked his phone, was surprised to find it dead, and was fairly certain he'd charged it as soon as he'd returned home from speaking to the police.

Yawning, then stretching hard enough to crack bones, Tony heaved himself out of the position he'd slumped into on the sofa. His back ached, his legs felt numb, and now he needed to go change his trousers. Today was certainly turning into one to delete from his memory.

With a heave, he managed to send his body forward with enough momentum to get to his feet. Then a wave of dizziness hit, and he stumbled. Instinct kicked in, and he thrust out his left foot to stop himself from toppling forward onto his face, only to feel it thump down onto the last couple of pieces of pizza still in the box on the floor.

Right then, Tony didn't care how much of the day was left; the safer option seemed to be to just go to bed. He was exhausted anyway, had no interest in watching another movie, and didn't want to leave the house, so what other option was there? Dropping back down onto the sofa, he pulled off the pizza-covered sock, then stood up again and headed for the lounge door. He would be in bed in a couple of minutes, and asleep soon after, and frankly, he could hardly wait.

In the hallway, at the bottom of the stairs, Tony reached out for the banister to help pull himself upwards. A yawn came upon him, and with zero control over it, his mouth opened wide enough for it to lock momentarily. The sensation of not being able to close his mouth sent Tony into an immediate panic. As he reached a hand up to physically force his jaw to move, the hairs on his arms and on the back of his neck stood at attention, his ears popped, and then there was Simon once again, before him, beside him, all around him.

'No,' Tony said, his voice weary, and cut through with as much frustration as anger. 'Not now. Whatever it is, just ... just no. I'm drained. I need to sleep. I'm going to bed.'

Tony lifted a foot to the first step.

Simon closed in.

'No,' Tony said, repeating himself, though this time his voice was louder, firmer.

He dropped his foot to the step, aimed for the next, only to find himself both pushed and pulled away from the stairs, then out through his front door, which was somehow open.

Tony came to a stop, saw his front door slam shut, and Simon was in front of him again. Before Tony could even muster the energy to tell him to just bugger off and leave him alone, Simon was gone. Then Tony's world dissolved into the horror of violent death, and when everything came back into focus again, he was already behind the wheel of his car and speeding away from his house.

THIRTY-FOUR

Arriving in Mells, Gordy made her way over the river and on towards the home of Maria Miller and parked on the gravel drive. Climbing out, she found herself in front of a house that exuded comfortable retirement, the kind of retirement where the house is paid off, the investments are doing well, and the pension is enough to make you smile on a daily basis. The Millers, she thought, had certainly provided well for themselves.

Mells itself was very much populated by plenty of other similar kinds of houses, and the village was certainly picturesque. It's clearly a haven for dog walkers as well, thought Gordy, as she walked up to the front door, seeing as she'd had to weave her way through a bevy of people and their hounds as she'd made her way towards, and then over, the bridge.

As she went to ring the doorbell, Gordy did a quick search on her phone for something, saved an image, then pressed the buzzer. A moment later, the front door swung open.

'Maria Miller?'

The woman in front of Gordy attempted a smile. Her mouth did well, Gordy thought, but the eyes really weren't putting in the effort.

Gordy introduced herself, produced a warm smile then allowed Maria to guide her into the house and through to the lounge.

'I was just about to make some coffee.'

'That would be lovely.'

Gordy plonked herself down in a comfy armchair and waited.

The room was furnished well, she noticed, and comfortable, though perhaps not quite as worn-in as she would like herself. It was as though everything was working really hard to feel homely, right down to the art on the walls, but something was still just a little off, like it was trying too hard.

Maria returned pushing a trolley. On the top, a cafetière clinked against a small jug and two coffee mugs as she walked into the room, and beneath it, Gordy saw a few slices of dark chocolate cake on a plate.

'How do you take it?'

'The cake or the coffee?'

Maria managed a more genuine smile.

'How it comes,' said Gordy. 'Black today, though, I think. The cake looks good.'

'Chocolate, Simon's favourite. Made a fresh one today, out of habit, really.'

'You were the cook in the house, then?'

'No choice,' Maria smiled. 'I don't think Simon even knew what a pan was, never mind how to turn on the cooker or a hob.'

Maria poured two mugs of coffee, then handed one to Gordy, along with a slice of the cake, on a small plate.

Gordy sipped the coffee, nibbled the cake.

'Not surprised it was his favourite,' she said. 'That's delicious.'

'Thank you.'

Gordy allowed silence to play its part for the next few minutes, as they both enjoyed the coffee and cake. As she suspected it might, the quiet became too much for Maria.

'Sorry about not being able to make it to the station earlier,' she said.

Gordy waved the apology away, finished the cake, placed the empty plate back on the trolley, then stood up.

'Toilet,' she said. 'Could you tell me where it is?'

Maria directed her to one downstairs, and Gordy found it to be a shower room as well, no doubt put in for those days where gardening has made you just too dirty to head upstairs for a shower or a bath instead.

Gordy didn't need the toilet at all. She was, for whatever reason, still bothered by the towel Tony had mentioned. It was stuck in her mind, and she couldn't shake it loose.

The towels in the downstairs shower room weren't white, however; they were a deep, soft ruby.

Flushing the toilet, Gordy walked back into the lounge and sat down.

'How's Amy?' she asked.

Maria's eyes went wide momentarily.

'Pardon?'

'Must be good to have a friend like that, who you've known for so long,' Gordy continued, ignoring Maria's look of confusion. 'I went to a school reunion once, you know.

Awful affair. I'll no' be going again should someone suggest it; there's only so much peacocking I can be doing with.'

'Peacocking?'

'Oh, you know.' Gordy smiled, batting the word away with a wave of a hand. 'When people get together and all they end up doing is talking up their own lives, comparing children's successes, holidays, houses, careers.'

'Amy's not like that at all,' said Maria. 'We've known each other since we met during fresher's week. We chat most weeks and see each other as often as we can.'

'Which university?'

'Cardiff.'

'What did you study?'

'We both did marketing. Amy was much better at it than I. One of those people whose ideas just fall out of them.'

Gordy sipped her coffee.

'You see Amy frequently, then?'

'Not as frequently as we would like.'

'It was just the two of you as well, yes, so nice and private?'

'We always have a lot to talk about.'

'Was Amy's partner with you at all?'

There was that nervous, awkward look again, Gordy noticed, and those wide eyes.

'Amy's divorced.'

Gordy managed an excellent look of surprise, just enough to show that it hadn't been the answer she had been expecting, and that there was a very good reason as to why.

'Must've been a mix-up, then,' she smiled.

'Mix-up of what?'

'Oh, I'm sure it's nothing.' Gordy held up her mug. 'Any chance of a drop more?'

Maria stood up and poured more coffee.

Gordy took a sip.

'Lovely,' she said. 'Now, where was I? Oh, yes, that was it, your husband, Simon ...'

The change of tack caught Maria sharp.

'Simon?'

'Yes, I'm sure it's tough right now.'

'I miss him.' Maria nodded, relaxing a little, sadness in her eyes. 'I can't believe he's gone. The house seems very quiet.'

For the first time since Gordy had arrived, Maria looked and sounded like she genuinely meant what she had just said.

'I'm sure it does,' said Gordy, going with that for a moment. 'What happened, it must've been a shock.'

'It was. It is. I don't understand any of it. I really don't.'

Gordy leaned forward, elbows on her knees, coffee mug clasped in her hands. 'Do you mind if I ask a rather difficult question? It's just that something came up in the forensic report.'

Maria said nothing, just stared, waiting for Gordy to ask whatever it was she was going to ask.

'Do you know what this is?'

Gordy placed her mug on the trolley, took out her phone, then turned it around to show Maria the image she had pulled up when she had arrived at the house.

Maria's eyes went wide.

'No, I mean, yes, of course I do, I mean, it's a mushroom, isn't it, but ...'

'Do you know what kind of mushroom? Though maybe it's more accurate to refer to it as fungi? I'm no' sure what the difference is myself.'

Maria's eyes drifted from Gordy's phone screen, staring into the middle distance.

'Just looks like one of those little mushrooms you see in fields around here in autumn,' she said.

'It is the season for them, that's true,' agreed Gordy. 'Was Simon into foraging?'

'What? Why?'

'We think he might have known what these actually are, you see. They're Liberty Cap mushrooms. They contain psilocybin.'

Maria's eyes were back on Gordy now, and she was fidgeting. Gordy pushed a little harder to find out why.

'Can you think of a reason why Simon would be consuming them?'

'He would never do that.'

'How do you know?'

'It was hard enough to get him to take a paracetamol,' said Maria, 'never mind anything like an antidepressant!'

Now that was a strange comment, Gordy thought.

'Simon was prescribed antidepressants, then?'

Maria folded into her seat, as though some great weight had just pushed her back into it.

'He had dark periods,' she said. 'Depression, and a bit of anxiety as well. Always struggled with his mental health. He'd be up sometimes, then hit these really black times, then he'd be all up again. I wondered if he was bipolar, asked him to go to the doctors. He did, had counselling. So, yes, he was prescribed antidepressants. Didn't take them, though. Or he did, but would then think he was fine, knew better than the doctors, and stop.'

Gordy paused, did her best to look thoughtful, then said, 'But if he didn't want to take prescribed drugs, then why would he go to the trouble of finding and consuming Liberty Cap mushrooms?'

Maria shook her head.

'I really don't know.'

'Also, you were the cook in the house, yes?'

Maria smiled.

'I didn't mind it at all. Simon was very generous.'

'No, what I mean is, you don't just eat the mushrooms as they are; you usually add them to food.' Gordy reached over for another slice of the chocolate cake. 'Like this, for example.'

For a moment, Maria's smile was a thing frozen in time, so much so, Gordy wondered if it might fracture and fall off. And then, little by little it actually did start to fracture, until, eventually, it was gone completely, and Maria was sobbing.

THIRTY-FIVE

Tony knew he was breaking the speed limit and really didn't care. He knew the Somerset lanes as well as anyone who had lived there their whole life. Probably better, actually, considering his job. Years spent navigating his way from address to address, down little-known tracks to out-of-the-way houses, had given him a deep and thorough understanding of where everything was. He never used satnav—what was the point?

The route from his home in Norton St Philip to where Simon was telling him to go, the village of Coleford, was an easy one; straight past Tucker's Grave, and without the time to stop for a pint of cider either, through the village of Faulkland, before crossing the main road between Radstock and Frome, and then on past the lake he'd caused such a disturbance at earlier that day.

Arriving in Coleford, he relaxed as best as he could, letting Simon direct him. It wasn't the easiest of things to do, handing over control to a dead person, but Tony was fully aware he had little choice but to do so. He did wonder if he was about to make a fool of himself by knocking on someone's door to make sure they weren't being murdered or anything, but he just had to go with it.

Driving through Coleford, he waited for some sign from Simon, not really sure what it might be. Then his ears popped painfully enough to make him blink, and something told him he needed to turn left. Not long after that, and just beyond what looked to be a small, village hall on his left, he heaved his vehicle off the road and up onto a kerb, then was out the door.

Looking around, Tony had no idea where he was. Coleford wasn't a place he'd ever really visited, so the fact that he was now smack bang in the middle of it and hoping for guidance from someone only he could not so much see, but at the very least feel, twisted his gut with worry. Was he mad? Was that really what all this boiled down to, that he was seeing and hearing things, and in doing so, losing touch with reality?

Tony walked away from his vehicle, willing Simon to come through again, to tell him where to go next, but the sun was bright, and the heat of it, despite it being autumn, had him narrowing his eyes, and he walked into a bush filled with thorns, before crashing his shins into a low wall.

Swearing, Tony stepped back, brought his hand up to his face and saw that it had been punctured by the bush, so much so, some of the thorns were still in his flesh. And his shin stung, too. Just what the hell was he doing?

Turning on his heel, and pulling the thorns from his skin, Tony made his way back to where he had parked, the worry in his gut turning to anger at himself. He needed to get control of things, stop allowing all this to control him. This was no way to live!

At his vehicle, Tony went to open the driver's door, only to have those hairs on his neck stand up.

'No,' he said, his voice low and quiet so that if anyone else was close or walking past, they wouldn't hear. 'No, I'm not doing it. Whatever it is, I'm out. I've had enough. I can't just go on like this, it's ... I mean, it's bonkers, isn't it?'

Then his ears popped, and an image smashed into his skull with the force of an axe splitting a log.

Tony tried to ignore it, closed his eyes to force away the pain the image was causing as it burned its way into his resistant mind. The image only burned brighter, so much so that Tony toppled forward onto his vehicle and screamed.

'Leave me alone! Just go, please! I can't do this, I can't! I don't want it, I never asked for it, go somewhere else, to someone else! Please!'

A hand rested on Tony's shoulder.

'You alright, there, love?'

Tony didn't answer right away. He was panting, his arms were bleeding from the thorns, his shins hurt, and now his knees did, too.

'Sunstroke, is it? Well, you should be wearing a hat. I know it's odd to have such a warm day like this considering the time of year, but you've still got to be careful, haven't you? Do you want a drink of water, maybe? I can get you some. I only live over the road. Was just taking Magpie here out for his walk. I called him that because as soon as I got him, he was always into things, wasn't he? Stealing this and that and either eating it or chewing it or ripping it apart? You know, one day, I was in the kitchen, and I'd left the fridge open, I don't hear so well, and I'd not heard that little warning beep to tell me to go over and shut the door. Well, when I eventually noticed, what do you think I found? Magpie here, headfirst inside the fridge, his little tail wagging like mad, as he troughed down half a pound of sausages. He was sick as can be, and serve him right, too, if you ask me. Now, about that glass of water ...'

Tony stood up to find a very small woman and an even smaller dog at his side.

'Oh, you did that too fast, really, didn't you?' she said. 'Don't want you getting dizzy, now.'

A name as well as an image was scorched into his mind.

'Gail,' he said. 'I'm looking for Gail Carpenter ...'

The woman narrowed her eyes as she stared up at Tony.

'Are you? And why's that, then?'

'I'm a friend.'

Those eyes narrowed even further.

'You don't look like any friend of hers I've seen here before.'

'Please,' Tony begged, 'it's important. She's in danger!'

The woman poked him in the chest with a tiny, bony finger, and her dog yapped at him with a single, sharp bark.

'If you're a friend, you should know where she lives, shouldn't you? Honestly, what do you take me for? Come on, Magpie!'

And with that, she was gone.

Tony thought about chasing after her, pressing the point that he really needed to know where Gail lived, but knew there was no point.

'Simon,' he hissed, looking around. 'You've got me here, so why the hell don't you—'

Then Simon came through, and Tony knew exactly where he was going.

He ran.

THIRTY-SIX

'I had to do something,' she said, her words making their way through the tears. 'He wouldn't take the drugs. I loved him, but when things got dark, he was awful, not to me, really, but to himself, and I'd heard about those Liberty Cap things, and I found some one day, just by accident. I was desperate, so I just thought I'd add them to his food, see if anything happens, just one or two, you know? I really didn't expect anything to happen, but then he was calmer. I mean, it was really noticeable. I tried it again, in some cake, a few more mushrooms, and Simon was happier. So, you know, I just sort of kept on doing it. I didn't mean any harm by it. I just wanted to help! I even sent him off to his bloody outdoor swimming sessions with it in the little snacks I'd send with him. Cake usually, sometimes in the hot chocolate.'

Gordy was stumped. This was someone breaking down about her husband, confessing that she had been drugging him secretly, which in itself was a serious offence, not least because picking, preparing, eating or selling the mushroom had been illegal since 2005, with Liberty Cap classed as a class A drug. But it wasn't the confession of someone who had then gone on to brutally murder him. And what about those boxer shorts found at the cottage, which was the real reason she'd come round in the first place? Just what the hell was going on?

'Who was at the cottage?' she asked.

Maria didn't answer straight away.

'Maria ...'

Maria looked up, her eyes red from the tears.

'Amy.'

'A pair of men's boxer shorts were found by the cleaners after you had left the property,' Gordy said. 'Now, you've told me that Amy was divorced, so I can't see how she could have taken them there by accident. You, on the other hand, there's the possibility that they were Simon's. Is it at all possible, Maria, that maybe some of Simon's underwear got mixed up with what you took with you?'

Gordy was giving Maria a lot of line here, she knew, but sometimes that was for the best.

Maria looked up at the ceiling, started crying again, and shook her head.

'I've been so stupid,' she said. 'I knew I shouldn't have gone. I mean, why risk ruining everything? And now he's gone, isn't he? And I can't put any of it right!'

'Maria,' said Gordy, her tone calm, serious, 'did you have anything at all to do with Simon's death?'

Maria gasped.

'I didn't drug him to death! I didn't! Why would I ever do that? I loved him. It's just that, well, it wasn't very exciting, and then someone else showed interest, and I kept putting it off and putting it off, until ...'

Gordy had no idea where any of this was going, if it was relevant or not, but she pushed anyway.

'Until your reunion with Amy? Someone else went as well, then, yes?'

'Not as well, instead of,' said Maria. 'Amy never went to the cottage. And now I've got her in trouble, too, haven't I? I asked her to just say she'd been with me, because I panicked, and because ... because ...'

'Because of what?' Gordy asked. 'I need to ask you again, Maria ...' And when she did, she was considerably more direct. 'Did you kill Simon?'

Maria was on her feet.

'No! No, God, no. Why would I kill Simon?'

'Then what are you saying you did, Maria?' Gordy asked.

Maria dropped back into her chair.

'I gave in to temptation,' she said. 'I went to the cottage with Danny.'

'And who's Danny?' Gordy asked.

'Couple of years ago, Simon bought me membership to a gym and spa over in Bath,' Maria explained. 'Danny's one of the massage therapists there.'

'And you were having an affair with him. Is that what you're saying?'

Maria shook her head.

'Danny was persistent,' she said. 'It was flattering. I would go for a massage, and it would always be him. He was exciting, but I didn't want anything, because I'm married. We got on well, talked about everything. He was really understanding about Simon's depression as well. God, I even told him about the mushroom thing. Then, something happened during one of the massages, things got a bit out of hand. I swore never again, but ...' Maria sighed. 'I had to have one last fling, didn't I? I can't explain it. I booked the cottage. Simon was none the wiser. I headed there the day Simon was …' Another pause. 'Maybe if I'd not gone, Simon would still be alive? I mean, I could've gone with him, couldn't I? Maybe? I don't know. There are too many questions. All I know is that the night Simon ended up in that pool, I was drinking my way through a bottle of wine, waiting for Danny to arrive. He was late, too; by the time he arrived, I was quite drunk.'

'Late?'

'I got to the cottage late afternoon, early evening. Danny actually turned up here, would you believe! Said he'd lost his phone and needed to tell me he was going to be late, because he had to cover someone at work. I wasn't happy, I mean, coming here? To our house? What if Simon had seen him?'

'You mean Simon was here when Danny turned up?'

Maria's nod was all panic and disbelief.

'He was upstairs having a nap. Usually does that after a swim; the cold water really takes it out of him. Anyway, Danny wasn't here long, thank God. Then I left for the cottage after Simon had woken up and headed off himself. Gave him the pack-up I'd made for him. The later it got at the cottage, the more nervous I became, which was why I just kept drinking. I didn't know if Danny was going to turn up. I told him in the end that it was a one-and-done thing, that we'd never do it again. It was too much. And it was wrong.'

Gordy asked, 'Has Danny been in touch since?'

'Every day,' said Maria. 'Keeps telling me he loves me, that he's here for me, that kind of thing, and that now with Simon gone, we can be together. It's really inappropriate. I made it very clear nothing else would ever happen, that it was just a bit of fun. I've stopped answering his calls. I should never have done what I did. Simon didn't deserve it, and now I've got to live with this for the rest of my life, haven't I?'

Maria started crying again, but the sound was different now, and there were no tears. Because she'd already cried them all out, Gordy thought.

As she waited for Maria to calm down again, something from what she had just said suddenly burned bright in Gordy's mind.

'Danny was late, but he was here first, yes?'

Maria nodded.

Gordy picked up a slice of the chocolate cake.

'What were you doing when Danny turned up?'

Maria frowned.

'Why's that important?'

'What were you doing?'

'I don't remember.'

'Think, Maria ...'

'I am! Bloody hell, how should I know? So much has happened. Simon's dead! I mean, I was probably in the kitchen, wasn't I? Fixing up Simon's snack and hot chocolate, and then Danny was there and—'

Gordy was on her feet, phone in her hand, number punched in. Her call was answered in two rings.

'Boss?'

'Patti, the massage therapist—'

'Mr Daniel Larson. Lives in Warminster.'

'And where is he today?'

'Home, I've been told. I checked with the spa he works at, and he does a bit of freelance as well, private clients, that kind of thing, so that's what he's on with.'

'I need someone over here right away to be with Maria,' said Gordy.

'I can get Travis and Helen over in ten.'

'Perfect. Do that. Then send me Daniel's address and meet me there. I need to bring him in for questioning.'

'Really? Why? He's just a name, isn't he, someone floating around on the edge of things. You think he's important, then, that he knows something?'

'I think,' said Gordy, 'that he has a thing for Maria, somehow convinced her to go away with him for a few days—'

'The boxer shorts?'

'My guess right now is that they're his. I also think his thing for Maria may well be a little more than just fancying a tumble in the sack behind her husband's back.'

'He killed Simon?'

Patti's voice had gone cold with those words.

'Just send me that address, Patti, and we'll go from there.'

'Well, I'm nearly there already, actually; thought I'd pop over and introduce myself. Picked up Pete on the way, because it's always safer with two, isn't it? And if you're thinking what I think you're thinking, then I'm even more pleased that I did.'

Gordy was as surprised as she was impressed to hear Patti say that.

'Be careful.'

'I'm never anything else. Especially now after what you just said.'

Gordy hung up, looked over at Maria.

'Officers are on their way.'

'What's happening?' Maria asked. 'Why do you need to

speak to Danny? I mean, you can't! Everyone will know, won't they? They'll know what I did!'

'Maria,' Gordy said, her voice flat calm, like a lake with no breeze at all, but her mind was working overtime, connecting so many things all at once, that it was making her head spin. 'You didn't kill Simon. But someone did. That's what matters right now, finding the person who killed your husband.'

'But why do you need to speak to Danny? It doesn't make sen—'

Maria's voice died, and then realisation sent her eyes wide.

'Oh, my God ...'

A few minutes later, Travis and Helen were at the door, and Gordy was already in her vehicle and wheel-spinning out of Maria's drive.

THIRTY-SEVEN

Gordy was racing out of Mells, lights and sirens blaring, when a call came in.

'What?'

'Gordy, it's Patti.'

'I'm on my way, just left Mells. You have Daniel?'

'He's not here.'

'But you said—'

'He's supposed to be. The spa checked his diary, and he's got bookings for today, at the therapy studio he has at his house, but he's not here.'

'You're sure?'

'We've rung the bell, knocked on the door, walked around the property, he's not here. Checked with neighbours a moment ago, which is why I've called; they saw him leave about half an hour ago.'

Gordy slowed down, pulled over, and stopped.

'Any idea where?'

'No one spoke to him, just saw him leave. That's all we know right now.'

'Description of his car?'

'Yellow convertible. I've already shared that with uniform, see if anyone gets eyes on something like that, because yellow convertibles aren't that common, are they? I'm on with getting the rest of the details as well. Soon as I have them, I'll send them.'

Gordy wasn't listening, she was thinking, and quickly.

'Gail,' she said.

'What about her?' asked Patti.

Gordy almost mentioned Tony but kept that to herself.

'I'm thinking aloud here,' she said. 'Gail recognised him at the river. What if he's gone there?'

'Why would he do that?'

'I think he may have gone there to then follow Simon, maybe find out what he was doing, where he was going. He was late that evening when he turned up at the cottage Maria had booked for them both. She thought he had to work late. I'm pretty sure that wasn't true.'

'You mean Gail's a loose end?'

'I think he attacked Charlie as well. She said something about seeing someone at the pool; what if it was Daniel? What if he saw her as well, followed her, found out where she lived, attacked her at the river? Only, it didn't go according to plan, did it? And Charlie, she has no idea who it was who tried to kill her, does she? And she's protected now, or at least for the moment, so he can't do anything about her, not yet. But Gail? Well, Gail he really can, can't he?'

'But how would he even know where she lives?'

'She booked in with him privately, remember? Some wood therapy or something, whatever the hell that is. Pretty sure part of the booking process is getting her contact details, home address.'

As Gordy was speaking, she was already turning around, and on a road she had learned a while back went by the delightful, and perhaps unnecessarily apt name, of Murder Combe.

'I'm going there now,' she said. 'You've got Gail's address as well; I want everyone there ASAP.'

'You can't go in on your own, you need to wait for backup!'

'Don't think I have much choice, do you?'

'Gordy—'

Gordy killed the call, then wheel-spun her way to face the right direction and headed to Coleford. The road was a blur of green as she sped by trees and bushes and fields. Patti called again, but Gordy ignored it; no time for a chat now. It was time for action.

The road pulled her on, and all Gordy could think about was everything that had happened since she'd gone on that speed date. The days had been busy, that was for sure, but in such a way she had been unprepared for. To have Charlie caught up in it all as well, that had caught her off guard, as had how quickly she'd found herself attracted to the woman, and not just because of her looks. She was fun, seemed utterly genuine, and had made her feel very at ease and comfortable with herself. Whether or not she was ready for anything serious, she had no idea, but then how would she ever know, if she didn't at least try and find out?

A T-junction raced up to greet her. Gordy turned right, found herself heading down a hill, the lane thin and windy, then through the hamlet of Vobster, up another hill, after which Coleford greeted her with houses, parked cars, and people going about their everyday lives.

They've no idea, she thought, no idea at all of the darkness that seems to hide just behind the normality of existence. And that's for the better, she thought; that was her job, and though the burden was a hefty one, she preferred it to be hers than someone else's.

Checking Gail's address, Gordy zipped through Coleford, took another left, then parked up. Following the directions on her phone, she slammed the driver's door, locked up, and then ran.

Down an alleyway between two houses, Gordy chased a surprised cat, which hissed at her as it jumped up a fence to get out of the way. At the end of the alleyway, she took a right onto a road lined with semi-detached houses, all of them with well-tended front gardens.

Spying Gail's house, Gordy pulled herself up sharp. Her heart was racing, her breathing fast, and she needed to be calm, in control, if she was going to have any chance of dealing with whatever it was she was about to deal with. And there was the problem right there; she had no idea what waited for her on the other side of Gail's front door. It was a hunch that had sent her to this address, nothing more. A good one, sure, but even so, still just a hunch. Gail wasn't alone, she knew that; Mike was with her. That was some comfort, except that Daniel, assuming he was the killer, had already disposed of Simon and attacked Charlie. He was a violent man and clearly willing to do what it took to get what he wanted, which seemed to be Maria.

Gordy wondered about waiting for backup. It was on its way after all, and probably wouldn't be too long, either. Warminster wasn't too far. Patti was probably only twenty minutes away, if that. But a lot could happen in twenty minutes, and something told her she couldn't wait.

The only thing she had to hand, which would offer any

protection at all, was the extendable baton she carried with her. Gripping it now, she made her way up to Gail's front door, which burst open so violently, one of the hinges snapped, as three bodies tumbled out and onto the ground in an almost playground display of wrestling and writhing arms and legs. The air filled with swearing.

THIRTY-EIGHT

In the split second it took for Gordy to register what was happening, she clocked both Mike and Tony in the fray. They were on top of another man with a tan only money could buy. Daniel, she suspected.

'Bastard!' Mike yelled, as Daniel kicked up hard enough to launch him into the air.

Then he was back into the scrap, his arms and fists whirring with all the skill and accuracy of someone who had clearly never been in a fight in his life.

Tony, on the other hand, was doing a damned sight better, Gordy noticed, as she now raced over to break things up. He'd managed to flip both himself and Daniel around, so that Tony was now on the ground on his back, with Daniel clamped between his legs. Tony's arms were around the man's neck, and Daniel was scrabbling his fingers at them, trying to break free.

'Enough!'

No one listened.

Gordy was next to the three men, now, could see no

weapons beyond the fists Mike especially seemed so keen to put to use, no matter how ineffectively.

She was about to yell again, wary of getting herself into the middle of the three men, when out of nowhere it seemed, a jet of water blasted into the moment, its tip directed mainly at Daniel's face. He spluttered, coughed, and tried to pull himself free, but Tony had him held fast. Mike was still on top of him, swearing, grabbing at his collar, heaving him left and right. Then the jet of water was directed at Mike, and he fell off Tony and Daniel, shock on his face.

'The bloody hell are you doing, Gail?'

Gordy looked over to where the jet of water was coming from. There, at the side of the house, standing on a path that led to the rear of the property, was Gail. And she was holding a hose.

'You heard what the detective said, enough!' she roared. 'Get off the ground and stop being silly buggers!'

'But he tried to kill you!' Mike spluttered back.

Tony, in the meantime, was making no effort at all to let Daniel go.

Gail pointed at her forehead, and Gordy saw a large bump there, already growing purple.

'Well, all he's done is give me a bloody good headache,' she said. 'And I don't think you and that builder chap trying to give him a good pasting is the best way to deal with it, is it?'

'We were just trying to protect you!'

'I don't need protecting!' Gail shouted back. 'I need you all to stop what you're doing!'

Gordy stepped in, pointing her baton at Daniel's face, then took her ID from a pocket and flipped it open for him to see.

'Hello,' she said.

Daniel stopped struggling. Tony still held him, though.

'I'm Detective Inspector Haig. And you, I presume, are Mr Daniel Larson.'

Daniel tried to speak, but couldn't.

'Tony,' said Gordy. 'Would you mind easing off a bit?'

Tony did, as the sound of footsteps racing towards them broke into the moment.

Gordy looked over her shoulder to see Patti and Pete appear at the end of Gail's garden.

'Need a hand?' Patti asked, as she and Pete walked over.

Gordy said nothing, knowing she didn't need to.

Pete and Patti grabbed Daniel and had him on his feet, with his hands cuffed behind his back, before he even had a chance to work out a way to resist the arrest.

'There, that wasn't so bad, was it?' said Gordy, as she helped Tony to his feet. 'Can't say I was expecting to see you here.'

'Can't say I was expecting to be here, either,' Tony replied.

'Simon?'

Tony gave a quick nod as Patti and Pete read Daniel his rights and led him out of the garden.

'What happened? And I don't mean with Simon, either, because I don't think I really want or care to know. That's not me being rude, either, it's just, well, you know, not very police and detective-y, is it? Not sure that's a word, but we'll go with it, eh?'

'Daniel was already here when I arrived,' Tony explained. 'Only just though.'

'He was in the house?'

'He'd already had a go at Gail with a mallet he'd brought

with him. Mike had managed to deflect him enough not to have her end up with a cracked skull. Still caught her hard, though. Knocked her out.'

'Then what?'

'When I turned up, Gail was coming to.'

'Who let you in, then?'

'Door was open, I just let myself in. Saw Daniel with the mallet in his hand, ready to have a go at Mike, who was standing over Gail, protecting her. Then, well, I don't really know what happened, exactly. Details are fuzzy. But Mike and I, we, well, you saw, didn't you?'

'I saw three men fall out of a house.'

'I didn't know what to do. Don't think Mike did either. We both just knew we had to stop Daniel doing what he'd turned up to do. So, we did. It's not an everyday thing, is it, to just put yourself between someone out to kill someone else, and the person they're out to kill?'

'Not really. Did you have any thoughts as to what you were going to do once the brawl started? Really, you should've called the police, waited for us to arrive.'

'There wasn't time, was there? He'd already attacked Gail, and I didn't want him hurting anyone else, or escaping. We just did what we thought we had to do.'

'You took the law into your own hands.'

At this, Mike stepped in.

'No, we didn't,' he said. 'We kept him busy and away from Gail while we waited for you to arrive.'

'But it's only by luck that we did,' said Gordy. 'You didn't call, did you?'

'I did,' said Gail, coming over to join them, her clothes wet from the water spray. 'While they were rolling around outside, I put a call in.'

'Then got the hose out,' said Mike.

'About that,' said Gordy.

'Well, you do it with dogs, don't you?' said Gail. 'If they start getting frisky or fighting. Same with cats.'

'We're not dogs or cats.' Mike frowned.

'Worked though, didn't it?' Gail shrugged, then stumbled a little and leaned against Mike.

Gordy put a call in for an ambulance, then guided Gail back inside and gave her a check over.

'My first aid is just enough to make sure you're okay,' she said, as Gail rested on a sofa in her lounge, 'but you need a proper check over.' She then looked around the room, looking for something. 'This mallet,' she said. 'The one Daniel hit you with.'

A hand appeared in front of Gordy, and in it, a carrier bag.

'Here,' said Mike. 'I used the bag to pick it up, because you'll need to get fingerprints and DNA won't you?'

Gordy opened the bag. Inside, she saw the large, wooden mallet Gail had been attacked with. Its surface was mostly smooth, though she noticed that it had been chipped in places, and she remembered the strange slivers of wood that Charming had found in the wound to the back of Simon's head.

'What actually is it?' she asked. 'Is Daniel into carpentry or stonemasonry or something?'

'Remember, I said I'd had a wood therapy massage?' said Gail. 'That's one of the tools he used. Felt really good, too, smoothing out my skin and massaging my muscles.' She then pointed at the bump on her head. 'Felt less good here, though ...'

Having waited for the ambulance to arrive to deal with

Gail, Gordy headed outside with Tony. Mike stayed inside with Gail.

'He's got more fight in him than I would've expected,' she said.

'I was happy to just restrain him,' said Tony. 'Mike, it seems, really wanted to pummel him.'

'Good job he threw punches like a drunk, then, isn't it?'

Tony smiled.

'You're going to want to talk to me again, aren't you?' he said.

Gordy gave a nod.

'Not today, though. Today, I think we've seen more than enough of each other, don't you?'

'I do,' Tony replied. 'Wouldn't want people to start thinking we work together or anything; imagine the gossip.'

'Oh, I don't have to imagine, I know,' said Gordy, and with that, she headed over to where Patti and Pete had Daniel in the back of their car, ready to follow them to the station.

THIRTY-NINE

Twenty-four hours later, or thereabouts, Gordy was sitting in an interview room with Patti by her side. Those twenty-four hours had been busy for everyone on the team, with the SOC team called in to not only go over Gail's property but also Simon and Maria's house, and Daniel's place over in Warminster. Additional staff and officers had been brought in, further witness statements taken, numerous photographs, reports, meetings ... Somehow, Gordy had managed to grab herself just enough sleep, so that she was plenty alert to question their key suspect.

Sitting opposite Gordy were two men. One was dressed in a dark blue suit designed to look expensive, but too shiny to be so. He had a floppy fringe and kept flicking his head to keep it out of his eyes. The other man was in denims, a grey T-shirt, and a nondescript hoodie. His well-muscled torso was more than apparent beneath his clothes, made more so by how he kept flexing his pecs, sometimes at the same time, sometimes separately, as though to a drumbeat only he could hear.

From the look in his eyes, which was all smug arrogance, Gordy sensed that he fully believed he was being provocative, sexually so, too. Pathetic, really.

Having already gone through the usual patter of switching on the recording equipment, then reading the man in the hoodie his rights, she stated the names of everyone in the room.

'Present for the interview are Detective Inspector Haig, Detective Sergeant Matondo, Mr Daniel Larson, and his legal representative, Mr Harrington.'

'No comment,' said Larson.

Gordy stared at the man just long enough to let him know she was neither amused nor intimidated by whatever it was he was trying to do or be.

Harrington had already said what he needed to say, his voice reminding Gordy of the sound a balloon makes when the air is allowed to squeal out of it. So, she got right into things.

'Mr Larson, you have been brought in for questioning in connection with the murder of Mr Simon Miller, in addition to an attack on both Ms Charlotte Apperly and Ms Gail Carpenter. Do you understand?'

No response, beyond staring off for a moment into the corner of the room.

'We have witness statements placing you at the River Avon, just outside Bradford-on-Avon, on the same day Simon Miller was killed. These outline that you went for a swim with Mr Miller and an associate of his. We also have witness statements placing you at the house of Mr Miller the afternoon of the same day, and then that evening at another address with his wife. Further, we have witness statements placing you at the house of Gail Carpenter, where you attacked her. Do you have anything to say to this?'

'No comment.'

Well, if that's the way it's going to be, then fine, Gordy thought. Sometimes she felt, saying nothing was as much an admission of guilt as yelling out, *I did it*. It just made her even more determined to line up the evidence. Gordy opened a large file and presented a photo.

'Do you recognise this man?'

Larson said nothing.

'For the record, I have presented Mr Larson with a photograph of Mr Simon Miller,' Gordy said, then slid a slip of paper over to Larson. 'On the evening of the day you were seen swimming with Miller, you were then to meet with his wife, Maria, at a little cottage she had booked for you both. This is the address of the cottage and a photo. Do you recognise it?'

Larson leaned forward, stayed silent.

'What about these, then?' Gordy said, and presented an evidence bag, inside which were a pair of boxer shorts, once again stating out loud what she was showing Larson.

'They're just boxer shorts,' Larson replied. 'Could be anyone's.'

'Are you saying that you don't recognise them?'

No response.

'Well,' said Gordy, 'we'll soon know for sure, what with the DNA samples we were able to collect from them. But I just thought it wise to give you the opportunity to claim them first.'

'DNA samples?'

Gordy looked at Patti.

'He'd be amazed what we can find on a piece of clothing like this, wouldn't he, Detective?'

Patti gave a nod.

'Sweat, pubic hair, urine, skin flakes, semen ...'

Larson shifted in his chair.

'Anyway,' said Gordy, 'let's track back a bit, shall we, back to a little pool in Somerset?'

This time, Patti laid various photographs in front of Larson and explained what she was doing and showing as she did so. They showed the crime scene as it had been found, minus Simon's body.

'Recognise this?'

'Looks like a pool in a woodland.'

'What about this, then?'

Gordy presented two evidence bags and more photographs, explaining each item. One bag contained a small number of white threads, the other tiny slivers of wood. The photographs were of each but magnified considerably.

Larson's silence continued, but Gordy didn't allow it to get to her; she'd been in the job too long to allow that to happen.

She pointed to the white thread and the relevant photographs.

'These threads were found at this pool. They are a match of towels found at your property, Daniel.'

Daniel, to Gordy's surprise, laughed, and she saw a look of horror at the outburst on Harrington's face as he reached out to rest a hand on Daniel's arm to stop the outburst.

'Something funny?'

'Everyone has towels,' he said.

'They do,' Gordy agreed. 'But then we'll be able to do a little bit of DNA magic on what we have, won't we? And who knows what that might show us? Now, on to this ...' She dropped her finger on the other evidence bag. 'Any ideas?'

'About what?'

'What these might be?'

A shake of the head.

'Patti?'

Patti reached for Gordy's file, shuffled through the contents—a little too dramatically perhaps, she thought, but it was a nice attempt to unnerve Larson—then she took out another photograph and placed it on the table.

'Do you recognise this?' she asked.

The photograph was of a wooden mallet, the one that had been found at Gail's house and used to knock her out. Thankfully, after a serious check over, she had been found to be suffering from only a mild concussion, so she'd come away from the attack relatively unscathed. It could've been a lot worse.

'I've seen something sim— I mean, no comment.'

'For the record, we have now presented Mr Larson with a photograph of the weapon used to attack Ms Gail Carpenter,' Gordy said. 'We have three witnesses to this attack, including the victim. Their statements support the fact that it was you who attacked her.' She pointed to the evidence bag containing the slivers of wood, then at the enlarged photographs of the same. 'These tiny fragments were found in a wound to Mr Miller's head. They match exactly where slivers are missing from the surface of the weapon used to attack Ms Carpenter. We can conclude, therefore, that the weapon used to attack Ms Carpenter was also used to knock Mr Miller unconscious before he was then drowned. Though, it's worth noting here that the blow to his head was enough to kill him, anyway.'

Larson yawned.

Gordy narrowed her eyes. Time to just lay it all down and crack on.

'I'm going to outline everything I think happened,' she said. 'Just so that we're all clear. And bear in mind, if you will, all the witness statements we have, the physical evidence, forensics. A couple of years ago, Maria, Simon's wife, joined the spa and gym you work at. She came to you for massages several times. She found you exciting, different. Whatever, really, it doesn't actually matter. Anyway, things got out of hand during one of her sessions with you, and despite her wanting nothing more, somehow you both ended up deciding to go to a little cottage for a few days of slap and tickle.'

Gordy let her words sit in the air for a moment or two before continuing. She ignored as best she could the look Patti was giving her for using the same phrase that she'd used in an earlier conversation they'd had.

'The thing is, Daniel, I think Maria only wanted a bit of excitement, nothing more. And I'm not here to judge that, mind. To each their own. You, however, wanted more, didn't you? Maybe you were excited about being with an older woman, and who could blame you? She's a looker, isn't she? And all that exercise has certainly had an impact, that's for sure. But instead of accepting things, you didn't just insist, did you? No. You decided, for whatever reason, to try and force the issue. By killing Simon.'

What followed that was a minute or two of protestations from Harrington, with lots of him telling Gordy she had no right to say that, and that his client really needed to keep his mouth shut. Where the hell Larson had found him, she had no idea, but she suspected that the man's details were readily available on noticeboards alongside adverts for scrap metal collection and window-cleaning.

Once everyone had calmed down, she continued.

'You wanted Simon out of the picture. You'd never met him but knew from chatting with Maria where he would be the day he was killed. You also knew all about her secretly dosing him with psilocybin, by adding it to the cakes she made him, but more on that in a bit. Now, where was I? Oh yes, that was it. You turned up at the river to chat with Simon. Maybe you planned to follow him home and kill him there, I don't know. Either way, you found out that he was heading to a little pool later that evening, and you just couldn't say no to the opportunity, could you? I think you learned a little about the pool itself as well, that people use it because they think it might heal them, help them have children, that kind of thing, so you even went to the trouble of turning up with some mistletoe.'

'Mistletoe?' exclaimed Harrington. 'What are you—? I mean, you've not mentioned that before!'

Gordy ignored him.

'Had me going for a while, did that, suspecting there was some kind of ritual thing going on, but it was nothing of the sort, was it? Anyway, you found out where Simon would be and decided to pop along to see Maria. Took Maria by surprise, that, you turning up at the house with that story about losing your phone and needing to tell her you would be late that evening. Now, back to the psilocybin …

'Like I've said, Maria had mentioned that to you, and you probably did just turn up to let her know you'd be late, because otherwise it would be a bit suspicious, wouldn't it? When you arrived, though, she was sorting some food out for Simon, and I think you saw what she was doing, maybe she told you which little bottle or pot or whatever had the psilocybin in, and with a bit of distraction, you put in an extra dose or three?

'My guess is that you then hung around, or parked up on the way to Simon's destination, so that you could follow him to the pool. Later on, when Simon is having his swim, eating the food Maria had sent with him, he's probably not feeling that great, a bit dizzy perhaps, and that makes him a lot easier to deal with, doesn't it, seeing as you've given him an overdose of the psilocybin? Which you then do, by the way, by knocking him senseless with that mallet of yours, before drowning him. Oh, and you stood on his back to keep him under the water, didn't you? We found bruises, took measurements, so we'll be checking those against your feet, I can promise you that.'

Larson, Gordy noticed, was staring at her, his brow furrowed, eyes narrow slits of darkness. Good, she thought, let him stare.

'Simon had actually booked himself in for a night at a hotel after his swim. A little treat for himself I think, what with his wife heading off for a few days. I know that detail's not really relevant right now, but it shows how oblivious the man was to what was going on, doesn't it? So, you've dealt with Simon, haven't you? But there's a problem. Two, actually. One, is that you recognised someone that morning by the river, and you couldn't be having that. Quite the surprise, no doubt, but you'd deal with that once you'd dealt with Simon. Then, of course, someone sees you at the pool, don't they? Your plan, it's unravelling, and before you know where you are, murdering one person becomes murdering three, or trying to, anyway. You followed Ms Apperly, and while she was taking an evening river swim at West Lydford, you attacked her. Didn't succeed, thought you'd got away with it anyway, and perhaps thought you might try again some other time? As for Ms Carpenter, you recognised her from the spa, didn't you? And you were maybe getting desperate by this point and attacked her in her own home, using the same weapon you'd used on Simon. Have I left anything out?'

Larson said nothing.

'I don't think so,' said Patti.

Gordy knew there were a fair few leaps and jumps and loosely tied knots in what she had said, but there was enough to be going on with. Some of it would change, she was sure, as the investigation was stepped up a gear, and everything brought together by everyone who had been involved, to take everything to court and prosecute. She looked at Larson, saw nothing but darkness in those eyes.

'Do you have anything to say?' she asked. 'This is your opportunity to—'

Larson was out of his seat with such speed that Gordy's reactions were instinctive more than clear thought. As he leapt forward, reaching across the table to grab her, she grabbed the table's edge with her hands and thrust it forward. Though Larson's chair was fixed to the floor, to prevent it from being used as a weapon, the table was not, because sometimes it needed to be moved. Right then, Gordy was thankful for that, as she drove it into Larson's waist and pinned him to his chair.

Harrington was out of his own seat in a flash, shock in his eyes. Then Patti was around to Larson, and before he knew what was happening, had his hands cuffed behind his back. He continued to struggle, and threw in a good amount of swearing, too, but Gordy was done.

'Daniel Larson,' she said, walking around to help Patti

with Larson, 'I am arresting you for the murder of Simon Miller, and the attempted murders of Charlotte Apperly and Gail Carpenter. You do not have to say anything, but it may harm your defence if you do not mention when questioned something which you later rely on in court. Anything you do say may be given in evidence.'

Larson said nothing.

Gordy glanced over at Harrington.

'Coming?'

Gathering his things together, he grabbed his coat.

'I hate this job,' he said, then was out of the room, tripping over the carpet on his way.

FORTY

'We're allowed to be here, right?' Gordy asked, standing on the bank of a river. She could feel the grass beneath her feet, cool and damp.

The afternoon was turning to evening, the air cool, and somehow, Charlie had persuaded her to don a swimsuit and go for a dip.

'Of course,' Charlie said. 'I know the farmer who owns this bit of the river, but there wouldn't be a problem anyway; loads of people come here.'

They were over near Evercreech, and the river they were about to enter was hidden well by a thick canopy of trees which lined its edges. Walking across the field towards it, the soft light of the failing sun had blessed their way with a golden hue. Now, though, Gordy was draped in shade, and she was very close to questioning her own sanity.

'The last time I did this ...'

Gordy's voice caught in her throat, her memories taking her north, to another river, another gathering, and the memory of scattering ashes.

She felt a hand rest on her shoulder.

'You don't have to if you don't want to.'

'It was my idea.'

'Doesn't matter. Only do this if you're comfortable with it. We can just get dressed, head back, it's fine.'

Gordy shook her head.

'No,' she said. 'I'm here. I want to do this.'

For a moment, Charlie said nothing, then she asked, 'Just out of interest, why?'

Interesting question, Gordy thought, because she wasn't entirely sure herself.

'I need the shock of it,' she said at last. 'I know what the water feels like, how it stings. I think it's what my body is desperate for, my mind as well, all of me, actually. Does that make sense? Probably not. Does to me, though. God, I sound mad ...'

Charlie laughed.

'Not at all. I get it, I really do. Sometimes, it's just hard to put into words, isn't it? That primal need to be in water, like it's calling you almost, beckoning you.'

'Something like that, though I've never thought of anything I do as primal.'

'Well, now's a first, then, isn't it?'

Charlie was standing beside Gordy.

'You ready?'

'No.'

'There's no rush. Just go in easy and calmly. Remember the breathing exercises we did before we stripped off as well, yes? That'll help. We won't stay in for long, either. This isn't about swimming around for hours, it's about being at one with the water.'

Gordy laughed.

'Being at one with the water? Come on, Charlie, you know that's not how my mind works. I know it'll do me good, but being at one with it? I'm no' so sure.'

In the gloom beneath the trees, Gordy saw a playful scowl on Charlie's face, then felt her hand slip into her own.

'Oh ...'

'Come on,' Charlie said, and with that, she led Gordy down into the water's cool embrace.

Dive into the next DI Haig thriller!

WANT to plunge straight into *Grave Omens*, the chilling fourth adventure in the DI Haig series?

Simply scan the QR code below.

You'll also be able to access free short stories and a regular newsletter. Contact me directly, see new book covers before anyone else, and get exclusive chapter extracts. Plus! Recipes, photos and a behind-the-scenes look at the life of an author.

ABOUT DAVID J. GATWARD

David had his first book published when he was 18 and still can't believe this is what he does for a living. Author of the long-running DCI Harry Grimm series, David was nominated for the Amazon Kindle Storyteller Award in 2023. He lives in Somerset with his two boys.

Visit www.davidjgatward.com to find out more about the author and his highly-acclaimed series of crime fiction.

facebook.com/davidjgatwardauthor

Printed in Dunstable, United Kingdom